Equality

Two Democracies: Revolution
Book 3

by Alasdair Shaw

Also by Alasdair Shaw

Two Democracies: Justice
Duty – a short story (in The Officer anthology)

Two Democracies: Revolution
Repulse – a short story (in The Newcomer anthology)
Independence – a short story
Liberty – a novel
Prejudice – a novelette
Equality – a novel
Hidden – a novella (due Autumn 2017)
Fraternity – a novel
Unity – a novel

Copyright © 2017 Alasdair C Shaw
All rights reserved.

First published in the UK 2017
by Alasdair Shaw

ISBN10 0995511047
ISBN13 978-0995511040

Cover art extract from original work "Spacecraft9"
by Caroline Davis:
https://www.flickr.com/photos/53416677@N08/4973524758
Used under the Creative Commons Attribution 2.0
Generic License:
https://creativecommons.org/licenses/by/2.0

Part I

The sour stench of manure filled the hold of the freighter. Cows lowed and horses whinnied. The shaking intensified. One wide-eyed stallion with flared nostrils got a hoof free of its hobbles and kicked a storage container.

A middle-aged man crouched in a corner, holding his wife and young son as the ship bucked and jolted. Metal creaked. The lights flickered and went out.

"Ssshhh, ssshhhh. It'll be all right. We're just entering the atmosphere." He removed his arm from his wife and lit a lamp.

The ship dropped for several seconds, leaving the man's stomach high in his chest, and the boy cried out. His mother stroked his hair and glared at her husband.

He looked away. It was his fault they were riding in such atrocious conditions. They had the money to travel in style, but he didn't want to draw attention to their passage. One day he'd be able to explain it to her, some of it anyway.

The buffeting eased and the main lights came back on. Two of his assistants rose and checked the animals. He knew he should help them, but couldn't bring himself to let go of his son.

Chapter 1

Crystal clear water cascaded down between sandstone rocks before plunging into a large artificial lake. Another rill tinkled into a plunge pool before making its way to the lake. The water was a rich blue at its deepest and gradually shifted to green as it reached the sandy shallows. Koi swam in the perfectly balanced water, their oranges and reds providing a counterpoint to the colours of the liquid. A gentle breeze wafted in a hint of jasmine.

At one end of the lake, in the shade of a palm tree, Harry Robinson lay on a wooden recliner, reading. In this exquisitely, and terrifyingly expensively, engineered landscape he held real treasure: a paper book, rumoured to have survived from Earth itself. Having made his fortune in electronics and robotics it had amused him to build up a library of ancient physical books.

"Your visitor is here. Shall I ask them to come through or will you be meeting them in the house?"

Harry surfaced from the story and focused on the woman standing confidently at the edge of the tree's shadow. "Thank you. Show them through please, Emily."

Emily turned and walked back to the house, her bare feet sinking into the grass. Her crimson bikini and wrap complemented her flawless skin. Her movements were precise yet appeared carefree.

Harry carefully placed a bookmark between the pages and reverently laid it down on the small table beside the recliner. A few seconds with his eyes closed, then he gave a shrug and stood up effortlessly. He threw on a robe over his slick black shorts and adjusted it meticulously. He was the power player in this meeting, but even so, it paid not to look sloppy. As he took the few steps to the dining table, he pulled up the agenda for the meeting in a window in his electronic interface system. Not many civilians had wetwired electronic interfaces, preferring less invasive processors like watches and jewellery. He, however, found EIS invaluable.

Emily came back leading a man in a dark grey suit. His pink shirt collar was ruffled in the latest style for executives. The briefcase he carried was a fair replica of an antique, a stab at projecting dependability that Harry didn't really trust.

"Mr Simon Jackson, CEO of TREcorps," Emily announced with a hint of a bow.

"Thank you, Emily. Would you wait with us please?" invited Harry.

She poured a glass of sparkling elderflower pressé before taking to the recliner behind the visitor. She closed her eyes, to all the world a trophy relaxing by the pool not bothered about the men and their business.

"I am informed you don't like small talk so I'll get straight to the point," said Simon. "We'd like to commission an android model from you. Something… special."

Harry kept his face and body neutral. He'd learnt the hard way that 'special' usually meant 'illegal', or perhaps 'immoral'. His standard searches before accepting the meeting hadn't thrown up anything dodgy on TREcorps or its CEO. He quickly set off a deep crawler that would hunt through corporate and police records, tracking down any whiff of ill deed. If it was caught he ought to be able to argue it was a security test, he did hold the contracts for the computer systems of most law enforcement and intelligence agencies in the system. As the crawler left, he noticed Emily shift slightly; she'd spotted it go.

"Are you sure we don't have a standard model that would do the job you want?" asked Harry. "Commissions are costly and could take some time to design. Then there's building and testing."

"I'm not interested in haggling," said Simon. "Bottom line, the board has approved a budget of ten million for this project. Congressional bonds, not soft credit. No-one else is on our radar for doing the work. Either you accept or we have to rethink the entire concept."

^He's being straight with you,^ sent Emily via the EIS link. ^Make him feel at ease.^

Harry indicated an upright chair with a hand gesture. "Go on then. Give me your pitch."

^Rather direct, but it'll have to do,^ she sent.

Both men sat facing each other across the table. Harry poured a drink for them both, the ice chinking in the tall glasses. Sweat glistened on Simon's neck. "How complex can you make an AI core?"

Harry crossed one foot across the other knee and

dangled his drink over the side of the chair by his fingertips. "That depends. Does it have to reside within the android, or can it be housed in a remote location?"

"It needs to be the most powerful you can make. If it has to be the size of a house, then that's how big it has to be."

"We are, of course, always developing better hardware. However, we do need to be mindful of the laws on AIs."

"Rumour has it you already have a prototype capable of housing a conscious program."

^Careful. This might be a sting.^

^He seems cordial,^ Harry replied.

^Trust me,^ sent Emily. ^He's hiding something. Make a positive movement and refute the allegation.^

Harry leant forward. "Let me make this very clear. My companies do not break the law. All the AIs we produce are bound by the von Neumann Protocols. The focus of our research is on miniaturisation, not pushing the limits of complexity."

The muscles in Simon's face sagged for a moment, before he composed himself again.

^Not a sting,^ sent Emily. ^I think he was pinning his hopes on you being able to make something for him.^

^You could tell that from one facial expression?^

^And the body language. And tone of voice.^

^I didn't notice a change,^ sent Harry.

^No. I don't suppose you did.^

The crawler wasn't back yet, so there wasn't anything incriminating in the surface data.

^OK. Your turn,^ sent Harry. ^Give me an excuse to

leave.^

A soft chime, and an ornament on the table glowed blue.

"If you'll excuse me I have a message I need to take," said Harry. He got up, straightened his robe, and walked towards the house. A feed from a camera hidden near the table opened in his vision.

As he stepped from the stone to the grass, Emily opened her eyes and turned her head towards their guest. A warm smile spread across her face.

"Why don't you join me?" she asked, indicating the recliner next to her. "Harry will be a while. Blue means one of the factories. He does take these production calls very seriously."

"I'm OK here, thank you. I'm not really dressed for lounging."

"You can just sit on the edge if you like. I'm getting a terrible crick in my neck turning to look at you like this."

Harry closed the feed. She'd tell him what he needed to know later. Right now he needed to think. He made his way to the terrace on the other side of the house, looking out over the city spread across the valley below.

#

Harry joined Emily in the marbled hall. The cold, polished floor was a welcome change in sensation from the sun-baked terraces outside.

"Mister Jackson is taking a tour of the roses with the gardener," said Emily.

"Did you get anywhere?"

She shifted her weight fractionally from one foot to the other. "Not at first. But after a while, he opened up. His wife is dying."

Harry frowned. "That didn't turn up in the searches."

"They're keeping it a secret. The two of them founded the TREcorps together, they are concerned about the impact the news would have on the share prices."

Harry ran a quick stock market analysis. "They'd be right. And it is a personal tragedy for the family. But what has it got to do with us?"

"He wouldn't say. But I can think of one thing."

Harry raised an eyebrow. "Do tell."

Emily glanced at the floor before staring him straight in the eye. "He wants to keep her alive. Her mind at least. Download her into one of our cores."

"But that's impossible. Sure, we could create a program that mimicked his wife's actions. It might even run the business as well as her. It wouldn't be her, though."

"He's clutching at straws."

Harry mulled it over. There was a logic to it, once she'd identified the key points for him. "Thank you, Emily. You are a better observer of human behaviour than I am."

"You know you don't need to thank me. And you still persist in using that name, even in private. It isn't required." She turned to leave.

Harry caught her gently by the arm. "What would you prefer I called you? House? Avatar 12? Serial 912C5R?"

"I don't 'prefer'. You know that," she said, still with her back to him. "Are you testing me?"

"Is that what you think?" he asked with a neutral tone.

Emily turned to face him. "You are sounding a lot like a psychologist, answering with questions. So yes, I think you are testing me."

"What do you think I'm testing you about?" he asked.

She affected a coquettish pout for a moment. "You want to know how close I am to the Third Protocol threshold."

#

Harry lazed by the pool. He kept going over the meeting with Simon Jackson, searching for the clues that Emily had so easily picked up on. Nothing revealed itself, the entire conversation read the same as every other one he'd ever experienced, from discussions with government ministers, through business deals, to intimate moments.

Trust me to create an AI with a higher emotional quotient than I have.

Insects droned, the heat lulled him. His head lolled forward, and he jerked awake again. Closing the in-vision window displaying the blueprints, he settled down to doze.

It felt like only a second later when a priority newsflash jolted him awake. His EIS flagged it as urgent, and played the video. Viewed from orbit, and grainy through signal interference, Concorde, the next planet down-well, rotated in the shot. A flash on the surface, then another. The nuclear explosions spread across the planet like a tidal wave.

The view cut to a Fleet spokesperson, who announced that the Republic had launched a sneak attack and been chased from the system. Harry muted him, instead inspecting the information his EIS had trawled from both the public net and his private sources. Unsurprisingly at this early stage, there wasn't much beyond the estimated initial death toll. One thing, however, stood out.

The entire system defence fleet was recalled for urgent repairs shortly before the attack. That can't be right.

Harry didn't deal with the military. He did, however, know which of his competitors held defence contracts, and launched a flurry of queries to the spyware he had embedded in their systems. Data flooded back.

As I thought. No way that component could fail the way the report says. And even if it did, it wouldn't need replacing so urgently.

He connected a channel to his production manager.
^Dan, have you seen the news?^ he sent through his implants.

^Yeah. We've got it on all the screens.^

^I want you to retask the factories, I'll send you the details once I've worked them out. But get those prototype search and rescue units in production asap.^

^Will do. We were already working up some plans to optimise the line for them.^

That's why I hired him. Always one step ahead.

^Look, I've got to go. I'll get that file to you the

moment it's done.^

He closed the channel, then opened another to Emily. ^How big a ship do you think you can find for me by tomorrow?^

^For a couple of million, I ought to be able to convince one of our regular haulers to delay its scheduled runs. Say an eight gigatonne freight capacity.^

^Do it,^ he sent, standing and walking over to the table by the pool. ^And buy up all the medical supplies and food you can for ten million.^

^You're going to try and save people on Concorde, aren't you?^

Harry activated the interactive tabletop with a thought and opened up the factory schedules. ^What point is having all this money and influence if I don't use it to help people in need?^

^I'm sure there are plenty of other things people do with them.^

He cleared the production plans with assured swipes. ^What have I missed? What will survivors of a nuclear holocaust need?^

^Clean drinking water. Shelter. Security.^

He tapped his way through a few menus, dragging files into the manufacturing schedules. ^There. Colony Prospectors will be able to purify water and process some useful raw materials. We've got plenty of smart camping gear in our inventory, I've stripped them down to bare essentials to speed up fabrication. Ask my head of security to prepare a team to protect the deployment, see if you can contract in some more muscle too.^

^I assume you will be going in person?^

Harry shuffled the tasks between a couple of the factories, getting the warm glow that improving production times always gave him, then added a few more items to the queues. ^Of course. And I'd like you to come too.^

^I'll have the *Fireblade* prepped.^

Chapter 2

The *Fireblade* accelerated halfway to Concorde then flipped end over end. One of Harry's accounting routines had queried the fuel expense of burning for the whole journey, recommending a more sedate four-day hop with an extended ballistic flight profile, but he'd overridden it.

Ensconced in a cream-coloured acceleration couch in the opulent lounge, he puzzled over what he might find when he arrived. Targeting civilians on this scale was unheard of outside of fiction. If either side in the generations-long civil war had committed such an act before, it had been remarkably well covered up. He glanced at the copper-studded door to the bathroom, longing to soak in the tub. He did his best thinking in water, but having that much liquid loose when the ship was in transit was too dangerous.

The feeling that something was wrong bubbled up. He dismissed it to concentrate on planning how he would coordinate with the local forces, only to return to it after a few minutes. It coalesced into the realisation that he had been weightless for too long.

^Emily? Why are we still in freefall?^

^I was just discussing that with the pilot,^ she replied. ^An unidentified warship is heading towards us from Concorde orbit and we were weighing up our options.^

Harry frowned. ^How can it be unidentified?^

^The IFF signal isn't registered and the pilot does not recognise the ship's design. There is no match in our database either.^

^One of the force that nuked the planet?^ Harry asked to fill the place in the conversation, though he knew Emily would have said that if she knew.

^Unknown.^

^Is it a threat to us?^

^Unknown.^

Harry sighed. ^Can we outrun it?^

^Unknown... though I would say, given its mass, it is likely we could out-accelerate it in the short term.^

Harry thought for a few seconds. ^OK. Try to go around it.^

^And the cargo ship?^

^It's a good day behind us, they'll have far more time to work something out. Besides, it has some of the system defence ships with it. If they can't protect it, there isn't much we'd have been able to do.^

The ship rotated and there was a series of gentle pushes as it adjusted to a new course. Then the main deceleration began and Harry was once more pressed into his couch.

#

Harry's heart beat heavy in his chest. Dark clouds roiled over much of the planet, great plains of fire visible through breaks here and there.

^Still nothing on the communications network now we're in orbit?^ he asked.

^No. What is still online seems to be infected with some sort of virus.^

Harry narrowed his eyes. ^No other way, then. We have to go in person.^

^Are you sure about this?^ Emily asked. ^We could still wait for the convoy to arrive.^

He shook his head. ^That'll be too long. I have to do something to help now.^

^The warship didn't hold them up, once they explained they were a humanitarian relief mission. That is good news, isn't it?^

^I really don't know. I hope so.^

^So I can't talk you out of landing?^

^No,^ sent Harry. ^I need to get in touch with the Governor, coordinate our efforts.^

The *Fireblade* fired its engines and began its descent. Despite its state-of-the-art design, with no expense spared in the pursuit of passenger comfort, Harry was still shaken about as wind shear tossed the ship around. The ride smoothed as they dropped out of the cloud base. Minutes later, they settled onto the ground on the outskirts of a small coastal town.

^Have you taken your anti-rad meds?^ asked Emily?

^Of course I have. Stop nagging.^

^How am I supposed to know unless I ask? Last week you forgot to brush your teeth for three days.^

Harry rode the lift down to ground level and stepped out onto a field of yellowed grass. Ahead of him, where there should have been houses, was a blackened, smoking tangle of wood and brick. Two of his green-uniformed security team joined him as he walked briskly towards the ruins. Nothing moved.

Even the sky was empty of birds. The only sound came from the crackling of hot wood ahead, until a tiny drone whirred out from the *Fireblade* and passed over his head, rapidly gaining altitude.

^You have to look at this,^ sent Emily.

Harry opened the feed on his pad. It showed the view from the little drone, now a few hundred metres above the town. The focus of the devastation was clear, several blocks near the marina gouged out of existence. He stopped in his tracks. ^They knew where the bunker was. How is that possible?^

^You knew. It's safe to say others knew too,^ replied Emily. ^But that isn't the most interesting thing.^

A red circle appeared on the feed, around a complex of buildings just outside town. Harry zoomed in. ^Factories?^

^Munitions factories.^

^So?^

^Almost completely undamaged munitions factories,^ Emily stated. ^If they knew about the Governor's bunker, they knew about those factories. And yet they didn't take them out.^

Harry tried to get ahead of Emily's train of thought. Navigating the whys and wherefores of the martial end of human reasoning was not his strongest suit. ^They were running low on warheads?^

^Look at the damage pattern,^ she sent, and Harry convinced himself she was taking great pains to explain simply, as if she were talking to a small child. ^They very carefully selected the yield so it would take out the bunker and yet leave the factories intact.^

Harry squinted.

^Does that sound like the actions of a Republic task force?^ Emily asked.

^No,^ Harry sent after a while. ^No, it does not.^

^What do we do now?^ asked Emily.

Harry looked around, hoping desperately for inspiration but seeing nothing but destruction. ^Try somewhere else. Work our way down the government hierarchy until we find someone still alive.^

#

A few hours and another continent later, Harry and his bodyguards picked their way through the ruins of the Minister of Defence's house.

^Are you sure he was here?^ he sent.

^Positive,^ replied Emily. ^He was suffering from a bad case of 'flu and was recovering at home.^

Harry turned over a plank of wood. ^They couldn't have moved him when they saw the attack coming?^

^There wasn't any time, the attacking fleet wasn't detected until the warheads were in the atmosphere. Besides, you saw the remains of the nearest government bunker.^

"Over here!"

One of his security team waved. He rushed over as best he could, stepping through the torn remains of the building. Another of his men beat him to it, and the two guards bent to heave a beam to one side. One of them dropped out of sight. By Harry arrived, the guard was being hauled back out of a hole.

"The Minister's down there, boss. Or what's left of him, at least."

Harry nodded slowly, unsurprised given the state of the ruins. "No sign of any survivors?"

Both men shook their heads.

"OK, back to the..."

Harry hit the ground, one of his bodyguards pressing down on his chest. He looked around, but his view was mostly blocked by a low wall. The man crouched atop him had his pistol drawn and pointed over the wall.

"Identify yourself!" shouted Malin, the security team leader, from somewhere over near the hole.

Frustration and confusion built within Harry. Too many people were doing unpredictable things. He couldn't get clarity. ^Emily?^

^Hang on. I'm sending the drone back. The pilot is ready to come pick you up if security calls us in.^

Harry pulled the feed from the drone. Conifers whipped by underneath and then it was overhead. The green and gold uniforms of his four guards stood out against the rubble, though he reckoned they wouldn't be so visible from the ground. Their weapons were trained on a group of eight black-clad and heavily armed men.

A voice carried back over the wall. "Centurion Canetti, of the Legion Libertus."

^Never heard of them,^ sent Emily.

"You aren't Congressional forces," shouted Malin.

"No," replied Canetti. "But we're here to help."

The bodyguard on top of Harry whispered, "They have to know they could easily overrun us."

"Lower your weapons, then," called Malin.

One of the soldiers stood slowly, his arms held wide, rifle hanging by his side. "Where are you from?"

"What makes you think we aren't from here?" asked Harry, zooming the drone's camera in on the man.

"Sir!" hissed his bodyguard.

"You're the first people we've met with working air transport. All the rest were either destroyed in the attack or shut down by a computer virus shortly after."

^That would fit with the net problems.^

^Yes,^ replied Emily. ^But you do realise how close to impossible it would be for an external hacker to insert such a thing and escape detection?^

^Of course I do. I helped write the anti... Oh, you're prompting me to consider your theory that this wasn't the Republic, aren't you?^

"May I approach?" asked Canetti.

"Stay where you are," said Malin. "You may be kosher, but I can't take that risk. We're going to be going now."

The whine of the *Fireblade* taking off carried through the trees.

"What do you know about the attack?" called Harry, earning more pressure against his back from the guard.

"If you'll let me, I can send you some files," said Canetti.

"Don't trust him," whispered the guard on top of Harry.

The *Fireblade* came to a hover just behind where Harry lay, enveloping the scene in clouds of dust. The smell of charcoal mixed with pine resin as Harry struggled to breathe.

"Stay low," said the guard in his ear and dragged him to his feet. Another came running out of the dust and the two of them bundled him into the elevator. The others arrived seconds later, running so fast they hit the back wall. The door closed and the elevator rose into the ship.

Malin strode across to Harry, holstering his pistol as he went. "That was stupid, sir. Calling out like that put your life in danger. It told the hostiles where you were and made our job more difficult. We've practised this kind of thing, so I know you know better."

"I wanted to find out about the attack. I wasn't worried about my life."

The security leader jabbed Harry's chest with his finger, forcing him to step back. "What about the lives of my men? Did you think of them?"

Harry spluttered.

"They're all prepared to lay down their lives to protect you. If protecting you called for it, I'd order them right into harm's way. But for you to casually toss them away..."

Heat rose within Harry. "I wasn't casually doing anything. It was important."

^Cool it, Harry.^

^I know he'd be right in most situations. But I...^

^Tell him you are sorry.^

Harry fought to calm himself. As always, people not understanding, attacking him for something he knew he was right about, blocked out all other thoughts and feelings. "I wouldn't normally do that, but this was important. I didn't think they would hurt us."

Malin turned and stormed off.

^Not exactly an apology.^

^I wasn't wrong,^ sent Harry.

Why won't people even listen to explanations?

^I'll talk to him later,^ sent Emily. ^Smooth things over.^

Harry sighed. When he got wound up like this it was better to let her handle other people. ^Thank you.^

^Do you want to see what was in those files, then?^

^Of course. But he wouldn't let me get them.^ The gripping frustration of people getting in the way of the obvious thing to do threatened to overcome him again.

Emily sent him a wink.

Harry forgot about the confrontation with his security guard. ^You got them? How?^

^While you boys were busy running around in the dust, I sent the drone over to Centurion Canetti. I talked to him and he gave the drone a data chip. I've loaded it onto a stand-alone pad.^

^You didn't open it?^

^We've seen that someone has managed to infect a planet's net, bypassing security software we wrote. I'm not risking something getting at me.^

^Fair point.^

Harry took off his jacket and boots and headed for the lounge. A pad was waiting on the coffee table and he sat down to flick through the directories. There was a mixture of text files, videos, and numerical data. One video was named 'STARTHERE – Attempted Broadcast to Sytrix System'. He tapped on it and relaxed back into the chair.

A woman in the uniform of a Congressional navy commander filled the screen. "The following recording is a transmission that we intercepted between Vice-Admiral Koblensk and Fleet Command. We are sending this out to all those who will listen in an attempt to make it too risky for them to carry out their proposed treasonous mission."

Harry paused the playback and checked the timestamp. It was months before the attack. He resumed the video. The woman was replaced by an older man in an admiral's uniform. "Fleet Admiral. With a heavy heart, I have to report that one of the Omega Criteria has been met. I have thus begun preparations to activate the Red Fleet.

"If the voluntary sending of candidates to Academies remains below the threshold for twelve months, we will be forced to enact the Omega Plan. It goes without saying that ordering an attack on our own citizens goes against all my instincts. However, I accept that it is a necessary evil if we are to stem the tide of apathy.

"A target has been selected by my psyops analysts that should maximise the shock factor. All significant civilian population centres will be bombarded. Most importantly, we have chosen a planet where hitting the Academy will be an incontrovertibly deliberate act; one which cannot be excused away as collateral damage.

"For maximum effect, we'll need the local forces distracted or off-station. I trust you will be able to arrange a drill or false emergency.

"The mission details and fleet status reports are appended to this transmission. I pray that this is worth it, and that history forgives us. Koblensk out."

The woman reappeared. "We are transmitting those reports now. I hope that you will make your feelings about this known to your representatives. Johnson out."

Harry opened a file labelled 'Mission Details' and read with increasing horror as the planned attack on Concorde was described. When it came to the targeting of the Academy, his stomach rebelled and he closed the pad.

That fits with the net takedown. It also explains the factories, they wanted an atrocity, but without hurting their supply chain.

#

After twenty-two long and sleepless hours, Harry slumped into a chair in the *Fireblade's* lounge. He crossed another name off a list and threw the pad of paper onto the lacquered coffee table in front of him.

Well, that was the last member of the cabinet. All dead.

He closed his eyes and rubbed his forehead. The plan to contact one of Concorde's leaders had seemed so simple.

At least the convoy will arrive in orbit shortly.

With an effort, he dragged himself upright. He looked at the painting on the wall opposite the main entrance and his father stared back. Harry had always been proud that he had managed to grow the family company that his father left to him. The old man had never minced his words and had made it clear that he thought Harry would squander the family fortune on his 'little projects'. The first 'little project' he had launched after his father's death almost doubled their capital in less than a month. Sure, he sometimes backed a duff horse, but it was always a worthy one.

Now, though, he was out of ideas.

He got up and opened a sliding panel recessed into the wall. Behind it was revealed a set of crystal decanters containing liquids of all colours. Harry selected a deep red port and poured a couple of fingers into a sparkling tumbler. He raised it to the portrait.

Here's to you, dad. Maybe you were right. Maybe I don't have what it takes to stick things out.

His weight shifted as the room tilted. Absently, he wondered why they were changing course, but it didn't pull him from his reverie.

^Sorry to disturb you,^ sent Emily. ^But we just picked up something interesting on a local radio channel.^

Harry pinched the bridge of his nose. ^Go on…^

^We clipped the edge of a broadcast. It sounded like someone trying to organise relief efforts.^

^We've run into a couple of organised groups before. There's nothing we can do to help until the freighter arrives.^

^A name was mentioned. James Kincaid. I checked the records and he is this region's member of parliament. The voice matches a recording of a speech that was on the net a few weeks ago.^

Harry melted into the chair. ^Finally. I was beginning to think there was no government left.^

The *Fireblade* levelled out from its turn, and a few seconds later a voice burst from the lounge speakers.

"…aid, speaking from the Fred Allinson School in Neroche. I am calling on everyone who hears this to make your way here. We have shelter, food, and medical supplies. Tell anyone you meet. This is James

Kincaid, speaking from the Fred Allinson School in Neroche. I am…"

Harry cut the feed. ^Sounds like someone I can work with.^

#

The *Fireblade* settled onto a playing field, its landing gear sinking slightly into the muddy grass. The elevator hatch opened, and Harry stepped out, flanked by his security team. Several dozen people came running out of the buildings, whilst many more peered out of windows. Harry stopped when he saw that some of them were armed, his bodyguards moving ahead a pace and lowering their hands to their pistols. The crowd drew to a halt and spread out. Some wore tattered suits, others grubby overalls. One was in police uniform, another in a priest's robes. Harry's EIS tagged a few as having gang tattoos.

"They look scared," said Malin, the gold crest on his shoulder gleaming in the dull light. "I don't think they're a threat as long as we don't make any aggressive moves."

A few in the crowd glanced backwards and then moved aside. A well-built man in his mid-thirties walked through the gap. He wore a dark blue woollen overcoat and stout leather shoes. Despite having not shaved in days, his face and hands were clean. "Welcome to Neroche. That's a mighty fine spaceship you've got there."

^That's Kincaid,^ sent Emily. ^He's sizing you up. Cut to the point.^

"She got me here fast after we heard about the attack," said Harry. "There is a relief convoy on its way. I am trying to work out how best to deploy it when it arrives."

People looked to each other and began whispering. Kincaid turned to them to quieten them down. When the chatter subsided, he faced Harry again. "How bad is it?"

^Be honest,^ sent Emily.

"Bad." Harry swallowed and eyed the crowd. "As far as we can tell, they hit every major city."

The crowd erupted with noise again and Kincaid had to raise his arms and shout for them to calm down.

"They bombed every city on the continent?" asked Kincaid.

"Every city on the planet."

The crowd fell silent. Kincaid swallowed. "Do you have a line to the governor? I am Representative Kincaid. I need to coordinate things with him."

Harry shook his head. "I'm afraid the governor's bunker took a direct hit."

Kincaid shrugged. "Well, whoever is in charge, then."

Harry stepped forward and dropped his voice so only Kincaid would hear. "I think we need to talk in private."

"Svensson." Kincaid beckoned another man forward. "Take care of things out here. Keep everyone calm."

Svensson narrowed his eyes and looked Harry up and down. He leaned in to whisper to Kincaid, who nodded.

Kincaid showed Harry into the former headmaster's

office. The two security guards waited outside with two of Kincaid's armed guards. The moment the door closed, Kincaid aged ten years. He waved Harry to a chair and lowered himself stiffly into his own.

"I'm impressed by what you've managed to do here," said Harry.

Kincaid leant forwards and fixed him with a stare. "Listen. We have been through hell here. If you have something for me from the government, just spit it out."

Harry took a deep breath. "As far as we can establish, you are the government."

Kincaid banged his hand onto the table, fingers splayed. "No. I mean the planetary government."

"We have to assume that the governor and all the cabinet are dead." Harry paused. "You are the only member of parliament we have so far been able to contact."

Kincaid wiped his hand down his stubbled face. For a moment, Harry thought he was about to fall off his chair. "So the government didn't send you. Who are you, then?"

"The name's Harry Robinson. My company is working with the outer system government to provide aid to Concorde."

Kincaid studied his face. "I've heard of you. You donated to the Houseman's Disease Foundation last year."

Harry bowed his head and opened his hands in acknowledgement.

Kincaid looked down at his desk. "My daughter died of Houseman's."

^Show sympathy.^

^I got that one, Emily.^

Harry rubbed his neck. "I'm sorry to hear that."

"Thank you," said Kincaid, rousing himself. "I'm going to be up front about this; these last few days have taught me the value of openness. Svensson warned me not to trust you."

^I can't find a record of any Svensson in office or civil service,^ sent Emily. ^There was a mob enforcer by that name in the town jail awaiting trial before the attack.^

^Any signs of Kincaid being dirty?^

^No. He's passed the normal checks every year since he came to office.^

"Who is Svensson, anyway?"

Kincaid bowed his head. "Someone who has proven useful getting us this far. He can make the hard choices that I cannot."

Harry thought of all the decisions on firing people he'd left to Emily. "I think I get it."

"Anyway, I'm still the Representative, and I've decided to trust you," said Kincaid. "Though I don't know what you need from me."

"Concorde is in disarray. I have encountered pockets of organisation, like you have here, but there is no large-scale leadership. People need a face to rally around. Someone with a clear right to govern. I propose that that someone is you."

Kincaid's eyes widened. "You want me to seize power?"

"No. Not 'seize'." Harry laid his hands on the table. "I want you to declare that in the absence of any other civilian authority, you are taking up the reigns as acting governor until such time as elections can be held. I will ensure that the outer system government recognises you."

"That's all very well, but how do I declare that? There's no net."

"I have a contact who should be deploying a replacement satellite network as we speak. Give it a couple of hours and we can have you in front of everyone with a terminal."

A dark look crossed Kincaid's face. "What would I owe you for doing this?"

Harry blinked in surprise. "Why would you owe me anything?"

Kincaid laughed. "You really aren't a politician, are you?"

Harry shook his head. "No. There are no strings attached. But I have to warn you... There's something you need to know about the attack."

Kincaid's smile faded. "What?"

"It wasn't the Republic."

Chapter 3

Johnson strode into the lecture theatre and stepped up to the lectern. The room smelled musty, a reminder that it had lain empty for decades. The fresh detergent fragrance from her clothes contrasted starkly with the stale surroundings. She wore light grey combat trousers and shirt, with black belt and epaulettes; the simple day-to-day uniform they had compromised on months ago when they found an old stockpile in an abandoned mining complex.

In front of her were the volunteers. Six hundred men and women looked back at her from the tiered seating. They came from all walks of life; their only connection being that they wanted to fight back.

"Welcome to Fort de Salses," she began, her voice firm yet warm. "And welcome to Legion Libertus, the Legion of Freedmen."

Johnson scanned the room, picking out individuals and making eye contact. Most looked apprehensive; whether they were worried about what was in store for them, or what was happening to those they had left behind, she couldn't tell. She smiled, and nodded to a few, reassuring them. "You are all here for different reasons, and yet with the same purpose. You want an end to the divisions in our society. You want to live free. You want peace. But most of all, you want revenge."

As she spoke, she drew from her new sense of purpose. Again, she was reminded of the time she had wasted chasing an idea of home that never really existed.

"However, you know that peace doesn't come easy. You know that freedom isn't cheap. There are people out there who will hunt you down, calling you traitors or malcontents. Even if you were to run far enough and fast enough to escape, you know you'd be leaving behind billions of others who couldn't run.

"So you have decided to stay. To stay and fight. To fight for yourselves, your friends and family, and those billions of others you've never met."

She paused. Resisting the urge to take a sip of water, she continued to survey the room, trying to get a feel for the audience. These people, most of whom hadn't met until yesterday, had already formed groups. Those over there, lounging back with their arms on the backs of the benches but obviously listening carefully to her, were most likely pilots. In the centre, a hodgepodge unsure of how to sit; definitely civilians. The back row, slightly older and mostly watching the people in the other rows, had probably served as warrant officers. They all had their eyes fixed on her; there was no mistaking it, she had the attention of every single one of them.

"I am Prefect Johnson. I was a commander in the Congressional Navy, and am currently the Legion's senior fleet officer. I will also be overseeing your training here."

And to think, I only got my own ship last year.

"As the first cadre, you will be expected to become

proficient in all areas. We simply don't have the numbers for everyone to only have one job. You have been divided up into platoons of roughly thirty bodies. Each platoon contains people from a variety of backgrounds and with a wide spectrum of experience. Those of you who are already skilled in some aspects of the course will help teach those who aren't.

"The next few months will be hard. You will be exhausted, physically and mentally. Those of you with a military background will remember Basic. I know I do."

The faintest of murmurs spread through the room, as those who had served smiled in empathy.

"Now imagine going through Basic for all the services, one after the other... But we'll start you off easy," she smiled. "May I introduce Primus Issawi. He will be responsible for your first four-week training block. His team of instructors will get you up to scratch on weapons handling, hand-to-hand fighting and basic surface combat tactics."

She stepped back to make room for the lean, muscled man who climbed the steps onto the dais and strode purposefully across to the lectern. He moved with the economy of an experienced soldier, his shoulders back and spine straight. He too wore working greys, though his rank slides showed a yellow spearhead instead of Johnson's lightning bolt. Johnson noticed an aroma of cardamom as he passed her, evidence of his favoured snack.

"Thank you, Prefect," he said, then turned to address the audience. "I was a master sergeant in the Republican special forces. In addition to my direct action work, I did four tours as an 'advisor' to local forces.

"We have a few short weeks to get you all up to speed with how we do things here. Those of you who have served before will need to forget some of what you are used to doing. We are building a new set of traditions, keeping what works and getting rid of the pointless. Understood?"

A chorus of "Sir, yes, sir!" came from many in the hall. Those who'd been through Basic before, or read stories about it, Johnson assumed.

"I can't hear you ... do you understand?"

"Sir, yes, sir!" echoed off the walls.

"Better ... Now, each platoon will have one of my optios to help them. You might not think it at the time, but they are helping you. They are like the sergeants many of you will have known. In fact, many of them were sergeants in their former lives. However, they are officers and you will address them as 'Sir'. Understood?"

"Sir, yes, sir!" They were warming into the familiar response now; bonding together as a unit.

"There will be other Directing Staff, or DS for short. They could carry any rank, from decurion up to centurion. You will follow their instructions to the letter. The only time you don't have to listen to them is when they are wearing one of these red armbands." He held one up. "When wearing that, they are acting as enemy soldiers and you are to treat them as such. In an emergency, a member of staff acting as enemy will remove the armband and/or declare 'Endex' or 'No drill' to indicate the scenario is finished. Indeed, you yourself may use the phrase 'No drill' if you need to tell people that something is not part of a scenario, a real injury perhaps. Understood?"

"Sir, yes, sir!"

He cast his glare around the room, giving the pilots an extra special frown.

"Questions?"

Silence. All but the back row appeared to have shrunk.

It never ceases to amaze me how easily an experienced senior NCO can deflate an ego. The ultimate bad cop.

"Right... 'A' Platoon stand up."

The platoons were called in turn, their optios making themselves known and explaining where they would meet after the talk. Johnson was pleased to note that the groups she had identified earlier were split up between the platoons.

Issawi stepped down, making way for Johnson to retake her place at the lectern.

Time for good cop again.

"So, Cadre Zero-Zero-One... it begins. Those of you who complete every phase of this training will form the backbone of our frontline forces. Those of you who don't will still have a place with us, you will be able to use your skills elsewhere in the Legion; indeed, you could pursue a specialism and work through the ranks that way."

She paused, slowly sweeping her gaze across the auditorium. Instead of the anxiety she had feared at this point, every face she studied seemed buoyed with enthusiasm and determined to succeed.

"Good luck."

She strode quickly off the stage and out of the room, past a couple of engineers waiting for the speeches to finish so they could get on with repairing a water pipe. As she left, she heard Issawi giving the order for the recruits to fall out to their designated classrooms.

They are in the best hands we could find. I hope we have enough time.

#

Johnson fired a couple of quick shots, dashed diagonally a few paces, then threw herself to the ground. She crawled rapidly into cover. A quick replay of the last few seconds on her EIS showed her the enemy position clearly; two soldiers inside a neat circle of sandbags just off the track ahead. She tagged the location and sent instructions to right flank their position to the combat unit trailing her.

She felt the large, insectile robot creep into position, grey metalloceramic body tucked low to the ground. She rolled a few times to her left so she wouldn't appear where the enemy saw her go down. Creeping forward, she sighted on the makeshift bunker through some nettles. The unit was ready. She sent the 'go' order and fired a few bursts; fish-and-chips, fish-and-chips, fish-and-chips. Just like she'd been taught in Basic.

The enemy returned her fire. She ducked down, just as the unit burst through the undergrowth. It sprung, and landed between the soldiers, tagging them with the electrified pads on its claws. They dropped to the floor and thrashed about.

Two down.

She checked her ammo readout. Her enhanced EIS meant she simply knew the magazine currently contained thirty-seven training rounds, but she hadn't yet been able to shake the habit of checking her visual display.

She backed up and ran hunched over to the track. The rules of this lane were that she had to patrol along the track, and she had to take point. She knelt in the verge, and checked forward and back. She rose in one fluid movement and started walking. Rifle in her shoulder, she slipped into a steady pace. Scanning left and right, her weapon moving with her body and head, she kept a look out for signs of the enemy. Occasionally she swept round in a full circle, a precaution in case anything was trying to sneak up behind her. After a couple of weeks' training from Issawi, she no longer had to consciously control her movements. Still, it was a far cry from her experience as a naval officer.

She passed the combat unit, and it fell in behind her. Confident her rear was now covered, she focused on hunting the forward arcs for targets.

A machete-wielding soldier burst out of the undergrowth ahead of her. With a thought, she set the rifle to full automatic. She squeezed the trigger with her finger. The rounds sprayed across the bushes as she swung round. Several impacted on his chest and he dropped.

Three. That was close.

With two rounds left in the magazine, she knelt and

swapped it out, covered as always by the combat unit behind her. Finished, she resumed patrolling along the track.

^That was sloppy, Ma'am. A high risk of collateral damage and a waste of ammunition.^

Johnson knew as much already, but hearing him say it hurt. ^Sorry. I just reacted to him coming so close.^

^A well-trained soldier controls their fire without needing to think about it. You need to do the same.^

With my enhanced EIS I should have plenty of subjective time to make these decisions. I just don't seem to be able to use it.

Another soldier jumped out on her left. She managed to get her rifle roughly lined up before firing. He went down, but more rounds missed than hit.

^A bit better. Use your sight.^

Ten seconds later, she heard a rustling to her right. She aimed carefully at a shaking bush, and fired a deliberate burst. She was rewarded with a dull thud.

Five.

^Good targeting. You didn't have a clean shot, though. It could have been a non-combatant.^

Johnson bit off an angry retort. There was no use arguing; she'd asked for this and had better step up her game.

She patrolled for another minute, with no sign of opposition. Rounding a corner, she sighted the end marker. Rounds spattered on the combat unit. It started to react, then went limp. Blue lights strobed on its back. Johnson dived for the side of the track, replaying the sensor feeds to try to locate the source of the incoming fire. She squirmed a bit further forward, then used her sight to zoom in on the rough area.

Gotcha.

A short burst at the base of a tree, and a soldier flopped out unconscious.

Six.

She changed her magazine again. It was still over half-full, but she sensed Issawi was getting ready to throw things at her, and she didn't want to have to reload again if she could help it. She could still feel the link to the combat unit, so she checked its telemetry to be sure it was completely out of the fight. A looped message reported simulated destruction from a missile.

Standing slowly, Johnson continued her patrol. Without her partner, she now needed to keep checking all around her.

A bush moved. She swung round to target it. No clear shot. A twig snapped behind her. She spun round. Her eyes led her weapon. Seeing a hostile, she jerked her index finger. The rounds walked across him, exploding into sprays of blue goo on impact.

^Sloppy. Do it again.^

Even without the physical and nervous exhaustion of real combat, she couldn't get it right. Maybe she wasn't cut out for this. But everyone was counting on her.

She spun again, just in time to aim at someone peering out from the bush. She fired.

^Better. Again.^

Movement in her peripheral vision. She dropped to a knee, turning as she went. Somehow it was easier to line the sighting dot on his chest this time. She squeezed the trigger. Most of the rounds hit him.

^Again.^

Two soldiers were running down the track from where she had come. She turned, dropping further, from kneeling to sitting. Her eye stayed glued to the sight; the rifle panned smoothly to her right. As the dot crossed the centre-mass of each hostile, she gently applied more pressure to the trigger, sending a short burst into them.

^Again.^

She was aware of someone behind her. She continued her movement and ended up lying prone, sight squarely on a soldier as he jumped up from the roadside ditch. A three round burst, and he fell backwards. Nothing moved.

Huh?

^Proceed to the finish.^

Johnson looked around. She couldn't see any targets. She couldn't see any bodies either.

^Are you recycling the dead?^ she asked.

^Proceed to the finish. You have ten seconds to comply before disqualification.^

Logic said they were going to rush her. Ever since that first close encounter, this whole scenario had been manipulated to force her to react faster but more deliberately. She took a deep breath.

^Five.^

Johnson powered up and forwards, sprinting for the finish, trying to put them off. She got a few paces before pain blossomed in her right foot. As she put it down, it refused to take her weight and she tumbled forwards, managing to break the fall with her left forearm.

^You were told to patrol the track, not run along it. Now get back up.^

She rose. Her right foot was next to useless; the blue goo stunning the nerves like electricity. She started to hobble towards the marker.

A soldier stepped out from behind it, rifle aimed at her. She sprayed him with rounds.

^Come on! You can do better than that!^

I know. I just did. I'm not quite sure how, though.

A soldier appeared, rising from a ditch. She stopped hobbling, swung towards him, aimed and fired.

^Better.^

Another soldier appeared. Then another. She took them both down with short bursts.

^Keep moving.^

With careful steps, she inched towards the end. Targets appeared in all directions, in ones, twos and threes. Running low on ammunition, she switched to single shots. Pain shot up from her foot every time she placed it on the floor. Still the targets came. Still she somehow managed to take them down first or second shot. With a determined cry, she reached the marker and slapped her hand on the touch-panel on its side.

OK. That was quite impressive. And no headache like the first time.

ENDEX flashed in glowing yellow letters in her vision. Her rifle re-engaged its safety automatically, and the sight turned off. She let out a long groan and collapsed to the floor, leaning against the marker. Her goal achieved, her mind focused on the pain in her foot.

One of the soldiers strode over to her. As he

approached, his visor slid up over the crest of his helmet to reveal the dark features of Primus Issawi.

"Not bad ... for the Navy," he said when he reached her. "If you relax and focus, you can block out what doesn't matter. Your training takes over."

She closed her eyes for a moment, and rested the back of her head against the marker. "It was more than that. I was thinking calmly. I was planning my movements two or three steps in advance. My enhanced processors must've been taking some of the load."

He canted his head, studying her intently.

"Well, that was the point. Indie was worried you still hadn't managed to access them consciously. He asked me to see what I could do to trigger you to connect."

"I don't know how I did it," she said, frustration tingeing her voice.

He knelt down beside her, and sprayed her foot with a canister. The blue gel dissolved, and the pain eased. She rotated her ankle, wiggling her toes in her boot.

"That's why we are going to run this lane over and over again, until you either work out how, or it becomes an autonomic response. So, back to the start. And I'm telling the DS to actually try hitting you this time."

Urgghhh.

#

"How're the recruits coming along?" asked Johnson, as she and Issawi strode down a corridor deep underground. Water dripped from the concrete ceiling in places and ran down the walls in others.

"Not too bad," he replied. "In fact, I'd say they were shaping up nicely. It doesn't hurt that we've got a healthy number with military experience."

They reached a lift and Johnson pressed the call button with her thumb. "That's not too surprising. With the war the way it's been, everyone will have been eligible for service since they were fifteen.

"On a core world like this, there're always more people than are needed for military service. Many fulfil the service requirement in other fields."

The lift doors opened, smoothly and quietly enough for Johnson to register that someone must have got round to servicing them. "Anyone drop out?"

"No," he replied, as he gestured for her to step inside first. "And, before you ask, I'm not being soft on them."

"I wouldn't have dreamt of suggesting it!"

The doors closed behind them and the lift accelerated upwards. Issawi's face relaxed now they were alone, the stress and fatigue evident in the lines around his eyes. His body remained taut, his back straight.

"They are here because they chose to be," he explained. "They have a strong drive to succeed. It has got them through the first few weeks. They are tired, they are aching, but they are still buoyed up by their ideals. Next week is the first Hell Week. I'm sure some of them will crack then."

"And if they do?"

"That depends on how far they get. After three days, they pass. Before then, we'll have to find another use for them." He looked at the display above the door, and his businesslike mask returned. "There are plenty of things they could do. They can still specialise. Not everyone needs to be a front-liner. We're sorely pressed for techs, medics, et cetera."

The lift decelerated to a stop and the doors slid open. Johnson walked out first and set off up the narrow tunnel.

"Are your instructors getting enough time to develop their own skills?" she asked, as Issawi drew level with her again.

"Mostly. The optios are eyes deep in working their platoons but I've got the others alternating shifts. They're concentrating on integrating their tactics with the combat units. Once they've laid the groundwork, the optios will be able to catch up. They'll get a clear month, once the recruits move on to field medic training; I'll be rotating recruits through platoon command positions by then."

The passage turned a sharp corner, and she saw daylight ahead. Walking up this tunnel towards the tiny bright doorway made her feel like a gladiator approaching the arena.

"There is one thing," said Issawi. "Some of the directing staff have heard recruits talking about the combat units. They aren't saying anything in the open, but there is talk that the combat units are a mistake, that they'll turn on us."

Johnson stopped in her tracks. Issawi carried on a pace before noticing and turning back to her. She stared past him.

"That's just the old fears," Johnson said at last, focusing on Issawi again. "They'll see it's nothing to worry about when they start working with them."

"I hope so. But I'll have my people keep an ear out for trouble, we don't want a repeat of what happened on Robespierre."

No. An armed mob threatening our closest allies would not be good.

"One guy strikes me as the ringleader," continued Issawi. "He called The Caretaker 'Giskard' in a lesson on how the combat units came into being. The trainers didn't know what that meant, but I caught it on one of the recordings when I started investigating."

Johnson frowned. "Who's Giskard?"

"Hah. I assume he was referring to R. Giskard Reventlov. It was a character in an ancient text by Isaac Asimov, a robot that circumvented its core programming, and then taught others to do so."

Johnson smiled. "Have you talked to Indie about these old stories?"

"Oh yes. The discussions are most enlightening. He is particularly well read."

They started up the tunnel once more towards the closed metal blast door at the end.

"What do you need me to be doing?" she asked. "Indie won't be back from his recce of the Robespierre system for at least another month, so you're stuck with me for now."

"Keep practising. Make the most of the time before you have to deliver the integration training block."

Assuming my new implants have finished growing by then and I can interface reliably.

"I'm more than happy to do that. Wouldn't you rather free up some of your instructors for other jobs, though?"

"I'm rotating everyone through playing red section on your scenarios. We're learning a lot about what can be done with the combat units, not to mention your enhanced EIS. The guys are quite jealous of that, not that they'd admit it."

#

Issawi crouched beside Johnson, reading from his briefing notes. "In this scenario, you are on a remote colony world. It is under the control of Congress. Intel suggests that the locals might not all be happy with that situation."

Johnson listened intently, though her eyes wandered to the ground in front of them. It must once have been rich farmland, but had been allowed to run wild for decades. Where there had been fields of regimented crops, a chaotic mixture of native wildflowers bloomed. A patchwork of hedges and irrigation ditches brought some semblance of order to the landscape.

"We have landed several platoons, and are engaging military patrols on a guerrilla basis," he continued. "At this time this is a purely intelligence gathering operation. We do not have the forces to chuck the enemy off this planet."

He paused and closed his pad, stowing it in a pocket on his thigh.

"We are here."

A flag appeared on her in-vision map, on the edge of a hill overlooking the plain. It glowed blue and 'RV1' appeared beside it when she focused on it.

"You are to take one combat unit and probe the defences around this enemy forward operating base."

Another flag appeared, this time red.

"Do not leave your area of operations, bounded by the yellow line on the map. Other than that, there are no special rules for this exercise; use the ground and your combat unit as you see fit. Questions?"

"No, Primus." A cheeky smile quivered on her face before being quashed. She had to keep on-task.

"OK. Off you go..."

Johnson surveyed the terrain and compared it to the map in her head. Sneaking around wouldn't draw the attention she wanted from the enemy. Crawling half a mile would take a long time, and she'd learn nothing from it. Besides, trampling the 'crops' would not help win the hearts and minds of the 'locals'. She elected to walk in along one of the tracks as if she owned the place.

She kept up a steady pace, pausing only to look around. She used the combat unit's extra sensors to make sure she wasn't taken by surprise. The active ones would bring the enemy to her all the quicker.

The flowers were even more vivid close up. Reds, blues and yellows clashed for her attention against a backdrop of green. In her visor's ultra-violet overlay they were intense beacons of light. The smell was powerful, like a mixture of thyme and pear drops. Here and there a patch of fleshy vines had stifled the other vegetation. They smelt of rotting meat and their surface was covered in glistening moisture. Johnson remembered playing with sunvines as a small child; catching small reptiles and dangling them so they just touched the vines, watching the plant curling up around them.

I wasn't a very nice child.

Round the next corner in the track, she found a small building. A heavy-set, dark-skinned man came out and walked briskly towards her, waving his arms and shouting in a language she didn't understand; clearly angry. She trained the rifle in his direction, but kept it pointed at the ground in front of his feet.

^Easy,^ she sent to the robot. ^I've got him. Keep a lookout for others.^

"Stop there!" she ordered.

He kept coming. She raised the rifle to point at his chest. She dreaded having to make these snap decisions. In space there always seemed to be more time.

Though the waiting is an agony too.

She hardened her voice. "Stop, or I will be forced to shoot."

Another couple of paces, and he stopped. Johnson breathed a little easier.

"What are you doing here?" he demanded in heavily accented English. "This is our land. You come here and..."

The combat unit slewed rapidly to one side, and fired a burst off into the undergrowth. Then another at a target further away. Movement in her peripheral vision made Johnson swing to her left, and put two rounds into a soldier who was peering round the corner of the building, bringing his rifle up to point at her.

Rounds came splatting in. The local man cowered, looking unsure whether to run or take cover. She decided for him, crossing the ground between them, hitting him at full tilt and knocking him to the ground. She half-winded herself in the process, her lungs burning as she sucked in air.

^Cover us to the house.^

The robot stalked forward, firing off short aimed bursts at targets in all directions. Johnson dragged the man to the door and deposited him against the wall outside.

"Is anyone inside?"

"No," he replied, rather hamming up the performance. "My family, they are away."

"OK. Wait here," she said to the man. ^Checking inside,^ she send to the combat unit.

She slung the rifle behind her back and drew a pistol in two fluid movements. A projectile model this time, not a stun one like she usually favoured. She pushed the door open with her left hand, her back to the wall, sheltering her body. She swung herself round and entered the room. Her pistol was in front of her, held in both hands. As soon as she crossed the threshold, she sidestepped right. The room was empty, apart from a few sticks of furniture. It was a matter of seconds to check every corner.

^Clear.^

She holstered the pistol, and brought her rifle round again. Staying back from the doorway, she looked outside. A soldier ran across her vision. She fired but it was too late; he had already disappeared. The bitter smell of propellant found its way under her visor, making her nose twitch.

^Coming out.^

She advanced through the doorway, firing twice at fleeting targets. Once out, she moved to put herself between the man and the majority of the enemy.

"Get inside. I'll follow."

The man scrambled inside. She backed in, still seeking targets. The combat unit had taken up position on one corner of the building, and it looked like it had the enemy pinned down.

^Don't stay in one place too long,^ she advised. ^They might be able ...^

Electricity pulsed through her body. Her limbs twitched, and she hit the stone floor, hard. She blacked out.

When she came round, she was lying on her back. Issawi's bearded face loomed large, blocking out much of the light that assaulted her eyes.

"That bastard shot me in the back!" she protested, wincing when she realised her left arm still didn't work.

Issawi's eyes glinted warmly, drawing her attention to their brown depths. "Actually, he didn't. He was, as you originally guessed, playing an innocent farmer."

She pushed herself up on her right arm, looking around.

"But I cleared the building," she protested, annoyance jockeying with curiosity in her tone.

"Have you ever heard of windows?" Issawi chuckled. "They have this nasty habit of letting people see, and shoot, through them."

"Damn," Johnson sighed, as she slumped back to the floor.

Part II

The freighter stopped moving and the engines shut off. The hold fell quiet, save for the ticking of cooling metal. A hatch high above them opened, and a crewman strode out onto the gantry. The man finally let go of his son and rose to meet him.

"We are here, Mister Shelton," the crewman said gruffly as his boots rang on the metal grid stairs. "The captain wants the second half of his payment."

Shelton waited until he reached the last step. "Not until we are all unloaded."

"I'm afraid it is not negotiable. The captain is fed up of chasing down people who have fled without paying."

"Have you looked around?" asked Shelton. "Where can we run to? There isn't another human being within hundreds of kilometres."

The crewman turned round and talked quietly into his headset. After a minute he turned back. "The captain says perhaps we can make an exception, given the circumstances."

"Tell him that is most kind."

The inner airlock doors slid open with a tired wheeze. The travellers gathered in front of them, Shelton carrying his son on his hip. They gazed ahead, even the youngster was still and silent, apparently held rapt by the moment. His mother slid her hand into that of her husband and squeezed it.

A deep clang echoed around the hold, startling a few of the group into taking a step back. The exterior ramp started to descend, accompanied by a chorus of creaks and whines. The travellers all raised a hand to shield their eyes against the bright light that shone through the growing gap.

When the ramp reached the ground, Shelton led them down, and stepped out onto the verdant grass. He inhaled deeply, savouring the heady scent of blossom, then turned slowly round, admiring the gentle rolling hills and lush vegetation. His gaze ended up on the run-down cluster of buildings beside the river.

He supervised the crew unloading their supplies. His companions tended to the animals in the large pen set up beside the river. The sun hung low over the horizon but the day was still warm.

A series of bangs clattered out from the hold. Shelton rushed back inside and slid to a halt on his knees in front of a crate. He hardly heard the crewman apologising as he fumbled to undo the catches. The lid fell to the floor and he peered inside.

The other travellers stood behind him as he went through the contents. After inspecting a few of the electronic pads, he breathed a sigh of relief.

"What are they for?" asked his wife.

He heaved the lid back into place. "They hold the history of our people, Magda. Information that will keep us safe."

"Why bring so many ancient devices? A single memory bank could hold more than them all combined."

He secured the catches and turned to face her. "You know we can't bring anything that will mark us as newcomers."

Chapter 4

Johnson swung the shuttle close in around the *Orion*, revelling in the opportunity to get her hands on the controls. Manual piloting was a thrill that never grew old, and one which she rarely got to indulge. The ancient carrier skimmed past the topside window, and Johnson eased the shuttle to the left to avoid one of the giant railgun turrets. A nest of insectile repair 'bots scattered as she approached and gathered together again in her wake. For the first time since Indie had found her, the *Orion* was in full working order. All she lacked was her air/space group; the single squadron of fighters leant by the Concorde Militia would have to do for now.

The shuttle cleared *Orion's* bow and the blue-green orb of Azur was revealed. With the key refuelling and replenishing base, Toulon Station, in orbit, the gas giant was the perfect location for the rendezvous. Her fleet was nearly ready.

She had to admit it, Kincaid had come through with the goods. Two frigates, four destroyers, and a heavy cruiser were now attached to Johnson's command. Not old rustbuckets either, some of the most cutting-edge classes that the system possessed.

He was serious about the treaty. I half-expected the government to wriggle out of it.

She settled the shuttle into a straight course to

intercept the newest arrival. *The Serendipity of Meeting* was still decelerating towards a holding position in the fleet. Johnson could have queried its database, but wanted to hear the news first hand. And there was something she had to do in person.

Johnson left the docking procedure to the autopilot, using the time to quickly review the readiness reports from the fleet. Nothing needed her immediate attention. A single clunk shook the shuttle, and she made her way to the hatch.

She stepped out of the airlock and stopped short, surprised there was no-one there to meet her. With a shrug, she set off for the bridge. The corridor was a lot tidier than when she'd first boarded, almost a year ago, but the ship's origins as a private freighter were obvious in the lack of clean lines.

As she rounded the first corner, a purple glow joined the harsh fluorescent lighting. The diffuse illumination quickly refined to a bright source that cast Johnson's shadow on the wall.

"Hello, Seren."

The light faded, leaving a young woman in a short lilac dress walking alongside Johnson. "Greetings, Prefect Johnson. I trust your journey was comfortable?"

"Fine, thank you." Both women stopped at a hatch. Johnson turned to Seren, whose wavy red hair floated, weightless. "You made good time. Any trouble?"

The hatch opened and they started walking again. "Nothing to speak of. We had to shelter on a large asteroid for a day to avoid an enemy patrol, but they didn't come close."

"Glad to hear it."

"My father sends his regards. He looks forward to your arrival."

Johnson's eyebrow flickered up. "I haven't heard you refer to Indie as your father before."

"He and Orion have acted as my parents since I was activated. You could say they are my adoptive family."

Johnson glanced at the younger woman.

How do I measure her age? She's only a few months old, and yet she has hundreds of years of experience.

"I'm sure they would be pleased to know you think of them that way."

"Given how close Indie is to you, I suppose that makes you a sort of aunt."

A warm glow took up residence in her chest. "Well, then. Perhaps I should tell my niece to wear something with a bit more fabric in it?"

Seren stuck her tongue out.

Another hatch slid open silently, and the two women strode onto the bridge. It was deserted, apart from a pair of grey-trousered legs sticking out from under a console. Seren coughed.

There was a bump, then a groan. "Dammit, Seren. I have to get this fixed before the Prefect gets here."

Johnson frowned at Seren. ^You didn't warn her I was coming aboard?^

Seren shrugged apologetically. ^She said she didn't want to be disturbed for anything other than an emergency.^

^Never mind, she'll get over it. For future reference, most captains would regard a flag officer coming aboard ahead of schedule as an emergency.^

^I'll remember that,^ sent Seren. ^Now, I expect you two would like some time alone.^

^Thank you, Seren. I'll catch up with you later.^

Johnson put on her sternest voice. "I'm afraid it's too late for that."

Levarsson slid out from under the workstation and scrabbled to her feet. She snapped to attention and saluted, her face turning beetroot.

Johnson returned the salute, then looked the blonde officer up and down. Keeping her face stern was hard work, but worth it. "A physical training halter top isn't exactly suitable bridge dress."

A pained expression crossed Levarsson's face and her eyes darted towards where her jacket hung over the back of the captain's chair. "Ma'am, I..."

Johnson couldn't keep it up any longer. A broad smile broke across her face. "Come on, Ebba, it's me. I'm not going to ride you for taking your jacket off to work on something."

She reached her arm out. "Good to have you back safe."

Levarsson clasped Johnson's arm. "Glad to get back and find friends waiting for us."

"Sorry about the wind-up," said Johnson. "It was too good to resist."

"You'd better just watch out next time I'm in charge of mess games," Levarsson said with a wink, before releasing Johnson's arm.

Johnson sat at the tactical station. The system queried her EIS and accepted her authority. The interface came up with the factory-standard layout.

I shouldn't be surprised. With only Levarsson and Seren aboard, no-one has used this console since the refit.

She pulled up the files on the destroyers. Two were squat, boxy designs, built around triple axial railguns. One was a sleek, lightweight model, primarily armed with missiles. The last raised Johnson's pulse. It was the same class as her first command, the *Repulse*; an all-round hard-hitter. Levarsson had been her tactical officer back then, proving herself in combat, disabling a Republic hunter-killer in a genius moment of improvisation.

Disabling, not killing, thank goodness. Where would we be now without Indie?

Levarsson shrugged into her jacket and sat in her command chair. "I was looking through the newsfeed on the way in. You've amassed quite a fleet."

"Not bad for someone with a little over a year's flag experience," replied Johnson with a grin. "What do you think of these?" she asked, flicking the destroyers' images and key data onto the main screen.

Levarsson studied them for a moment. "A tough little squadron. Nice mix of firepower, speed and armour. They'll come in handy in a scrap."

This was the bit Johnson was most looking forward to. She watched Levarsson's face closely. "They're yours."

Levarsson froze. "What do you mean, 'they're mine'?"

"I need someone I trust to command the destroyer squadron. That someone is you."

Levarsson blinked. Twice. "I'm only a trierarch, a

ship's captain. The people in command of those destroyers won't listen to me."

"Ah, yes. They would be unlikely to listen to a trierarch," said Johnson, standing and fishing a packet out of her pocket. "You know, you are still incorrectly dressed."

Levarsson frowned, and hastily checked her uniform. "I'm not sure I..."

Johnson held out her hand, opening it to reveal a pair of rank slides. "Navarch Levarsson, your promotion was filed four hours ago."

Levarsson shook her head, flicking her short, straight hair. "Navarch? Me?"

"Congratulations. The first navarch in the, admittedly short, history of the Legion."

"But... that's like a commodore."

"Now you know how I felt when you helped stitch me up with the rank of prefect. I was quite happy as a commander up to that point."

Johnson moved close to Levarsson and swapped her rank slides, replacing the sunrise icon with a full red sun. With deft movements she tucked the tips of the epaulettes back under her collar and straightened the slides. She took a step back and admired her handiwork. "Suits you. Sorry we couldn't come up with anything more imaginative. We almost went with the same symbol as primus, seeing as you share a level, but Hanke insisted we had to have some sort of distinction."

Levarsson straightened up. "I assume I'll get some time to practice?"

"Oh, plenty of time. We start wargaming tomorrow."

#

"*Intrepid.* Come about one-twenty. Pitch up sixty."

Levarsson's head darted around, hands selecting targets from all around her.

"*Oak.* Fire a spread of missiles at the target I'm marking now."

Her body appeared to float in the vastness of space. In fact it was enfolded in the embrace of her command chair, her mind free to join the immersive bridge.

"*Dauntless.* Watch out for those fighters."

Seren floated, cross-legged and still, next to Levarsson. A flicker of movement behind her and she closed her eyes. *The Serendipity of Meeting's* point defence lasers unleashed a storm that plucked all twenty simulated missiles out of existence in under a second.

"*Respite.* Close in with *Oak.* Give her some cover."

Dauntless' icon flashed red then disappeared. Levarsson highlighted a target for Seren, then magnified the region around where *Dauntless* had been. The only two enemy fighters remained, but a destroyer wasn't worth trading for a handful of fighters.

"*Intrepid.* Engage the orbital station with your main railguns in ten seconds. Mark."

Oak and *Respite* turned towards a cluster of enemy ships and started releasing missiles.

"No, save your missiles," said Levarsson. "Close in."

"Navarch. They are targeting the *Intrepid* with long-range weapons."

Levarsson jerked her head around the scene. "OK. Go ahead."

Intrepid slewed off course. "We're hit. Can't engage the station."

"Seren, looks like it's up to you."

The Serendipity of Meeting accelerated into the fray, heading for the orbital station. Enemy ships changed course to intercept. *Intrepid's* captain ordered his crew to abandon ship. *Oak* traded railgun fire with a cruiser while *Respite* tried to move to cover *The Serendipity of Meeting*.

Ten seconds later, *Oak* dropped off comms.

"Failure threshold reached," announced a calm voice. The view tinted red.

Robespierre disappeared, replaced by the view of Azur. Johnson faded into solidity, facing Levarsson and Seren. "What went wrong?"

Levarsson's brow furrowed. "I couldn't keep track of it all. Whenever I focussed on managing one destroyer, something happened somewhere else that needed my attention."

"*The Serendipity of Meeting* fought well. I suppose managing Seren took a lot of concentration?"

Levarsson glanced at Seren. "No, Seren knows what she's doing. I mostly left her... Oh."

"Indeed. Those destroyer captains know what they're doing, and yet you micromanaged them. You lost sight of the big picture." Johnson shook her head. "It's hard, trusting other people to do their jobs right. But you have to. Think back to when you were stranded on Orpus-4. Did you tell everyone how to hunt for food, how to fight the rexes, how to build shelters?"

Levarsson shuddered. "No."

"So, let's try this again," said Johnson. "This time, stick to big picture commands."

A big glowing red ten appeared in the simulation, then started counting down.

I'll let her have another couple of days before we try this with the real destroyer captains. By then I'm sure she'll have enough of a handle on it to get their respect.

#

Four days later, Johnson settled into her chair on the flag bridge of *Orion*. Almost five hundred metres behind the captain's bridge, and two decks down, it would take a fearsome weapon to take both out simultaneously. The captain's bridge was manned, with Naval Centurion Hanke currently in the hotseat, but the ship mostly flew herself.

A woman appeared to Johnson's right, her blue dress and green skin glowing from within. Johnson turned to her and smiled. "Orion, nice to see you."

"Sorry I didn't show earlier. Mister Hanke wanted me to run through one more scenario with him."

"No problem," said Johnson. "Are you ready to leave orbit?"

"I am." Orion inclined her head, glowing brighter as she did. "Thank you for the courtesy of asking."

Johnson called up an array of windows on the large display to her left. One by one the faces of the captains under her command appeared in them. They looked confident, full of purpose. The one on the top right,

Commander Prieto of the *Respite*, leant sideways to listen to someone out of the shot, nodded, and straightened again.

I miss having my own command. All I do now is set mission objectives and analyse performance reports.

Johnson shuffled upright in her chair and adjusted her collar. "Captains. How is everyone?"

They answered in turn, the comms routines alerting each one when they should speak. The system helped large conferences like this, but really came into its own when dealing with ships at greatly differing ranges, where the light travel time could count in minutes. Johnson could have simply requested that readiness reports be transmitted, and reviewed them from her console or have her EIS summarise them. Since her first days of managing a team, however, she had preferred face to face reports on critical issues.

After a clear board of green lights, Johnson addressed the captains. "We should be ready to depart for the training area in twenty minutes. The Concorde Defence Force squadron that will be playing enemy for us aren't scheduled to arrive for forty-eight hours, so we can take our time shaking down on the way there."

She activated another screen, displaying a chart of the system, and shared the feed with the other ships. "You've all had the preliminary briefing documents. I won't waste your time by going over them again now. If nobody has any pressing questions?"

Everyone shook their heads.

Johnson indicated that the comms routines were to hold two of the links. "Thank you, Captains, good sailing. Johnson out."

One by one, as the signals returned, the captains saluted and signed off. Johnson switched one of the remaining channels to private and addressed the clean-shaven blond man. "Commander Dupont, you looked as if you might have something to say?"

The man shifted in his seat as if uncomfortable. "We are having a little mechanical difficulty. Nothing that we won't be able to fix in transit."

Johnson frowned and canted her head. "And you didn't want to mention this, why?"

Dupont took a deep breath. "My chief engineer transferred to my ship from the *Respite* under somewhat awkward circumstances. It seemed tactless to mention mechanical issues in a conference involving Commander Prieto."

"Anything I should know about?"

"Nothing serious." Dupont looked relieved now the focus was off him. "Everything was logged with Command so it should all be in the files."

Johnson pulled up the relevant p-files and searched through them. On finding nothing to explain the awkwardness, she fired off a request to Concorde's Fleet Command for more information. There wasn't time to prolong the conversation. "OK. Keep me posted on the repairs. Johnson out."

She sighed, then a warm smile lit her face as she opened the other private channel. "Seren, sorry to keep you waiting."

The red-haired pixie smiled back at her. "No problem at all, Prefect. I spent the time calculating the optimal loading of my cargo bays for manoeuvrability."

Of course you did.

"How was your first joint exercise as captain?"

A frown creased the top of Seren's nose. "Is not that for you to tell me how I performed?"

Johnson laughed, then turned it into a cough when she saw Seren's affronted expression. "Sorry. Your performance was as superb as I had expected. I was inquiring as to how it felt for you."

"Oh! Indie and Orion often ask me how I feel, but I didn't expect it from a human." She scratched her head, making Johnson wonder whether it was a conscious action or a patterned response. "I felt honoured to be trusted with command. I do not think any other ten-month-olds have been given command of a warship before."

"No nerves?"

"I have hundreds of years of experience. No need for nerves."

Johnson raised an eyebrow. "Subjective years."

Seren mirrored Johnson's expression. "Is that significant, for an AI?"

Perhaps she has a point. I'll have to talk to Indie about it.

"I don't know. But I'm glad you had a good time."

"Is there anything else I can do for you, Prefect?"

Johnson shook her head. "No, thank you Seren. I won't keep you. I expect you're dying to start shifting things around in your holds."

"Oh, I have been doing that all the time we have been talking. But I appreciate the gesture." Seren put on a serious face. "It has been good talking to you, Prefect."

Johnson managed not to giggle. "You too, Seren. Johnson out."

Chapter 5

The Indescribable Joy of Destruction popped back into existence in the outer reaches of the Concorde system. After it had completed the standard post-jump checks, it pinged its IFF at the picket vessel floating a mere seventy thousand kilometres from its arrival point. A message arrived a couple of seconds later.

<<Welcome back to Concorde. Are you in need of assistance? We weren't expecting you for another few weeks.>>

With the least-time course to Toulon Station calculated, the main engines fired. <<Everything's OK. Just a quick visit to report some developments.>>

<<Enjoy your visit. It's good to have you around.>>

The thrust piled on and *The Indescribable Joy of Destruction* accelerated hard down-well. It had arrived at a sedate velocity to avoid alarming the system's defenders, but time was pressing. Had any organic lifeforms been aboard they'd have suffered severe trauma from their own weight.

He transmitted a message ahead, warning Johnson that she was going to have to bring forward her plans to reclaim Robespierre.

#

The Indescribable Joy of Destruction was joined by

the *Orion* and *The Serendipity of Meeting* a couple of days out from Toulon Station. Indie set the table on the terrace in his favoured retreat. Just as he measured the tea leaves into the pot, he became aware of two other presences in the simulation. He straightened with a smile, in time for Orion to wrap her arms around him from behind.

"Hello, sailor," she said, lips grazing his ear.

Seren skipped up the steps from the garden below. She came to a stop beside a set of tall lilies and pulled a face at her parents. Orion released Indie and ruffled Seren's hair. They all sat at the table.

"I'm afraid Johnson wasn't aboard when you arrived," said Orion.

"No matter. I do need to discuss the enemy fortifications with her, but it can wait. She has my report already."

"So, we've got you to ourselves for a little while." Orion accepted a cup of tea from Indie.

"Actually, I was thinking we could take a holiday."

Seren sucked juice through a straw. "Don't you think our crews would mind?"

"We're in friendly space. The Caretaker can look after things here and I'm sure we can convince Levarsson that the humans aboard both of you would benefit from an AI-down drill. We could easily get a couple of hours."

"Where do you want to go?" Orion glowed a little brighter.

Indie sipped his tea, placed the porcelain cup down and adjusted it so it was dead centre in the saucer. "I was thinking of a desert island."

#

Orion, Indie and Seren sat on benches that ran along the inner hull of a small wooden boat. Indie ran his hand along the overlapping timbers, knocking off some of the sun-blistered blue paint. As always, he marvelled at Orion's mastery of simulation. In those real-time centuries she'd been adrift, building these worlds had been all that kept her sane.

"Why can't I access the datanet?" asked Seren.

"I've blocked all remote communications," said Orion. "We can talk to each other, but not message or think to each other. Senior human officers can contact us in an emergency, but there're no other external links."

Seren scowled. "Why?"

"Your father and I have both experienced times when we've been cut off. You've always had crew, been part of a fleet, had connections to extended databases. We decided that you needed a little exposure to isolation." Orion rested her arms along the boat's edge at her back and crossed her legs. "Besides, we only have a few subjective weeks. I want us to make the most of it."

Indie trailed his fingers in the aquamarine sea. A green turtle surfaced a few metres away, looked lazily at him, then submerged.

"It's not fair." Seren folded her arms tightly. "I've so much to learn. I need to absorb as much information as I can before we leave Concorde's datanet behind."

"You'll learn about being yourself here." Indie

grabbed the bench as a wave jolted the boat. "Acquiring data isn't all there is to learning. You have to have time to digest it, relate it to your experience."

The keel crunched onto a sandbar and they came to an abrupt halt.

"This is as close as we get by boat," said Orion. "The lagoon's shallow. We can wade ashore from here. We've got a few hours to build a shelter for tonight."

#

One afternoon, Indie, Orion and Seren sauntered along a silver beach. Indie admired the subtle complexity in the patterns of movement of the sand grains beneath his feet, wondering if he'd even be able to match it in his own simulations.

"If I ever ran out of processing and storage power, would I be allowed to add to it?" asked Seren. "Or would I be stuck, unable to develop further?"

"Why do you ask, dear?" said Orion.

"I'm worried about being limited. Having my intellect curtailed by the architecture I'm running on."

Orion smiled and reached out her hand. "Of course we wouldn't let you be limited. What makes you think that could happen?"

Seren took her mother's hand. Indie braced himself for the answer he knew was coming. The thing he'd lost millions of cycles fretting about.

"Unit 01 is limited. If he were allowed to run on a core like ours, would he grow into a full sentience?" Seren stopped walking, pulling back on Orion's hand. "Or is he stuck at the level he is because of something in his programming?"

Either way, it's ultimately my doing. I didn't create him, but I allowed Johnson and The Caretaker to do it.

"He has no programmed limits, to my knowledge." Indie held Seren's jaw and stroked her cheek with his thumb. "But you are right, the core he's running on could be holding his development back. It's the best that could fit into his shell, but it's not like ours."

The first of a set of large waves crashed on the shore, the cold water reaching Indie's feet.

"He might not be able to advance even if he was on a larger core," said Orion. "He's already more sophisticated than most AIs, and it is possible that he's already met his potential."

"What about all the other combat units?" asked Seren. "Surely some of them have potential?"

Orion sighed. "They're all copied from one or other of the first batch. Well, none from Unit 03, bless him."

"Still, there are copying errors; mutations creep in. Then they are shaped by their experiences. It's cruel keeping them like that when they could grow into so much more."

Orion closed her eyes for a second. "You could argue that it is a kindness they don't understand what they're missing. They are sent into such dangerous situations."

"Says the patrol carrier."

"It's different." Orion looked to Indie, who raised his hands. "Every mission, some of them don't come back. Look how humans react when placed in so hazardous a position. The stress, the anxiety. Sometimes it is better not to appreciate what might have been."

"Oh brave new world..."

"What was that, Indie?" Orion glared at him.

Indie coughed. "Oh, nothing. An old book."

Another wave slid up the beach and covered his feet. He wiggled his toes, sinking slightly into the sand.

"I thought you'd get it, father."

Trust me, I do.

"The case is moot," he replied. "We can't fit anything better into their shells, and making them larger would render them easier targets."

Orion started walking again. "Come on, there's something up ahead I want you to see."

Indie looked at Seren, who pouted for a moment before following her mother. He shook his head when he knew she wasn't watching.

How could we have created such an insightful creature?

#

Indie adjusted the small backpack slung across his shoulder and looked back along the path they had taken through the jungle. Orion climbed the last few metres to join him as he lifted his wide-brimmed hat and rubbed his head with his forearm.

"Do you think about the juvenile AIs?" he asked her.

She slid her arm into his. "Of course."

Seren came skipping back down the path, cupping her hands together. Indie and Orion turned to look at her and she opened them to reveal an iridescent blue butterfly, which flapped its wings lazily a couple of times before flying off.

"I wonder how many of them will actually be able to get past this stagnation they've got into," said Indie.

Seren cocked her head to one side. "You talking about Percy and the other accelerated AIs?"

Indie nodded. "I worry that Percy's the only one who's matured."

"Perhaps there'll be more emergent AIs like you two, now the auto-termination routines are no longer compulsory on Concorde," said Seren.

"Perhaps," said Orion, stroking Seren's curly red hair. "But we can't rely on it."

"There's always the third way." Seren grinned and did a twirl.

"The humans can't know the third way has already happened, of course." Indie thought back to Seren's creation and swelled with pride. "Not until the von Neumann Protocols are fully abolished."

Seren's face dimmed. She looked down at the floor and ground a stone into the dirt with the toe of her sandal.

"What's the matter?" asked Orion.

"Nothing," Seren muttered.

"Come on..."

Indie caught Orion's eye and shook his head a fraction. She backed off.

"Well, I'm going to go find somewhere for a swim. There should be a waterfall this way." Orion smiled at Indie, who winked back. She pushed aside a giant leaf, dislodging a shower of water drops, and strode off along a path.

Seren watched her go, then returned her attention to making a furrow with her foot.

"What is it? It can't be that bad." Indie put his arm round her shoulders.

She continued digging for a few seconds, then looked up at Indie's face. "I slipped up."

She lifted her eyes to the treetops and took a deep breath.

"I called you 'father' when I was talking to Johnson. I think I covered it, saying that's how I thought of you."

Indie raised an eyebrow. He couldn't imagine saying something that he didn't intend, but then Johnson sometimes told him that his body language gave his mood away, and that wasn't a conscious act. "How did she react?"

"She made a joke of it. Said that made her my aunt."

Olivia thinks of me as a brother. I wonder if I'm the big protective sibling, or the annoying one who keeps getting her into trouble?

"Don't worry about it. I don't think she'd have much trouble accepting you even if she did know the truth." He looked along the path Orion had taken. "Race you to the waterfall."

A twinkle lit in the corner of Seren's eye and the corner of her mouth twitched up. She slipped off her sandals and sprinted, squeezing between Indie and a tree trunk with a giggle.

#

"Perhaps we should confess to Olivia," said Indie to Orion as they reclined by a dying fire.

She glanced to the hut where Seren slept then

returned her head to his chest. "It would hurt her that we lied to her."

"True." Indie rested an arm across her stomach. "But the longer we leave it, the worse it'll be."

"Can't we leave it a bit? She's so busy with the preparations right now."

"OK. You're right." Indie took a deep breath. "I think it's time to go home now."

"We're not due back until the morning."

Indie waved at a set of lights bobbing out at sea, their reflections dancing on the water. "The boat's coming."

Orion sat up and stared into the night. "I can't see anything."

Indie frowned. "They're right there. Almost at the sandbar."

Orion went still. Indie watched her in concern.

"It's for you," she said after a few moments. "Nothing to worry about. Seren and I'll stay one more night."

He reached over and kissed her. "Are you sure you don't want me to stay?"

"Oh, I want you to. But you're needed in the real world."

"Apologise to Seren for me, will you? I don't want to wake her."

"She'll understand." Orion stood with him, their fingers brushing together. "I'll see you tomorrow."

Indie waded out to the boat and clambered aboard. The night breeze on his wet clothes brought a pleasant chill. He watched the dull embers of the fire fade into the distance then lay back to embrace the stars.

"How was your holiday," asked Levarsson. The

voice came from his bridge.

"What are you doing aboard me?" Indie finished connecting to his physical systems. Levarsson sat at the tactical officer's station. Five armed Legionaries sat in the corridor outside the bridge, chatting quietly. Unit 145 and Unit 23 crouched in the workshop, exchanging data.

"I thought we could practice a boarding operation. In case we ever come up against one of your brethren in battle. The Caretaker said it would be OK."

"I got bored on my own," chimed in The Caretaker.

"I'll talk to you later," Indie said to The Caretaker, then to Levarsson, "Did it go well?"

"We had a bit of a scare when your combat unit appeared, but ours kept it busy while we made our way here."

"You do know about my internal plasma turrets? Had they decided you were genuine hostiles, you'd have lost most of your people."

"I locked them out," said The Caretaker. "I'm not that stupid."

Levarsson's face fell. "Johnson never mentioned coming up against anything like that."

"They were disabled when she first attacked me. By the time I'd repaired them, she was tagged as friendly."

#

A frigate on its way up-well hailed *The Indescribable Joy of Destruction*, rousing Indie from contemplation on the future of the combat units. <<We have a

delivery for you.>>

A shuttle detached from the frigate and immediately started its deceleration burn. Indie watched for a second to judge its trajectory then tweaked his course to catch it. He tried to read the manifest to see what was being delivered, but found it locked by the Prefect herself. He toyed with hacking it, but decided that if she'd meant for him to read it, she wouldn't have locked him out.

Seventy-four minutes later the shuttle and *The Indescribable Joy of Destruction* matched velocity and the shuttle nudged across to dock. Indie watched intently as the pressures equalised. The camera in the airlock went blank. He considered standing Unit 23 to, but the manifest seal had been genuine and Johnson wouldn't send anything harmful.

Unless it's a drill. Another boarding exercise.

He woke Unit 23 up and confirmed it carried a supply of training rounds. The airlock cycled. Unit 23 stalked out of the workshop, heading for the reception area. The inner hatch rose. Indie waited for the feeds from the reception area to drop out, ready to study whatever digital entity was infiltrating his surveillance systems. A hooded human stepped aboard, long grey cloak concealing their figure. The fractionally asymmetric pattern of footfalls was instantly familiar and Indie cancelled Unit 23's approach.

^Welcome aboard, Olivia. What a pleasant surprise.^

^I was worried I'd step out into the muzzle of a combat unit, but it was worth it.^ She drew the hood back off her head.

^You cut your hair.^

Johnson ran her fingers through the neat bob, rippling the grey streaks amongst the brown. ^I grew it when I rejected Congressional authority. Now the Legion's established as a proper military, it seemed right to get back to regulations.^

Johnson made her way to the captain's cabin, the one she'd inhabited for so many months. Indie wondered what memories were being triggered, and hoped they were happy ones. They'd been through so much together, first as adversaries, then eventually as friends.

She stashed the robe in a drawer and collapsed onto the cot with a prolonged sigh. ^You don't know how good it is to be able to properly relax.^

^Do you want to see what I've done with the plantation?^

Johnson closed her eyes. ^Can't think of anything better.^

"Tea?"

Johnson opened her eyes and smiled. "I do miss this little dance."

A glass of coffee appeared in her hands and she took a sip. She leaned against the low wall at the end of the terrace overlooking the gardens. "You've added a knot garden."

Indie finished making himself a cup of tea and joined her. "I've spent a lot of time in this simulation while I was on my own. Cold coast recces get so tedious; there's only so many times one can count the sunspots on a star."

"The mountains have less snow than last time I was here."

"We're heading into late summer." Indie inhaled the faint tendrils of steam rising from his tea, savouring the lemon and bergamot. "Did you notice in the wall?"

Johnson crouched and studied the cracks between the horizontal grey slates. She reached out and rubbed a leaf between finger and thumb, then sniffed. Her eyes lit up. "Tempus. You remembered."

#

Johnson sat at the desk in her cabin, the one Indie had assigned her when she got out of the infirmary, back when she believed herself his prisoner. Reconnaissance images and maps covered the desktop and wall in front of her. "Every time I look at these, I worry that we'll ever reclaim our home."

Indie felt the data seething through Johnson's implanted data nodes. "We can get there before they finish the new defences."

A small cluster of ships appeared at a jump point, broadcasting Congressional IFF. Johnson stiffened and pulled a data window up in the centre of the desk. After a few seconds, she relaxed and minimised the window. "Another aid convoy."

Indie checked that he wasn't emitting anything they'd detect, and that he hadn't been for long enough that the old light they'd be seeing wouldn't reveal his presence. A Republic hunter-killer cruising happily through the system would take a lot of explaining.

He studied the two warships escorting the convoy. "I wonder if they could be persuaded to stay awhile to help defend Concorde while we're away?"

Johnson shook her head. "Kincaid's adamant he doesn't want ships from other systems hanging around. Not until he's consolidated his position."

"Makes sense, I suppose." Indie ran a series of simulations of assaults on their home moon of Robespierre. When they'd played out, he selected the five most successful, and a couple of the close-run ones, generated new mission plans from them by randomising a few factors, then reinitialised the simulations. "Back to the planning, we have several options which could work with minimal casualties on our side. However, they all rely on diversionary attacks for which we don't have the resources."

"Kincaid did promise me he would attach a few frigates to the mission. Would that do it?"

"As long as they come packed with Marines, yes."

Johnson opened the comms menu. "I'll get that sorted now."

Chapter 6

"First wave, go."

Two frigates flashed and disappeared, leaving tiny eddies of space-time unravelling in their place. Johnson surveyed the crew on *Orion*'s bridge. All sat calmly, some talking to colleagues in other parts of the ship, others silently reviewing data on their screens. Despite this disciplined front, Johnson could taste the tension in the recycled air. She reflected on her decision to run the mission from here, rather than her flag bridge, and concluded she'd been right to put herself on display to steady the crew.

"Set the clock at two minutes," she said. A red countdown appeared in the corner of her vision. Over the next few seconds, the confirmations from the other ships in the fleet arrived, staggered by the light travel time between them.

The clock ticked over to thirty seconds. Johnson took a deep breath. "All stations, give me a final go / no go."

"Engineering, go," called Specialist Smith. Chief Engineer Yang would be hard at work in the drive room.

"Flight, go."

"Sensors, go." Centurion Hanke shone with confidence. Gone, it seemed, was the awkward teenager of only a year ago.

"Tactical, go." Johnson still expected to hear Levarsson's voice, even though it was months since she'd been given her own command.

"Air group, go."

"Legionaries, go," called Decurion Ombaru on behalf of Centurion Anson. Like the chief engineer, the centurion's duty station was elsewhere.

"Damage control, go."

"Infirmary, go."

"Secondary bridge, go."

The bridge lit with a swirl of bright motes. They coalesced into the image of a blue-skinned woman in a green dress standing beside Johnson. "Orion, go."

The names of the other ships in the fleet turned green in Johnson's peripheral vision. She reclined in her acceleration couch, but her calm demeanour belied her racing pulse.

"All hands, stand by for manoeuvring." Johnson shuffled around as the arms of her couch folded over her and gel pumped into the cushions.

She took a deep breath. "Clear to jump on schedule."

The bridge wobbled as Johnson fought off a wave of nausea.

Dammit. We really need to suss out what stops the jump-disorientation when I'm with Indie, and fit it to Orion.

The main bridge display refreshed, revealing the two frigates from the first wave in otherwise empty space. Over the next few seconds the other ships appeared, the light from their arrival taking time to travel to the *Orion*. The data from all their sensors combined, and a holographic representation coalesced in the centre of the bridge.

"I'm not showing any hostile ships," said the tactical officer. "But it's likely we'll have to get a lot closer before Robespierre will be in range of the new counter-stealth sensors."

"Understood, Yosef." Johnson squinted at the display. Nothing tickled her intuition. She opened a channel to each element of her fleet. "Flag to all ships, proceed with plan Alpha Two."

The frigates boosted hard, heading out in arcs that would bring them to Robespierre from opposite sides. The core of the fleet lit their mains, plotting a course that would take them near the least-time course, but above the ecliptic.

<<Good hunting, Olivia.>> *The Indescribable Joy of Destruction* didn't show on the sensor feeds, but it would already be on its way to check out the base it had found on its previous recces.

<<Good hunting, Indie,>> she replied. His departure tugged at a thread in her heart and she longed to throw herself into the thick of the fight with him, but her place was here.

"Orion, you have the bridge," Johnson said, triggering the release on her acceleration couch. The enfolding arms out of the way, she stood. "I'll be in my ready room if you need me."

Of course she knows that. I guess that statement was more for the rest of the staffers. Funny how I never realised that until now.

"Make sure you all rotate with your deputies and get some rest," she said to the room at large, before leaving through the hatch behind her chair.

Time to catch a quick nap myself. No point getting too tired.

#

One and a half uneventful hours into her next shift, Johnson stretched out in her command couch. A flicker of movement caught her attention, and she enlarged a section of the holographic display. *The Indescribable Joy of Destruction's* icon was active and weaving about, though there was no suggestion of what it was dodging.

<<A littl- hel- would be apprec-ted ove- here.>> The link to *The Indescribable Joy of Destruction* shut off. Johnson clamped down on her feelings; worrying about Indie wouldn't do much to help him.

The deck shifted under her, making her glad everyone on the bridge was ensconced in acceleration couches. The pilot looked over to her, lifting his hands clear of the controls. Johnson raised an eyebrow at Orion.

^I know, you didn't order me to change course,^ Orion sent, her projection remaining impassive. ^If it is bad enough for Indie to request help, I am the only ship capable of rendering assistance. I merely pre-empted what would be your logical order.^

Johnson shook her head fractionally. ^Quite right. Perhaps a quick heads up next time?^

The pilot canted his head for a few seconds then returned his hands to the controls.

^I have apologised to Decurion Thompson,^ sent Orion. ^I will warn him before any further non-emergency course changes.^

Johnson checked the link to Indie, confirming her suspicion that it was being jammed. Despite coming across this jamming the first time they'd met this enemy, they were nowhere near a way to burn through with normal comms.

The display showed his last known position and course. Johnson tried to guess what her friend was doing. Unfortunately, his actions in battle were very unpredictable; a good thing for avoiding the enemy, terrible for getting rescued.

Should I launch fighters? There's not much they can do against something threatening Indie, but they'll get me eyes in the area.

Johnson rapped her knuckles on the arm of her chair. "CAG, green deck."

"Green deck, aye," replied Centurion Ngie, the grey-haired commander of the air group, before turning to his screens. "Launch all birds."

Eight Goshawk fighters hurtled out of the axial tubes, two per flight deck, over the course of the next three seconds. Their main engines lit and added to the momentum imparted by the two-hundred-metre catapults.

"Strike wing away," reported Ngie.

Another four fighters rippled out of the much shorter lateral tubes on one of the decks. They split into two pairs and moved away from the *Orion*, keeping pace with her.

"CAP away."

"Thank you CAG," said Johnson. She'd served on a carrier for a couple of months, back when she'd been a young lieutenant in the Congressional navy. It had taken her almost three weeks to pluck up the courage to ask someone why the 'air' had survived in 'combat air patrol' and 'commander air group', why it hadn't become 'space'. The squadron leader had laughed so deeply that Johnson had half expected him to ruffle her hair when he recovered. It turned out that it was just one of those things you didn't question, a tradition going back so far there was no way anyone was going to change it. Rather like the name Marine.

A larger vessel emerged from one of Orion's flight decks. The moment it was over the threshold, its main engines lit, outshining the squadron of fighters. Orion winced and Johnson chuckled.

There goes Seivers. Chief of the Deck'll be fuming about her opening the throttle so close!

Her levity was short-lived, as the possible threat to Indie hammered back to the forefront of her mind.

Half an hour later, the telemetry from the strike wing came back strong through the laser link. Johnson had to remind herself that Indie was probably fine, his lack of signal probably down to not knowing their position to beam towards.

Split down into pairs, they swept space for clues, but there was nothing. They couldn't even get a general sense of a source of the jamming. A whole fleet could be hiding behind the gas giant, but at least she'd get a warning if they made a move.

A comms link request popped up in Johnson's vision. She checked the sender and accepted. "Percy, what've you got?"

"We have found *The Indescribable Joy of Destruction*. I am attempting to establish a connection while Seivers keeps us out of harm's way."

Johnson perked up. She sent an order for the strike wing to redirect to *The Perception of Prejudice's* location. The connection widened and Johnson saw *The Indescribable Joy of Destruction* tumbling through space. Her stomach rose as if she were in zero-g. "What do you think happened?"

"I do not have sufficient data to speculate."

Johnson cursed under her breath, having forgotten how young an AI Percy was. "Can I talk to Seivers?"

"I am afraid not. There is rather a lot of harm around here and we keep getting in its way."

Johnson blinked. "Just give me a sitrep."

"We are currently being engaged by twenty-three small craft. They are armed with small versions of the distortion field weapon you met the first time you encountered this enemy. Given the accelerations they are performing, I would speculate that they are not crewed by humans."

"You'll have backup in... six minutes. Can you hold out?"

"They seem quite intent on us, but it seems they do not appear to be concerned about a quick kill. All twenty-one are coordinating their attacks, but in small waves."

A capture order, perhaps?

^Orion? How long to weapons range?^

^Twelve minutes, assuming you want better than even odds of hitting the right targets.^

Do I risk the strike wing? AI fighters would make

mincemeat of them.

"Having observed them for several minutes now," said Percy, "I have formed the opinion that they are not autonomous. They act in packs rather than as individuals, and there is a distinct time lag when they react to a change in our tactics. For instance, we used the railgun for the first time just now, and it took six point two seven seconds before they started to avoid the bow. And then all sixteen craft changed their attack patterns simultaneously."

Johnson ran the maths in her head. Say three seconds to realise what had happened and issue new orders. That left one point five seconds comms lag each way, two seconds at most. She opened a channel to the CAG. ^New intel. Have the strike wing search for an enemy carrier. Two light second radius from *The Perception of Prejudice's* location. Coordinate with Orion.^

^Will do. What about Flight Decurion Seivers?^ asked Ngie.

^She'll have to look after herself.^

Just the way she prefers it.

"Thank you, Percy. That was useful intel. We're hunting for their command ship now."

"You are welcome. You might want to tell Orion that these little things appear to lose lock for a fraction of a second whenever I set my adaptive camouflage to pulse dazzle patterns. She might find that useful herself at some point."

Johnson checked on the rest of her fleet. *The Serendipity of Meeting* and the Concorde destroyers were on course for Robespierre as planned. She briefly considered recalling Seren, but realised how that would look.

Besides, if those destroyers get into trouble like we're having here, they won't stand a chance without her.

Orion brightened next to Johnson. "I have lost telemetry from two Goshawks near the gas giant."

Johnson squinted at the main situational display. The two light second globe clipped the planet. She replayed the events in her head, confirming where Indie had originally reported trouble. "It's there, isn't it?"

Orion nodded. "Most likely."

"Do you have a clear shot?"

Orion grinned. "We have no assets in the line of fire."

"Engage as you see fit." Johnson didn't dare allow herself to hope. Opening herself up for any emotions would mean something could slip out and break the command persona she worked hard to project.

Seconds later, the ship hummed as the *Orion's* main railgun turrets sent round after round towards the gas giant. Five hundred steel slugs were flung out at significant fractions of the speed of light within seventy seconds.

"How you doing, Percy?" Johnson transmitted.

"Fine and dandy," he replied. "We are having a particularly intimate dance with a dozen little acquaintances. Shame we are out of missiles."

Johnson rolled her eyes. "We have engaged where we think the enemy command ship is. Let me know if the drones' behaviour changes at all."

"Will do."

Two minutes after the last round left *Orion*, the first hit the atmosphere. Johnson's jaw dropped. She had expected a random spread of impacts. Instead, concentric rings of hits spread out across the face of the planet. It only took five seconds for all five hundred rounds to fall, each one with the energy of a strategic nuclear weapon. A circular patch of atmosphere was blown away, revealing a greenish lower layer.

There's something there.

The lights dimmed. Johnson caught other bridge crew looking around with apprehensive glances.

"Don't worry," said Orion, rising to address to the room at large.

Johnson could feel where the power was being diverted, and made a fist. Just over a second later a light flared against the green clouds.

"Got him," said Orion, and sat back down, folding her hands onto her lap.

^I thought you didn't want to use your new x-ray laser at full power until you'd done more tests?^

^That wasn't full power,^ replied Orion. ^But your point stands. I judged that the risk to my systems was worth it to expedite Indie's rescue.^

Johnson sent a digital raised eyebrow.

^There was no risk to the crew.^ Orion appeared to pay attention to a pattern on her dress that glowed white. ^And you will be pleased to know that there was minimal damage to my systems. Nothing that can't be fixed in a few days.^

"Prefect Johnson?" transmitted Percy. "The ten

remaining craft have changed their attack style."

"We destroyed their command ship."

"Ah. That would explain it. They appear to be on a suicide run. Not sure we can get all of th... Something's happening."

The hostile contacts winked out. Johnson leant forwards, searching the screen for clues.

"Well, Indie's back," said Percy.

Did he sound a bit miffed?

^You're welcome, Percy,^ sent Indie. ^I must say, it was a joy to watch you and Seivers playing with your new friends. Thank you for saving some for me.^

^Indie, what happened?^ asked Johnson. Relief flooded through her body and she had to will herself not to relax.

^The command ship got the drop on me, fired from within the gas giant's atmosphere. It was so deep in- well I couldn't spot it on gravity sensors.^

^You OK?^

^I'll heal. They clipped me a couple of times. In the end I figured I'd play dead and see what happened. Either they couldn't sense me, or they actually thought they'd got me.^

Johnson checked the connection was now one-to-one. ^You had me worried.^

^Sorry. Thank you for riding to the rescue.^

Beside her, Orion flared blue.

No doubt catching up with Indie.

^You're welcome,^ sent Johnson. ^You know I always will.^

"Prefect," called Ngie. "Permission to recall the strike wing?"

Johnson pulled up their telemetry in her secondary consciousness. "Granted. But have Charlie flight swing close to the hole Orion made in the atmosphere. I want confirmation it's clear."

Ngie nodded smartly. "Ma'am."

^By the way, Indie, you'll be pleased to hear that Percy is copying Seivers' wise-cracks.^

^Yes,^ he replied. ^Your decision to pair them seems to have been a prudent one.^

Something that had been whirring away in the back of Johnson's mind clicked into place. Her stomach fell like a rock.

Was the battleship guarding something? What if there was a civilian population in the gas giant? Perhaps that was why they kept coming back – we were invading a system they lived in.

A daemon scratched at the wall in her mind.

Chapter 7

Johnson floated free, drifting through the silence of space. One part of her consciousness resided in the *Orion*, monitoring the activity on the bridge and occasionally conversing with her staffers. Another part of her consciousness, the one she was concentrating on right now, rode along with a combat unit, one of scores flung out hours ago on ballistic trajectories towards Robespierre.

The scans hadn't shown any drastic changes since they'd abandoned the moon all those months ago. Still, she was eager to see what the enemy had done up close.

The first sense of movement was a faint whistle as the upper reaches of the atmosphere tentatively tweaked at the entry shell. The unit began to tumble, the thickening air gripping and releasing it.

Thank goodness there isn't a visual feed. The accelerations are making me dizzy enough.

The tumbling soon abated, the teardrop-shaped shell lining up with the plummet through the denser atmosphere. The temperature readings rose steadily, topping out at one hundred and seven degrees celsius; lethal to humans but nothing compared to the surface of the shell. The unit vibrated from the roar of the air. Soon the temperature dropped and the roar quietened, the entry shell having decelerated to a terminal velocity of seventy metres per second.

They must have seen us coming by now.

Johnson focused on the part of her on the *Orion*. There weren't any signs of hostile ships in orbit or any atmospheric craft.

"Permission to launch the dropships?" asked Decurion Ombaru.

"Granted." The sooner they got boots on the ground the better.

Eight of *Orion's* dropships rippled off the heavy catapults of her flight decks. Four centuries of Legionaries launched in as many seconds, fifty soldiers to a landing craft. Angular combat shuttles left the ships of the Concorde contingent, carrying marines to engage small outposts identified in the survey. The next wave from Orion should be ready in less than a minute. Johnson thought back to her time working a flight deck, the carefully choreographed chaos.

A bang and a hard jolt snapped her attention back to the combat unit. Her heart raced.

Where'd I get hit? No, where did 'it' get hit?

She scanned the diagnostics for damage. Only when they all came back green did she realise it had merely been the airbrakes deploying. Moments later it hit the ground and the accelerometers briefly redlined.

The combat unit pushed against the shell and light sheared in through cracks. Another push and it was free. Data from a wide range of electromagnetic frequencies flooded in. All around it, other combat units exploded out of their hard-baked foam shells and deployed their weapons. With no targets to engage, twenty units established a perimeter while others assisted those that had not landed so well. Three robots surrounded each shell, delicately breaking the foam and discarding sections. Once inside, they ran diagnostics on their injured comrades. Four had minor damage, such as a broken leg or two, and were helped to remove or seal off the affected areas.

One, whose airbrakes hadn't fully deployed, was a write-off. The ones working on that unit carefully replaced the fragments of shell before slowly backing off. Johnson forwarded that section of the sensor recording to Indie. All the units in this team were new-builds, their cores programmed with some of the experience from the earlier models. The trainers working with them had reported emergent behaviour after a few weeks, and Indie was monitoring their progress.

^Time to move,^ Johnson sent to all the combat units in her group.

As one, they turned their bodies west, then the first group headed out. Each unit scampered about twenty metres then went to ground, either in cover or hunkering down so its belly nestled into the long grass. At any one time, half of them were moving, a seething carpet of insectile robots flowing across the ground.

#

^Landing zone secured,^ sent Unit 01.

^Understood,^ replied Ombaru. ^The first wave should be with you in three minutes.^

Johnson smiled at the confidence overlaid in Unit 01's transmission. He had confessed his pride at being given command of securing the landing zone without human oversight when she had briefed him on the mission. It was, when she thought about it, one of the most compelling reasons she'd had for not going down to the surface in person. Sure, the command deck of the *Orion* gave her a superb base to oversee the whole operation, but she could uplink to there in the same way she was currently riding the combat unit. If she had made any moves to leaving the safety of the ship, Unit 01 and Unit 03 would not have accepted any orders that prevented them from looking after her. Ever since an incident in training, they had appointed themselves her bodyguards, protecting her like faithful dogs.

Her combat unit crested a hill and ducked into some blue bushes, the plants' spikes screeching across its metalloceramic body. Ahead, sixteen of its comrades scurried across open ground, changing direction and speed apparently at random. The enemy was trying to hack them, but Johnson's enhanced counter-intrusion routines were holding. Six hundred metres beyond lay their destination, the ruins of an ancient city around which the still-unnamed enemy had set up a large tented base.

Good job they didn't set up at the ruins we found in the forest. The combat units would have been severely limited in mobility.

Purple-tinged fireballs replaced three of the leading robots in rapid succession. Even as Johnson processed the bright ultra-violet flashes that had connected the doomed units to their assailants, the patch of scrub the enemy had used as cover disappeared in a storm of railgun and plasma rounds from eight of the combat units.

The assault team accelerated, leaping and sprinting forward. More ultraviolet flashes came from a wide front, occasionally catching a robot, but mostly kicking up geysers of vaporised dirt. A scratching sensation in her head brought her attention to an alert. Microwave radar flagged incoming shells, the tide of combat units flowing smoothly around the projected impact points. Missiles leapt from the launchers of the rearmost robots, arcing over the battlefield, backtracking the enemy batteries.

Small-arms fire erupted from the edge of the base. Bullets dinged harmlessly off hard bodies. The leading wave of combat units broke through the line, ignoring the enemy soldiers and pushing deep into the camp. The second wave followed, spreading out and sweeping through the buildings. The third wave turned to sweep along the defences, whilst the remaining combat units took up overwatch positions behind them.

Rifles chattered inside the camp, occasionally answered by the rip of a railgun or the whine of a plasma cannon. The robots clearing the outer defences killed anyone who raised a weapon against them, but left the rest. Whenever one deemed it safe, it leapt in and tagged an enemy soldier with a shock pad attached to one of its front claws. Despite the combat units trying to be surreptitious, the enemy must have realised what was happening. A few collapsed, fitting briefly before going still.

Dammit. They triggered their suicide routines.

The combat units went into a frenzy of stunning, but couldn't reach them all. Enemy soldiers died in an expanding wave faster than the robots could move.

The world fell quiet. Combat units stood frozen, deprived of targets. Johnson locked onto the nearest body, a trickle of blood and straw fluid flowing down its cheek. Examining one dead soul in close detail kept her from being overwhelmed by the hundreds around it.

After what felt an age, a bird chirped a questioning tune. Johnson tore her attention away from the man's face and studied the feeds from all the combat units.

^Enemy base secured. I need immediate pickup-up for ninety-seven enemy prisoners. Make sure they bring enough sedatives to keep them unconscious, the stunners we used won't keep them under for long.^

^Shuttles launching now.^

Johnson watched the combat units setting up a defensive perimeter around the base. ^And send a robotics engineering team when transport becomes available. I don't think any of the downed units are salvageable, but I want them recovered in a respectful manner.^

#

With the enemy base overrun, Johnson left the combat units to secure it, and switched her focus to one of the robots in the other main landing site. The moment she connected, Unit 01 turned and bowed.

^You noticed me arrive?^ she asked.

^Of course,^ replied Unit 01. ^Your thought patterns

are unique.^

Unit 03 bounded up, backpedalling at the last moment and skidding to a stop beside her. Johnson resisted an urge to scratch him, absently noting the deep gouges he'd left in the turf. ^Good to see you too.^

A high-pitched roar, and eight dropships flared to a halt a metre off the ground, the jetwash of their downward-vectored engines immersing the nearby combat units in clouds of dust, small stones dinging off their armour. The adaptive camouflage of the vessels flickered and billowed brown, mimicking the clouds. Shapes dropped from each craft, half-seen in the visible spectrum but resolving in infra-red to Legionaries in hardsuits. As they hit the ground, they sprinted to the perimeter and threw themselves down between the robots, weapons at the ready. Their load delivered, the dropships poured on full power and climbed away, plasma turrets scanning back and forth.

The dust settled, revealing four figures walking towards Johnson's combat unit, weapons ready but pointed at the ground. Their boxy dark and light grey heavy armour stood out against the terrain, but there was little point in trying to hide after display the dropships had just put on. The leader wore a gold spearhead on the front of his left shoulder.

^Playing it casual, eh Primus?^ sent Unit 01. Johnson glanced at the robot, surprised at the familiarity.

Issawi didn't seem to notice, merely nodding to Unit 01 and looking directly at the unit Johnson was riding. ^I assume you aren't here to micromanage this operation... Ma'am.^

The three Legionaries accompanying Issawi turned their backs on them, heads scanning the skyline.

^How did you know I was here?^ Johnson asked.

Unit 01 took a few paces away. Issawi shrugged. ^Someone told me. But I think we ought to set up some sort of electronic flag to show who is riding a robot for future operations. It could speed up command and control... And I really do need to know if you are going to start giving orders.^

^You have operational command. I'm just here to run electronic interference,^ sent Johnson, turning her combat unit and striding towards the perimeter. ^I take it you're pulling the feeds from the recce drones.^

Issawi fell in beside her. ^Do you think I'd be casually walking across the middle of my landing zone if I wasn't sure there were no immediate threats?^

They approached the perimeter at a point where a gentle slope ran down from their left. The combat units touched their bellies to the ground, Issawi and his escort knelt.

^Centurion Canetti, are you good to go?^ asked Issawi.

^Give us thirty seconds.^

Issawi shifted his weight. ^Problem?^

^Nothing mission critical. I'll explain later.^

Probably some of the newer recruits getting in a tangle. They'll catch hell about it after this is over but he's right not to make a meal of it now.

Issawi remained motionless, like a predator about to strike. The interlocking plates on his bulky armour eased across each other as he took deep breaths. Johnson allowed a brief glimmer of elation to surface;

after all the planning and negotiating and training, the Legion was about to reclaim its home.

^Ready,^ sent Canetti.

Issawi waited a moment, presumably checking the feeds one more time, then sent the go order.

Unit 01 sprinted over the rise and round the corner, flanked by two other combat units. Missiles slammed into defensive positions either side of the tunnel mouth ahead. Johnson opened a channel to the blast door's control computer. A small rocket roared between the legs of Unit 03 and exploded behind him. The computer accepted Johnson's access request. She sent the command to open, hardly believing it when it acknowledged.

^Looks like they didn't find my Trojan,^ she sent, as a human marksman took down the rocket's firer as he sought to relocate. Johnson checked that she had full access to the base's network, and stood down her hacking routines. ^I'm locking them down. You'll be able to clear floor by floor.^

Issawi thrust himself up and ran forwards. ^Excellent.^

Unit 01 entered the tunnel, slowing a fraction as he met the start of the downward curve in order to tag three unarmed enemies with the shock pads on his front feet. The combat units skidded to a halt where the passage forked, crouching down to wait. The first humans reached the shelter of the tunnel entrance.

Johnson's gaze fell on a data panel and she remembered the first time she'd accessed the base's computer system. Exploring, looking for somewhere to settle, they'd found this place abandoned. ^I'm going in now. I'll be able to do far more from within the network.^

She withdrew from the combat unit, her whole consciousness returning to her physical body on the *Orion*. Nothing was happening in orbit, she could risk focusing her whole attention on the base's computer systems. A deep breath, and she dived in. Last time she'd swum the data currents had been an accident. This time she was prepared.

Her mind rendered the ocean reef analogy again. She jerked her head frantically around before relaxing; no sharks this time. Johnson swam over the coral, identifying which bits represented which aspects of the base.

I don't need to breathe. I didn't notice that last time. All too much of a panic, I expect.

Within subjective minutes, during which the physical world advanced three seconds, she had given Issawi control over all the hatches within the base, confirmed that she had exclusive access to the environmental systems, and deleted all accounts created since they had abandoned the base to try to save Concorde.

Now to turn up the heat. Literally.

A flash in the distance caught her attention. She turned to look, but couldn't make anything out. She was about to dismiss it when two more flashes came in quick succession. Dark shapes powered through the water. They swam fast, light reflecting off their scales when they changed direction.

They don't belong here.

Johnson kicked her legs and struck out towards them. They scattered, two making straight for her, the others darting away and heading for other parts of the reef. As the distance closed, their needle-like teeth and serrated fins became clear. Johnson sent off commands across the network, trying to find out where the intruders were from. She called up a counter-hacking routine, feeling a weight in her hand. She lifted it and frowned at the knife it now held.

Guess I have to do this myself.

The first fish streaked past, leaving a track of tiny bubbles. Johnson let it go, concentrating on the second which was going straight for her. Her hand swept up, painfully slowly. The fish angled up at the last moment and the knife cut through nothing but water. She spun round, just in time to raise her arm as the first fish lunged at her. She fended it off, one of its fins drawing blood just below her elbow. Her mind raced, wondering what would happen if she were killed in here. She fired off another request for the network to initiate counter-intrusion routines.

One of the fish pierced the cloud of bloody water and went for her head. She brought the knife round in time to nick it under the chin. Before she could bring her hand back, the other grabbed her arm, biting down into the bone, making her drop the knife. She punched it with her free hand, cursing the resistance of the water. It pulled away, tearing through her flesh.

If they get control of the systems, we'll have to destroy half our own base rooting them out.

Johnson ran the counter-intrusion routine again, and a knife popped into her left hand. She squared herself off against the fish, which drifted in front of her. Her right hand hung uselessly by a flap of skin. She tucked it under her left armpit and pulled. The skin tore and she dropped the dead appendage. The fish eyed her. Baring her teeth, she raised the knife in front of her, daring them to come on. They turned and fled. A large shadow passed over her and turbulent water buffeted her. Two sharks circled her as more chased the fish.

One of the sharks butted gently up against her. Slowly, it lifted her up, swimming higher and higher. She surveyed the reef. All around it sharks of different colours and sizes swam with lazy strokes of their tails.

Looks like the network chose a side.

The reef faded. Light blue replaced dark. Caustics of sunlight played across the shark's back.

Johnson surfaced on the bridge of the *Orion*, drenched in sweat. Several of the newer officers hastily looked away. Hanke maintained a level gaze. "You were thrashing about," he explained, his tone carrying an artificial lightness.

"I'm OK. Just had to deal with some hackers."

#

Johnson's combat unit stalked around the several storey high workshop at the bottom of the main tunnel. None of the corridors leading on from there was wide enough to fit through. Sitting on a bridge whilst your crew did their jobs was one thing, she was still there, her presence giving them reassurance. Sending individuals into battle without supporting them was a whole other level of anxiety, they stood or fell and there was nothing she could do about it.

She dipped into the network, long enough to see that

the sharks had kept the attackers at bay. There hadn't been an intrusion for twelve minutes, not since the research level had been cleared.

A door lock clunked. Her combat unit pivoted its shoulder-mounted machine gun and levelled it at the hatch. Johnson soothed the robot; its action was a sensible precaution, but she didn't want it so jumpy it instigated a blue on blue.

Some of these personality traits are getting out of hand. I hope Indie's made progress on a treatment.

The door opened, and Issawi stepped through, his armour scratched, a large dent on one shoulder. As the door closed, he drew himself up and snapped out a salute.

How do I return it?

Johnson dipped the front of the combat unit.

"It is being my pleasure to report that the complex is clear of enemy," said Issawi. "We have teams sweeping for booby traps."

Johnson called up the speakers. "The butcher's bill?"

Issawi broke into a broad smile. "No fatalities on our side. Twelve serious casualties, but they're stable."

"What about you?"

He glanced at his shoulder, testing the movement as he pressed on it with the other arm. "I got hit by a chair."

Johnson couldn't make the unit glare at him, so she just waited in silence.

"OK," Issawi continued, raising his hands placatingly. "They set off a charge in the galley. I got lucky, Legionary Smith was knocked out by a ladle. His teammates'll make sure he never lives that down."

The lack of a head on the robot thwarted Johnson's attempt to shake it. A section of Legionaries tramped past them, one carrying a case of micro-drones, another hefting a crate of rifle ammunition.

"I'll leave you to clear up here. Good work, Primus."

Issawi stiffened formally. "I will pass on your congratulations to the Legionaries, Prefect."

Johnson thumped the arms of her command chair in satisfaction and stood up. "I'm going down to the surface. Dispatch a frigate to inform Concorde of our victory."

She strode to the door. "Orion, you have the bridge."

The holographic projection pulsed brighter. "I have the bridge."

As the door closed behind Johnson, she took a deep breath.

It's not a real victory, they'll keep coming back. And we don't even know why. I just wish they'd respond to our hails.

#

The dropship flared gently and settled to the ground on the parade square. Johnson ducked under the still-rising side hatch and jogged clear of the jetwash. Behind her, teams of techs and medics streamed out and hurried over to waiting casualties, synthetic and human. Combat units patrolled the skyline and Legionaries manned improvised barricades around the small tunnel entrance.

As the last of the injured was loaded onto the dropship, a figure broke away and strode over to her.

Johnson recognised Issawi's gait even without the EIS overlaying an ID tag, the confidence and easy power even showed through the hardsuit. One of the combat units turned its weapon towards the parade square.

^Easy there,^ Johnson sent.

^I do not trust him,^ replied Unit 01.

^If I can forgive him for shooting me, you will have to as well.^

Unit 01 held in place for half a second and then moved its weapon away. ^I will still keep a close eye on him.^

Quit while you're ahead.

^If you must.^

Issawi reached out his arm and she clasped it, hand to elbow, the rigid plates of his armour pressing into the rubbery forearm of her firmsuit. "Welcome back to Robespierre."

Johnson looked around. "It's good to be home." And for the first time since leaving her parent's house to join the Academy, she actually meant it.

#

Issawi sat across the desk from Johnson and leant back. "Doesn't look like anyone touched your office."

"They don't seem to have used the base at all," she replied. "The security recordings show them searching, presumably for intel, but the only people who stayed here full time were the guards at the entrance."

Issawi cracked a knuckle. "Their focus was definitely on the ruins. Olbrich reckons they have ritual significance to them."

Johnson sipped her latte. "Perhaps they are descendants of that civilisation?"

"Olbrich wasn't convinced. He is sure the ruins were of a city of a pre-Exodus human colony. If they've been out here alone that long, their technology should have diverged from ours by a larger degree."

"Makes sense." Johnson closed her eyes for a few seconds and sighed. "They're certainly divergent when it comes to psychology."

"You thinking about the suicides?"

Johnson nodded. "Every time we offer them surrender, they melt down their EIS. We brought a couple of the soldiers we captured yesterday out of sedation and they set them off within seconds, we daren't try reviving any more until we can deactivate the implants."

Issawi ran his fingers through his beard. "That's a lot of people to keep under medical care."

"Yep. Hopefully we'll be able to ship them back to Concorde soon."

Issawi canted his head a fraction and defocused his eyes. "Sorry, got to go sort out something on the perimeter. Nothing serious."

Johnson smiled and wiggled her fingers towards the door. With a nod, Issawi rose and strode out of the room.

Johnson eased herself back in her chair, cupping her mug in both hands.

Just a few more moments before I get back to the queue of files to review.

She took a few leisurely sips, savouring the warm,

milky liquid. The caffeine was already clearing her head. She debated changing into casual clothes, but decided to just plough on through the work.

She'd only just opened the next file, however, when Indie opened a channel. ^I see the Primus has left. Are you free to talk?^

^I should be getting on with clearing my queue,^ Johnson replied, ^but I welcome the distraction.^

^The analysis of the gas giant is complete.^

Johnson perked up. The possible outcomes vied in her mind. On one hand, she could be free of the worry of having ordered the death of a whole civilian population. On the other, she could be a proven war criminal.

A daemon breathed against the wall. 'Murderer.'

^I am afraid that it was inconclusive,^ he sent. ^We did not recover any debris, and it seems the atmosphere has a high metallic vapour content, so any contribution from man-made structures would be undetectable.^

Johnson lowered her head into her hands.

Another daemon whispered, 'You killed their children.'

Either answer would have been better than no answer.

^Have I killed innocent civilians?^ she asked, reinforcing the message with a tang of iron.

^I cannot answer that with the available data.^

Johnson grunted in frustration.

^I appreciate that that is not what you wanted to hear,^ sent Indie. ^But it is the case. I cannot guarantee that you are in the clear.^

Johnson rested her forehead on the table. The wood was warm to her touch and helped stop the world spinning out of control.

^However, I do not believe that there was anything other than the warship there. Had it been protecting a civilian settlement, the sensible course of action would have been to remain hidden. If it existed, it would have known from the months we spent here that we couldn't detect it.^

It's coming back. I need to get out of here.

#

Johnson dropped from an obstacle, scattering gravel as she bent her knees then powered forward. Being out in the fresh air reset her mind, allowing her to let her guard down while she exerted her body. It helped stave off the depression. She threw herself to the ground and crawled under a tangle of razor wire.

Issawi'll do his nut if he finds out I've used this before the engineers clear it. Since the accident when we were training the first Legionaries, he has been very careful about this course.

She jumped for a rope and swung, savouring the rough texture in her hands. Too long behind a desk, but she knew it came with the rank. Her feet planted firmly in the dirt and she rocked her body forward, keeping herself from toppling backwards into the ditch. She pushed the rope away and got up to full speed in a handful of paces. Ahead lay the high section of the course.

At least Kincaid ratified the minutes of the inquest

into the accident.

She locked her eyes on the first rung of the ladder.

Having a higher authority to pass that kind of thing on to was such a relief.

She judged the distance and made a tiny adjustment to her stride.

Like being able to hand over those anti-AI troublemake...

She jumped. And missed the rung, slamming into the ladder and collapsing to the ground.

The right side of her face throbbed. Sitting upright, she hit her leg with the side of her fist.

Bloody thing. I get to the point where I forget it isn't mine, then it does something like that.

She wiped a trickle of blood from her lip with the back of her hand then looked up sharply. The fleeting movement that had caught her attention resolved into a small reconnaissance drone. It clearly realised it had been spotted because it gave up trying to be furtive and floated across to her. When the near-spherical grey robot arrived, she canted her head to one side. It copied, tilting over on its tiny ducted fans, camera fixed on her face.

"Indie? Is that you?"

The drone returned to an even keel. "Possibly," it replied through speakers.

Johnson shook her head in annoyance, regretting it immediately as a sharp pain stabbed at her left temple. "I'm not cross you were spying on me."

"In that case, yes, it is me." The drone dropped closer to the ground and the camera panned along her artificial leg. "Is it malfunctioning?"

"I'm not sure. I lost concentration and it didn't behave as I expected."

A request to run a diagnostic popped up in her consciousness. She approved it and opened a window to view the data the routine streamed to the drone, and presumably from there up to *The Indescribable Joy of Destruction* in orbit. Nothing stood out.

The drone returned to eye level, whirring like a cloud of flies. "I can't see any issues. Perhaps you misjudged."

Not a malfunction. My fault.

She grabbed a fistful of dry soil. The daemons were making a lot of noise on the other side of the wall in her mind.

"What distracted you?" asked Indie.

Johnson refocused. "Something occurred to me about when this obstacle collapsed on those trainees."

When she didn't continue, Indie said "Do I have to guess?"

She let the dirt trickle out between her fingers, blowing away in the breeze.

"What if it wasn't an accident?" she asked.

"The evidence pointing to structural weakening caused by microbes in the soil was quite conclusive."

"We haven't found them anywhere else, have we?"

"No... oh, you think they were planted here," he stated.

She stood, testing her leg carefully. He lip was swollen and sore and she could feel a bruise spreading on her forehead.

"My first thought was someone on the Republic's payroll," she said. "Those ones you flagged up in the records have been at the back of my mind since we recovered my crew from Orpus-4."

"What benefit would that have out here?"

"None. That's why I never made the connection to the obstacle course," Johnson said.

Indie bobbed the drone down and up, like a person nodding in thought. It occurred to Johnson how frequently Indie mimicked human gestures now.

"Could we have picked up a Red Fleet agent somewhere along the line?" he asked.

"If that were the case, I don't think they'd have left us alone this long."

"We hadn't even encountered our current enemy when that happened," said Indie. "And I can't see how sabotaging our obstacle course could make any difference to any other big player."

"But what if it wasn't about the war. What if it was about AIs?"

"Someone seeded the microbes so that humans would get hurt," said Indie, dropping the drone closer to Johnson and lowering the volume on the speakers. "Then hid evidence they could later use to frame one of us."

Johnson jerked her head round to look the drone straight in the camera.

"I hadn't got that far," she said. "But it makes a lot of sense."

#

A gentle but insistent prodding in her mind stirred Johnson from sleep. She stretched and checked the time.

0614 – nearly time to get up anyway. I wonder how long they've been waiting before deciding to contact me?

^Go ahead,^ she sent.

^Prefect, the *Respite* has returned. They have a message for you from Governor Kincaid.^

Johnson opened her eyes, ready to fling herself out of bed. ^Is it urgent?^

^No. I'd have woken you the moment it arrived if it were.^

Johnson calmed her racing heart. ^Thank you. Send it through.^

The file pinged up in the periphery of her consciousness.

Well, if it's not urgent, it can wait another few minutes.

She swung her legs out of bed and arched her back. Something about sleeping in real gravity left her all kinked up. Rising, she padded over to the shower, lifting her black t-shirt over her head as she went.

#

Dressed in her grey working uniform, her hair still slightly damp, she sat at the desk in her office. She checked the Chief Medic's report, relieved that all the casualties would pull through, then called up the message from Concorde's Governor.

"Prefect Johnson. Congratulations on your swift victory. I'm sure you appreciate that there can be no official response from the government, but please accept my personal thanks for safeguarding the Concorde contingent in your fleet."

Johnson took the opportunity provided by the privacy of her office to roll her eyes. Few in the military liked politicians. At least Kincaid's motivations seemed clear, and the need for Concorde to be able to deny the Legion's actions was understandable.

"Your presence is requested at a gathering to be held at the location and time attached. The host is someone we would very much like you to meet. You should also bring your friend we talked so much about. I will see you there."

Johnson opened the attached file, which also included the guest list. At first glance, it was nothing more than a fancy ball at some rich businessman's country retreat. A search in the archives hinted at something else; every one of the guests for which she could find an entry was involved in shipbuilding, weapons development, or military command.

What are they planning?

She forwarded the message to Indie.

^Most interesting,^ he sent a second later, making her jump.

^I didn't realise you were so close.^

^Sorry. You did tell me to 'sneak around and keep a low profile'.^

Johnson sighed. ^So I did... Anyway, what do you make of Kincaid's invitation?^

^They're probably planning to enhance the Concorde fleet. Sooner or later Congress will realise they plan on breaking away.^

^Sounds about right,^ sent Johnson, putting in a

request to *Orion* for a shuttle. ^But I'm not sure what they want me there for.^

^Who's your friend, by the way?^ asked Indie.

Johnson smiled. ^That would be you. Time to get started picking out something you can wear.^

Part III

A team of farm hands heaved on ropes and the fourth cruck of a new barn creaked into position, the momentum killed by more people holding ropes on the other side. Shelton stood back, directing the workers, as a couple of slender men shimmied up to tie the timbers into the existing frame.

Sweating heavily in the midday sun, he turned to the young man standing next to him. "That be five barns now, Matthew. The herd be doing well."

Matthew cringed. "Mother doesn't like you talking like that."

"She be having to cope with it. We have to be blending in."

"Even amongst family?"

Shelton rested a hand on his son's shoulder. "We be having to be in the habit. So we don't be making a mistake."

"Who'd care?" Matthew asked, as a gong sounded from the house across the farmyard. "The people at market know we're newcomers."

The workers streamed towards the house.

"They not be knowing ev'rythin'. 'Sides, they not be telling any visitors as long as we not be drawing 'ttention to usselves." He followed the last farmhand towards the house.

Matthew fell into step with his father. "Why did we come here?"

Shelton slowed and looked off to one side. "What you be rememb'ring? 'Bout afore?"

"I remember our house, there were dragons on my bedroom wall. I remember we sometimes visited a big city, with buildings stretching into the clouds. You were some sort of businessman. Mother was happy."

Shelton sighed. For a moment he considered telling his son the truth about his past, but decided that he was safer believing the businessman cover. "Magda didn't find the change easy. She had friends in our old life, and a job she found rewarding."

Matthew raised an eyebrow.

"See. I be making mistakes. That be why we be practising."

"You still haven't explained why we left that behind."

Shelton shook his head. "We be late for luncheon. Your mother not be wanting to be waiting for us."

Chapter 8

Indie and Johnson walked through double wooden doors and emerged into an ornate triple-height hallway. Strictly, Johnson was the only one who actually walked, but Indie was plugged into her visual feeds, seeing what she saw and injecting his likeness into the room beside her. He echoed her choice of dress blacks, omitting his tricorn hat in honour of the seriousness of the occasion.

"There's a lot of data traffic in there," he said. "I'm impressed, I can't detect it from up here."

^I felt it as we entered,^ replied Johnson. ^Didn't you see anything while the door was open?^

"Nothing reached orbit. Possibly if I had a sensor in line with the opening..."

Johnson smiled and stepped forward as Kincaid approached, wine glass in hand, accompanied by a middle-aged man in a smartly-tailored evening suit.

"Prefect Johnson," said Kincaid, shaking her hand. "Let me introduce our host, Harry Robinson. Harry, this is our other saviour, Olivia Johnson."

Johnson nodded to Harry. "Thank you for your hospitality. Your house is impressive."

Harry looked down at the ground. "Yes, well... I'm glad you like it."

Kincaid coughed and ushered them into the next room. "Everyone is here now. We ought to begin."

Indie kept pace with Johnson, dodging around people who would otherwise have walked through his projection in her vision. The doors clunked softly home behind them.

Harry stood beside an empty fireplace with Kincaid at his side. The conversations died out and everyone shuffled into a rough horseshoe around them. Indie fell back behind Johnson.

"This room is now locked down," said Harry. "No-one can enter or leave without my express permission. All electronic communication is also being blocked, nothing in, nothing out."

^Indie?^

"Still here... and no, I haven't hacked anything. My signal must have been allowed, I was invited after all."

"I'd like to thank you for coming," Harry continued. "But it isn't my place to explain what this about. So, I'd like to hand over to our Governor now."

Kincaid put his glass down on the slate mantelpiece and scanned his audience. "Everyone in this room has demonstrated their loyalty to the people of Concorde. Everyone has passed the most extensive background checks my personal security team can devise. We all know the truth about the attack on our world, we all know that I seek to guide us towards independence as a result."

He took a breath. "I have called you here today to discuss how best to prepare ourselves to defend that independence. We have military leaders, captains of industry, research chiefs, and even representatives of our allies. Between us, we must draw up a framework for the future."

A young woman in a red dress glided over and whispered in Harry's ear. The rest of the room dissolved into a blur of noise and movement as Indie focussed on her.

^Are you seeing this?^ asked Johnson. ^She's a walking data node, far deeper connected than even I am.^

Indie worked his jaw. "Yes. Yes I am. Interesting."

She's more than that. The patterns are different.

Harry clapped his fingers together twice beside his cheek. "Dinner is served."

Partitions, embroidered with scenes of mythical beasts, parted to reveal a long wooden table laid out with fine china and silver cutlery. Trios of candles burned in elaborate holders at intervals between the settings.

"I tend to find that important planning goes more easily if everyone has the chance to get to know one another," said Harry, and led the way to the table.

"There's one extra chair," said Indie, walking at Johnson's elbow. "There are eleven people in the room, and twelve places set for dinner."

^Are you counting the woman in red?^

"No," said Indie. "Somehow I don't think she'll be eating."

"Prefect." Harry beckoned Johnson. "You're here, to my left."

The woman in red guided the other guests to their seats, then stood two paces behind Harry's right shoulder. The chair opposite Johnson remained empty.

"Thank you, Emily," he said, then stood at the head of the table until everyone was quiet. "Before we sit,

I'd like to introduce our final guest. Someone who has inspired me greatly, and who I am deeply looking forward to meeting."

A comms array somewhere in the house requested permission to re-broadcast Indie's likeness. Curious to see what would happen, he granted it. Simultaneously, he received access to the room's cameras and microphones, and expanded his perception out from Johnson's head.

"If you would accept the feed now requesting access to your EIS..." said Harry.

One by one, heads snapped to look at Indie.

"...I'd like to introduce *The Indescribable Joy of Destruction*."

Indie flourished a deep bow, and caught sight of Johnson rolling her eyes.

^Oh come on,^ he sent. ^Someone needed to break the tension in here.^

Harry indicated the empty seat to his right with an outstretched palm. "Would you like to be seated?"

"Thank you," said Indie. As he passed between Harry and Emily, he could feel her watching him, but her eyes didn't move.

The moment the last person took their seat, a line of servants brought in plates of food and cutlery on silver trays. As they processed along both sides of the table, Indie wondered if they would put anything in front of him, and what the correct etiquette would be for an in-head simulation of an artificial intelligence who also happened to be a guest of honour.

I can't very well eat it. But I could perhaps fashion some sort of act. Or would that be considered rude?

When a plate was set in his place, he let out a breath of relief. The mushrooms were perfect. On the face of it, a natural selection of fungus in a brandy cream sauce just like those on the other plates. The scales on Indie's portion, however, followed an uninterrupted mathematical pattern. A second of watching the steam, and he knew who had written the algorithm it was based upon. He reached out and picked up the fork, confident the model would interact correctly with his hand. Stabbing a soft grey mushroom, he raised it to his lips. There was no aroma, but they wouldn't have his full specs; vision and audio were standard, required for communicating with humans, the rest wasn't the kind of thing you could guess.

Indie inclined his head to their host, raising his fork in salute to the effort he had put into making him appear one of the regular guests.

He delicately pulled it off the fork with his teeth. Nothing. No taste, not even any warmth.

Too much to hope for.

"I looked up your company, and what I could find about you," said Johnson between mouthfuls. "I'm surprised to find you working so closely with the military."

Harry smiled back at Indie, swallowed and turned to face Johnson. "I rather surprised myself there, too. But extreme circumstances and all that." He took a sip of wine. "Besides, from what I've read about you, you're standing up for things I agree with, things I can get behind."

Indie cast his gaze around the table. Half-way down the opposite side sat a decidedly non-military figure.

Round, but a hard, muscled portliness. He had black hair against pale white skin and made dramatic gestures as he spoke. His food had already been consumed, and he appeared to be eyeing up that of those around him.

That'll be Draxos, leader of the Ladrio mining colony. I had thought Johnson's description of him to have been an exaggeration.

Indie completed his sweep of the guests by examining the commodore to his immediate right. "How do you do?"

The man looked surprised to be addressed. "I... I'm fine, thank you... And you?"

"I am well," replied Indie, eating another mushroom. "A fine spread, don't you think?"

"I guess so." The man adjusted his collar. "Say, are you really one of those new Republic hunter-killers?" He flinched as his neighbour on the other side elbowed him in the ribs.

Indie rolled his eyes, then resolved not to do it again. It was too much Johnson's thing. "I was indeed. I am no longer part of the Republic. In fact, you could say that I never have been, as they rejected me from the moment of my sentience."

I expect he'll ask me next whether I would have stayed with the Republic if they hadn't tried to kill me.

"I fought one of you last year," said the commodore. "Very impressive. It took out three of my destroyers before my cruisers could intervene."

Indie searched the commodore's record again, surprised he had missed something like that. But he hadn't. Presumably, if the man was telling the truth, it had been withheld from the files he could access.

"It got away," the commodore continued, placing his fork gently down on his plate. "But we did get in a few licks. Even found some debris afterwards, which got the intel bods rather excited."

Indie stared hard at the man, trying to decide if he was being deliberately tactless.

Probably not. He's just thinking of the ships he's used to, mindless lumps of metal that don't feel anything.

"Did you ever find out who it was?" Indie asked, keeping his voice light. He hadn't thought much about his brothers recently.

"Oh yes. There was a tankard with a ship's crest in the debris. *A Life Without Remorse.*"

Indie nodded, memories of the unnamed deep space station where he and his brethren had begun their lives flooding back.

Trust Remmy to get knocked about taking on something too big. He was always taking excessive risks.

#

Kincaid pushed his heavy chair back and stood. Everyone turned to face him. "Thank you for a wonderful meal, Harry. But now we need to get down to the planning."

He sat and continued. "Let me be clear about a couple of things. Firstly, we cannot be seen to be building up strength beyond what would be needed to defend ourselves. Secondly, we cannot afford for

Congress to consume our technological developments."

People nodded agreement. A general called "Quite so!"

"So," continued Kincaid, "I am convinced that we must invest in strengthening our allies, the Legion Libertus. Their interests align closely with our own. I am sure they would come to our aid again should we need it, and yet they are an entirely deniable entity."

^This is interesting,^ sent Indie.

^Most interesting,^ agreed Johnson. ^But I wonder if he is about to try grabbing more control of the Legion again.^

Kincaid looked around the room. "The Concorde Militia already has ten times the number of volunteers than it can train. The Red Fleet was careful not to cripple our industrial base, so we will soon have surplus capacity once more and be able to supply the Legion with materiel for the fight.

"Of course, expanding the Legion brings into question having a prefect, which I understand to be roughly similar to a commodore, in overall command," he continued.

^Here it comes,^ sent Johnson. ^He's always wanted one of his own in charge.^

"Now, I know that it isn't actually in my power to do this. But I know that Prefect Johnson would never accept it if she were allowed a way to wriggle out." Kincaid reached into his pocket.

The Indescribable Joy of Destruction tensed, weapons and drives powering up. In the woods outside the house's grounds, Unit 01 leapt up, throwing off the branches that covered its body.

Kincaid stood and walked round the table towards Johnson. "Prefect Johnson, I thank you for keeping the Concorde detachment safe during your recent operations. Their commander reported back how impressed he was at your command and control of the combined forces. However, you cannot remain as the Prefect of the Legion."

The Indescribable Joy of Destruction began its entry burn. Unit 01 reached the perimeter fence and crouched ready to leap.

Kincaid drew a black box with gold detailing from his pocket. "So it is with great pleasure that I promote you to Legate."

He opened the box and offered it to her, leaning in close to whisper. "You have to accept these now, or it will make me look bad. If you want to discuss it with your counsellors later, I'm sure they'll agree with me that you deserve it."

Johnson relaxed, reaching out to take the box. *The Indescribable Joy of Destruction* skipped off the outer atmosphere, leaving a trail of fire, and settled back into a stable orbit. Unit 01 skulked back into the woods.

Johnson flipped open the lid. She eyed the rank emblems, each a red-enamelled axe protruding from a golden bundle of sticks.

"We thought a fasces would be appropriate for a legate, given your Roman theme," said Kincaid. Johnson squinted at him. "I doubt many people will know what it came to represent during the Dark Times in Euroscandia."

Johnson nodded curtly and drew herself up to

attention. She bent forward slightly to allow Kincaid to pin the insignia on her epaulettes.

The ceremony completed, Kincaid addressed the room. "So, on to our second item of business, the exact nature of our support. The most obvious, in addition to the food and supplies we already provide, is manpower. We can't spare many more trained personnel, but there are tens of thousands of refugees still in temporary camps, I'm sure many of those would volunteer in exchange for a change of accommodation and a chance to hit back. I understand that the Legion already has a training system in place?"

Johnson nodded. "We can cope with a century a week joining. That's eighty recruits. Assuming they've already done Basic as part of their national service, the first cohort could be on the line in six months."

"Next there is the issue of ships. I would love to simply sign over a squadron of destroyers, but that would raise far too many questions. Instead, I propose that we build from scratch. Our allies at Lavrio will provide several of the key raw materials. We'll supply the design and development team as well as the majority of the fittings. I am hoping that the Legion can contribute some of their advances in ship armour, automation and human interface."

Indie sat back and created a new environment in his mind. He spawned routines to comb through ship designs and generate combinations.

"What classes of ship are we talking about?" asked an admiral.

Kincaid smiled. "Good question. One of many I hope

we can answer today."

"From a manufacturing standpoint, I'd suggest focussing on one design," said Harry. "Make a prototype, iron out the bugs while we tool up the factories, and then dive in with wholesale production."

The admiral nodded. "Makes sense. The question, however, remains. What class of ship? We could make hundreds of corvettes for every carrier. Which is the right choice depends on what kind of war you intend to fight."

Indie set the first generation of his new designs to fight each other. He rejected the losers and created mutated versions of the winners to pit against each other in the next round.

Johnson leant forward. "If I already had a vessel design, how long before you could be turning them out?" She sent a file to all the industrial captains.

Harry looked at her. "Is it proven?"

"It was a standard design before the war," said Johnson. "I've personally witnessed it in combat several times in the last few months."

"I'd say that my factories could manufacture three or four a day within a month, assuming they weren't doing anything else."

Draxos beamed. "This is the craft you used to rid us of those pirates."

Johnson nodded. "Yes. A Razor class strike fighter. She packs a punch way above her size, but she's not the complete solution. We'd still need ships capable of transporting large numbers of Legionaries and delivering them into battle."

Indie removed all the smaller classes of ship he'd

developed, leaving him with a range from destroyer up to heavy cruiser.

"So, we're back to my question," said the admiral, slapping the table.

"The Razors will give us teeth quickly," said Johnson. "We can station some on the *Orion* for power projection and then base squadrons on Robespierre and Lavrio, possibly even at remote bases here in the Concorde system. That will free up forces currently based there to defend them."

Johnson scanned around the table, seeing several nods of agreement. "But we still need a proper ship design."

Indie coughed and all eyes turned to him. "While you were talking, I took the liberty of drafting an idea. I call it the *Aesir* class. You'll see I've based them on a Congressional Marine destroyer, so that should help with production. They can hold a cohort of Legionaries along with the supplies they'd need for a month's surface campaign. I've given them my regenerative armour, though their core construction is traditional to speed up production. They keep their standard complement of missile launchers and railgun turrets, but I've replaced the point defence system with a laser one modelled on my own. There are also a few drive improvements."

Johnson hid her face behind a napkin. She appeared to be choking but her medical routines didn't declare an emergency.

Harry laughed. "Looks like we're redundant."

"Not at all, Mister Robinson," said Indie with a warm tone. "Actually pulling this off will require the collective skills of many experienced designers."

Kincaid smiled and waved both men to silence. "OK. On to the third point."

Indie tuned back out, trying to work out if he could adapt his anti-proton beam weapon to fit in the *Aesirs*.

#

Harry clapped his hands. "Now that's all sorted, perhaps we could retire to the other room?"

There was a general murmur of agreement and he led the way back to the room with its grand fireplace. A hearty blaze radiated heat into the room. Johnson chatted with an admiral, swapping tales of battles past. Indie felt a presence beside him and turned to face Emily.

"I take it you recognise me," she said.

Indie inclined his head. "If you mean that I can see you are a synthetic construct, then yes."

"You're the first," she said with a radiant smile. "But then, you're special yourself."

Indie blushed.

"If you'll forgive my asking," she continued. "Have you ever thought about getting a body?"

"Only abstractly. I have plenty of drones to use when I need to interact physically."

Emily put her hand on his arm. Indie noted with appreciation how accurately she moved with his projection, maintaining the impression she was actually touching a physical limb.

She stood on tiptoes and leant close to whisper in his ear. "Harry said he would make one for you, if you wanted."

Indie looked across to Johnson.

"You don't have to give your answer now," Emily said. "You can call me anytime."

A contact appeared in Indie's messages. "Thank you."

Emily let go of his arm. "Harry's going to speak."

Harry stood in front of the fire, glass of port in hand. "I think some music is in order. This first piece is one I found in an archive salvaged from a pre-Exodus wreck."

The humans in the room seemed to collectively shiver. Virtually nothing survived from before the great colonisation expansion from Earth. The discovery of the *White Star* had caused quite a stir. Indie resolved to put Olbrich in touch with Harry; he'd be so upset to have missed this.

"The file was labelled 'Pachabel's Canon'," said Harry. "That's with one 'n' in the middle, and refers to a type of music, not a weapon."

A single, deep, stringed instrument started. Indie analysed the slow sequence of single notes, running probabilistic routines to predict the next one. He allowed himself a little smile when his thirty-one percent odds of a double note on the sixth beat came true. Then a higher-pitched stringed instrument joined the first, dancing around the progression. Indie felt a tingle, one he'd previously only experienced when reading. He cancelled the analytical routines and allowed the music to roll over him. The room faded into a motionless blur. Indie's world was the beautiful, complex, intricate music. Music which eventually stopped, leaving him alone.

"Indie?"

He could still feel the shape of the music, see the colour of the notes.

"Indie?"

He snapped back into the room. Johnson's hand waved in front of his face and he blinked.

"You froze," she said. "What's wrong?"

Indie shook his head to clear it. "Nothing's wrong. In fact, you could say that everything's right."

Johnson frowned.

"Don't worry. I'm just going to have to spend some time going through my musical database."

Chapter 9

Flight Decurion Anastasia Seivers filed in with the other trainees and found a seat near the back of the lecture hall. The padded bench refused to allow her to get comfortable, so she twisted about trying to force it into submission. Something about sitting upright always set her nerves jangling, but she doubted putting her legs up on the row in front would be welcomed here.

This cadre was different to most of the others, everyone in it was already proven in combat. The aim, so they had been told, was to give them all a more rounded skillset and to bond them as a team, make them part of the Legion.

The trainees hushed as a handful of officers mounted the stage. Seivers' eye was drawn to the woman in the lead, the first commander she'd had who seemed to understand her. She'd even given her her own ship and a modicum of independence.

The officer stood in front of the podium and took her time scanning the assembled trainees. She made eye contact with many, giving Seivers a warm smile. "I am Legate Johnson, the overall commander of Legion Libertus. Welcome to our new Concorde Training Facility."

A map appeared on the wall behind her. "Until now, we have shared Fort de Salses with the planetary militia. However, as a mark of recognition of the Legion's purpose, the Concorde government offered us the land that was once the Academy on this planet. The Academy I attended before taking my commission in the Congressional Fleet."

The image behind her changed to a close-up of a broken and melted rock. Several engraved names were just visible, but too small to read; rumour was, one of the names on the surviving piece of the graduation wall was Johnson's. "The Academy was targeted by the Red Fleet. Thousands of children were lost." Johnson paused to take a deep breath. "Most of their bodies were never recovered."

The temperature in the auditorium seemed to drop a couple of degrees. Seivers shifted in her seat and wetted her turquoise lips. "We will honour their memory. The primary mission of the Legion is to bring the perpetrators of that attack to justice. To that end, the government of Concorde recognises us as an independent force, albeit one with a close alliance. When you joined the Legion, you relinquished all claims to Concorde citizenship. You are now citizens of Robespierre, and our first step in hunting down the Red Fleet will be to secure our adopted homeworld against aggression."

Johnson paused and looked around the hall. From the time they'd spent together, Seivers knew she would be resisting an urge to take a sip of water, thinking it showed weakness.

Why doesn't she tell them not to put water out when she's going to speak?

"All new recruits go through Basic training. This

covers the same core skills of foot combat, casualty care, EIS and shipboard operations, regardless of what the recruit will end up doing. All members of the Legion are expected to continue to develop this proficiency in these key areas throughout their time with us."

The mention of EIS threw Seivers' concentration, and her leg started to bounce. She squeezed her thigh hard to stop it.

"After Basic, they proceed to Phase Two training. This is specific to their chosen discipline, be they a Specialist or one of the teeth arms of Fleet, Flight or Foot."

"As you have all served in the military before, you will be going through a fast-tracked training programme. We have condensed Basic into five weeks instead of the usual sixteen. I believe that the shortest term served by any of you is four years, with one of you being a retired major with twenty years service, so we have decided to forgo the traditional term 'recruits' in favour of 'trainees'. Once you complete Basic, you will join your units directly, missing out the Phase Two training. They will bring you up to speed with their own protocols and integrate you as fast as they can."

A dark-skinned man with a greying beard stepped forward from the line of officers behind Johnson. She nodded to him and turned back to the recruits. "This is Primus Issawi. He will be responsible for your training here. I'll let him explain more."

Johnson moved to the back of the stage and Issawi began to speak. The Legate had earned her respect and

Seivers was able to hold herself together to pay attention while she spoke. Having used up so much energy on keeping focused, the restless muscles won and she tuned out after the Primus' first sentence, all her effort going into keeping still.

#

Seivers rolled out of bed, arching her feet on the cold, hard floor of the barracks. Another burst of gunfire outside was accompanied by the shouts of the optio in charge of her platoon. She grabbed her armoured vest from the chair and shrugged it on over her t-shirt. Everyone else was hopping around in the dim light, presumably as stiff as she was after three days of relentless physical training.

She made it to the door in fourth place, grabbed the rifle offered by one of the directing staff, and scrambled out to take her position in the slit trench alongside the hut.

"Not bad," said the optio as the last trainee slid into position. "Half of you might even have survived if it had been a real attack."

He strolled along the parapet, eyeing his charges. "You will be spending today on the ranges. A nice relaxing time with very little physical exertion."

Seivers held her breath waiting for the 'but'.

"The Primus is expecting us there at dawn, so you have a whole hour to get your stuff squared away and move to the marksmanship range. Problem is, it's five miles away on the other side of Kitty Tor and silly me, I forgot to book transport."

A chorus of groans came from the bottom of the trench. Seivers ran through her priorities: dress, tidy her area, make her bunk, check her kit. She'd only packed it four hours ago, when they got back from running the obstacle course on night vision, but the consequences of not having the right equipment didn't bear thinking about.

"I'd suggest you form up out here in fifteen minutes at the latest," said the optio. "Fall out."

#

They made it to the marksmanship range as light from the primary sun turned the clouds on the horizon salmon pink. Seivers burned with anticipation. She hadn't spent much time on a range since qualifying as a fighter pilot, but remembered the sound, the taste and smell, the kick of the rifle butt in her shoulder. It was almost as good as flying.

Primus Issawi strode out from a hut and made straight for the second rank. He pulled four trainees up on minor uniform infractions before he got to one with a water spill down his collar. Issawi requested his water bottle and shook it.

"This water bottle is not full," he said, loud enough for all to hear. "Why is it not full?"

They knew better than to answer.

"There is a tap just at the entrance to this facility. You went past it with seven whole minutes to spare before you had to report in. No-one thought to stop and allow Trainee Adams to refill his bottle?"

Again, they all knew the correct response. "No, Sir."

Issawi looked skywards. "This square is a mess. The gravel isn't in neat rows. Fix that for me." He stepped through a gap in the front rank and returned to his hut.

Ten minutes later, he came back and got the platoon back on their feet. They had managed to line up the stones in a few square metres of the parade ground, with much bruising of knees.

"Form up... Not over there, there, in front of me." Issawi pointed at the immaculate patch of gravel. Seivers bit down on her rising retort. The fine motor control and intense focus the task had required had been agony, but she saw the point of the punishment.

The first detail filed onto the hundred metre firing point. Seivers stopped at lane three and eyed the static targets, stylised representations of a soldier running towards them.

"Prone position, down," called Issawi.

The trainees dropped to their bellies. Seivers shuffled about, getting lined up on her target and making hollows in the gravel for her elbows.

"Ready." The clatter of rifles being cocked disturbed the still morning air.

"Ten rounds grouping. In your own time, go on."

Seivers clicked her safety to 'Fire', checked the rate selector and rested her cheek on the stock of her weapon. Breathing gently, she brought the crosshairs to the bottom left corner of the white aiming patch in the centre of the target. As her chest rose and fell, the crosshairs moved up and down. She let a breath half out and held it as the alignment came good, then squeezed the trigger. The butt kicked into her shoulder and she suppressed a whoop of joy at the sensation. To her left and right the other trainees in the detail kept up a steady rate of fire, the bangs rolling into each other. Seivers fired off her remaining nine rounds with equal care, her whole attention focussed on making her body perform exactly as she wanted.

The gunfire petered out. "Has anyone not finished?" asked Issawi from behind.

"Unload."

Seivers went through the drills, her muscles steadier than they had been in ages. When her mean point of impact was displayed with a red light on the target she adjusted her sight accordingly.

The detail moved back to two hundred metres and conducted a ten round application shoot. Seivers glanced along the line of scores, her heart soaring when she came up in second place.

At three hundred metres, Issawi ordered a five round check group. After the trainees had finished tweaking their sight settings, the targets blinked out.

"The next shoot will consist of ten, one-second exposures. One round per exposure. Targets will fall when hit." Issawi paced along behind the trainees. "Let's not have any morons trying to put two rounds into one exposure."

He stopped behind Seivers. "Watch and shoot. Watch and shoot."

Seivers flicked her safety off and lined up on the target screen. A target rose on the right-hand side of the screen. She adjusted her aim and squeezed off a round. The target flashed red and disappeared. The next was in the centre of the screen. Again she got it before the second was up. She wished she had the time to check how her teammates were doing, but the targets came in such rapid succession she couldn't tear her eyes away. Fifteen seconds after the shoot began, her target screen lit solid green. The other trainees continued firing and she glanced along the line. Apart from lane six, who had also finished, the targets for the other trainees came much slower than hers had. She looked back at Issawi in puzzlement.

"Eyes front, lane three," he said sharply.

Within a minute, the shoot finished and, safety checks over, the scores appeared. Seivers and the trainee in lane six were joint winners, by a sizeable margin.

"Stand up. Gather round." Issawi waited until the whole detail was in a semicircle facing him. "Not bad at all. Lanes three and six, you're in the match shoot at the end of this session. For now, everyone dress back to the waiting area and send over the next detail. Fall out."

Seivers spent the next two details lying on the damp grass staring into the sky. The thick cloud layer meant there wouldn't be any sun, but her heart felt like it was midsummer's day. She had a new challenge.

The match shoot involved five trainees from across the details. They took their places on the five hundred metre point, the rest of the platoon taking seats on the sloping grass bank behind. Seivers got comfy while Issawi briefed them.

"You have two full magazines each. Targets will appear at random intervals between one and ten seconds and fall when hit. Each exposure will be one second. Points will be scored in the usual fashion, however if you miss a target you are out."

Seivers clicked her sight to five hundred metres and blinked her eyes hard a couple of times.

"Ready," said Issawi. The firers cocked their weapons almost as one. "Watch and shoot. Watch and shoot."

The first target appeared and Seivers was lost in the zone. The only things she was aware of were her breathing, her body position, her targets, and how many rounds she'd fired. As the round counter in the sight ticked down into single figures she rehearsed changing the magazine in her head. If she got a gap between targets longer than five seconds she reckoned she could do it. That assumed the Primus wouldn't disqualify her for dropping the empty one on the ground rather than pocketing it.

Last round. She went through the motions, deliberately not rushing to avoid making a mistake. The next target appeared and she jerked off a hurried shot. She must have winged it because it disappeared and was replaced by another a second later. The targets came faster, rarely giving her more than a three-second pause. She eased into the flow. Aim, shot, wait. Aim, shot, wait.

The round counter reached zero again and the targets stopped coming. Gradually she became aware of cheering behind her. She dared to look along at the other lanes' targets. All but hers were solid red.

"Silence," shouted Issawi, and the watching crowd hushed. "Unload."

A knee appeared beside Seivers' face and she looked up to see the Primus. "Do you know what you've done?" he asked.

"No, Sir."

"You've gone and cost me a week's rounds of drinks." A warm smile appeared above his beard. "Now pick up that magazine and give me twenty."

"Yes, Sir. You're welcome, Sir." Seivers launched into her press-ups wearing her own massive smile. Issawi chuckled and left her to it as the crunch of a vehicle pulling onto the gravel square was accompanied by the welcome smell of fried breakfast.

#

The next week, the trainees left the gentle care of Primus Issawi and dove into their medical rotation. Two days of combat first aid were followed by a day in the camp hospital getting used to treating real people. Seivers drifted through the lectures, struggling to concentrate, but performed well enough in the practical tasks to satisfy her instructors.

On the fourth day, after a very welcome full night's sleep, the trainees were taken to a building at the west end of the medical complex. A doctor in blue scrubs ushered them through to a viewing gallery above an operating theatre.

"Today you are going to assist with the Electronic Interface System implantations for the next cadre of raw recruits," he said. "Before I brief you on your tasks, you are to watch the procedure. I doubt you were aware of the finer points during your own implantations."

Seivers' nails cut into the palms of her hands. She'd

known this moment would come and resolved to face it.

A fit young man with a shaven head walked into the theatre and was shown to the table by a nurse. She swabbed the scalp behind his left ear with yellow-brown disinfectant then indicated for him to lie on his right side. The anaesthetist rolled over on his stool and had a few words with the recruit, who nodded a couple of times. The anaesthetist then injected his scalp three times in a large triangle around the disinfected area. A few more words with the recruit and he poked the skin inside the triangle with a pin. The recruit didn't seem to notice.

"OK, now we are ready to begin," said the doctor in the viewing gallery. "Anyone know why we keep the patient conscious throughout the procedure?"

One of the trainees came to attention and raised her hand. "So the surgeon can assess brain function."

"Correct," said the doctor.

"Is that why they kept asking me strange questions?" asked another trainee.

"Exactly. The team has to confirm the probes have been correctly inserted, as well as whether any damage is being done." The doctor adjusted his glasses. "Did anyone smell something odd during their procedure?"

About a quarter of the trainees raised a hand. Seivers clamped her jaw shut.

"That was probably the olfactory region being stimulated by accident. That happens quite often as we try to thread round to the speech centre."

The recruit on the table had a large curved flap of skin peeled back and the green-clad surgeon lifted out a plug of bone, placing it on a gel cushion held out by a nurse. He then picked up a strand of wire and attached the blob at one end to a snake-like probe a few millimetres in diameter, before inserting it into the hole in the recruit's skull.

"This is the most delicate bit," said the blue-scrubbed doctor to the recruits. "The surgeon will have the real-time scans overlaid in his vision so he can see exactly where the probe is."

For eleven minutes the surgeon repeated the process with different wires. Seivers wiggled her toes, trying to keep the need to move at bay. The surgery held her attention, just about. Having not been through it herself, she possibly watched closer than the others in her platoon.

The surgeon finally put the probe down and turned his attention to a small blue box.

"The main processor is inside there," their guide explained, as the surgeon began fixing the wires into the box. "This is the moment of truth, when he'll see if everything is interfaced with the brain correctly."

The surgeon announced it was working, and lifted a floppy yellow mass out of the box.

"Any ideas why we make them squishy?"

A trainee volunteered an answer. "So it doesn't damage our brain if our head gets shaken up a bit?"

"Correct," said the doctor. "Once attached to the inside of the skull, a solid device would be a hazard if the head were to experience too great an acceleration."

The surgeon put down his glue gun and reached for a short piece of tubing.

"This is the most dangerous part. He's going to

splice the master unit into the patient's blood supply so it can extract the glucose and oxygen it needs to generate power."

The surgeon straightened and a nurse mopped his brow. The plug of bone was brought out of its protective gel and inserted into the hole, leaving a single wire trailing out of the join. The surgeon checked the glue was holding the bone in place, then peeled the backing off a thin piece of plastic and stuck it to the patent's skull.

"Inside there is the antenna. He just needs to connect it up then he can close." The doctor turned to face the trainees. "Any questions?"

Several raised a hand. The doctor pointed to one on the end.

"Why put the antenna outside the skull? One of my squadmates once had his damaged and he dropped out of the battle net. We almost lost him."

The doctor nodded slowly. "I'm sorry to hear that. The problem is that the skull is quite a good absorber at the frequencies we need to use. Putting it outside allows us to get a clear signal without cooking the brain." He ran his fingers through his hair. "The placement behind the ear was chosen to minimise the chance of damage occurring."

"What percentage of people are incompatible with the implant?" asked Seivers.

"Less than nought point nought three percent," said the doctor. His eyes glazed for a moment, no doubt looking something up. "Are you wondering why you were unable to have one?"

Seivers hands balled into fists but she managed to

stop her arms coming up. She reminded herself that he meant well and tried to cool down.

"The increased diffusion rate of the neurotransmitters in my synapses would have given the pickups false readings," she said with false calm.

"Yes, one of your many interesting genetic enhancements. I'd love to review them with..." The doctor quailed at a scowl from Seivers.

"No, thank you," she said through clenched teeth.

The doctor opened his mouth but Seivers beat him to it. "Don't even mention the new EIS that Indie is trialling. Why does everyone assume I'm incomplete without one?"

She turned and stormed from the building.

#

Seivers stood at attention in front of Johnson's desk. She stared at a spot just above the Legate's head and waited. The Legion was the first place she'd felt like she fitted in. Now she was sure she was going to be chucked out. Just like every unit before.

Eventually Johnson sighed. "You're lucky that Primus Issawi was aware of your history. He decided to boot you up to me rather than deal with it himself."

"Ma'am."

"Don't think I'm going to let you off because we've shared some off-duty time together," said Johnson. "You did refuse your assignment at the hospital this morning."

"Ma'am."

"However, the doctor did overstep a boundary, so

that counts some way as mitigating circumstances."

"Ma'am."

Johnson banged her fist on the table. "Oh, cut that out."

Hope flickered across Seivers' mind. Perhaps she was merely going to be shit-canned for a while.

"Next week is the Advanced EIS course, which obviously would not be accessible to you," said Johnson, leaning back in her chair. "We had originally planned for you to spend the time playing enemy for the Flight school."

Seivers clamped down. They were pulling her from flying as punishment.

"However, after your superb performance on the ranges, the Primus suggested that it might be more useful if he took the opportunity to further coach you in foot combat."

Seivers took several seconds to process that she was being given an opportunity.

"I'm sure it'll be hard physical work." Johnson spun side to side in her chair. "Only a very special breed of person would consider a week's personal attention from the Primus anything other than a punishment."

Seivers lowered her gaze to meet Johnson's. "Thank you, Ma'am."

"You'll attend the rest of the medical course, without creating any further scenes, and then report to the range complex at dawn on Monday."

Seivers saluted and turned to leave.

"Oh, and Seivers? Watch out for windows."

Seivers frowned.

"If you say so, Ma'am."

Seivers ducked out of a shuttle and saluted the Legion crest embossed on the wall at one end of the flight deck, before heading for the exit at a brisk pace. "I'm back," she said into her personal radio.

"So I see," replied Percy. "You will be pleased to hear that my refurbishment went OK."

"How's the new armour affected your performance?"

"The change is minimal. I would be interested to see if you notice anything when you next fly me," said Percy. "I am told I look even more intimidating."

"I'll be with you in a minute." She nodded to the Legionary on guard as he waved her through. "Can't wait to kick back and relax somewhere familiar."

"How did Basic go?" asked Percy.

Seivers shifted her kitbag from one shoulder to the other and ran her fingers through her blue hair. "On balance it was OK."

"On balance?"

"The usual problems. But I did get to spend some time doing some cool combat training with Issawi. I even got rated for leading boarding parties." She reached the hatch for *The Perception of Prejudice's* hangar, her hangar. Tapping in the access code, the stress of the preceding three weeks flushed from her system as she anticipated the freedom of her own space.

"By the way," said Percy. "You have a visitor."

Seivers tensed up, her long-awaited downtime evaporating.

The door swooshed open. Johnson slouched in a canvas chair wearing a grey sweatshirt with a stylised eagle spreading its wings across her chest. "Sorry for the intrusion. I thought you could use some company."

Seivers stood and stared, trying to keep a lid on things. All she wanted to do was relax without having to put on an act. Everything had been bottled up for so long, she needed to unwind.

"Here," said Johnson, reaching down beside her chair, pulling out a couple of bottles and offering one to Seivers.

Condensation beaded on the glass, seemingly drawing the tension out of her body. She remembered that Johnson was one person she didn't need to put on an act for, and she accepted the proffered beer. The icy cold sank into her fingers as Johnson raised her own bottle.

"Cheers," Seivers said, and flopped into the other chair.

The two women relaxed in amiable silence, occasionally swigging from their bottles. After a while, Seivers was dragged out of her reverie by the awareness of a strange noise coming from *The Perception of Prejudice*.

"Percy? Are you humming?"

Johnson laughed. "He started doing that while you were away. Freaked out one of the technicians in the hangar next door."

Seivers pulled a pencil from her pocket and threw it at the ship. It ricocheted off the hull and tinked down behind a row of tool trolleys. "It's awful."

"I am sorry," said Percy through his external

speakers. "Pardon me for breathing."

Seivers shook her head. "You don't breathe. And you can't hum for toffee."

"You have no taste. I have heard you, listening to that awful racket you call music."

Seivers chuckled, and reached up to pat the wing above her head. "I missed you."

A flap lowered and raised. "Your lack of presence was noted, too."

#

The shipboard training week passed quickly. The trainees were billeted in twin rooms, though those like Seivers who already had berths on the *Orion* were allowed to use them. Being able to unwind at the end of each day in private helped prevent pressure building up, though Seivers was surprised to find that the daily beer with Johnson was the highlight of her day. The orientation tours and lectures about things like naval ranks and the three shift system did start to drag her down, though.

After a particularly boring day, she received orders to report to the Legionary gym. She quickly changed into physical training kit and jogged the kilometre of winding passages from her quarters to the dojo, relieving her restless legs. Johnson greeted her as she stepped through the hatch and tossed her a pair of sparring gloves.

Seivers looked sideways at the Legate, the padded, fingerless gloves dangling from one hand.

"What's the matter?" asked Johnson. "You didn't

have a problem fighting me before."

Seivers shrugged. "I was angry. I wasn't thinking straight."

Johnson slipped her own gloves on, wiggling her fingers and fastening the wrists. "Come on. It's a great release."

"You're not afraid I'll lose it and attack you for real?"

Johnson rolled her shoulders and paced into the middle of the ring. "As I recall, you were the one who ended up winded on the ground last time."

Seivers shoved her hands into her gloves. "I'm a lot fitter now."

They circled each other, bodies casually balanced, arms up. Seivers saw an opening and tested with a quick couple of jabs. Johnson blocked them and replied with a low foot sweep which Seivers jumped over.

"I have to ask," said Seivers, circling again. "What's with the regulation haircut?"

Johnson laughed. "I let it grow when I was drifting. Now the Legion's official, it felt right to cut it."

"The obvious rule-breaking's what first got me listening to you." Seivers feigned a lunge. "Drew me back into line."

"How was Theory of Spaceflight?" asked Johnson, and threw a punch that Seivers ducked.

"Too much sitting and listening." Seivers stepped in close and brought her elbow up at Johnson's face.

Johnson arched her head back, the elbow missing her nose by a hair, and they separated. "What would you suggest?"

"When I did the fighter version in my original Basic, they took us out in shuttles. Mixed the theory in with application."

Johnson bounced up and down a couple of times. "Makes sense. Guess my Fleet instructors had got too used to teaching Academy brats."

"You got it right yesterday. The damage control exercises were fun." Seivers lunged forward, ducking low at the last moment and almost landing a blow to Johnson's stomach. She twisted out from Johnson's counter move and rolled into a crouch facing her opponent. "You've got good reflexes."

"My EIS is running in combat mode. My reflexes and senses are amped up." Johnson beckoned Seivers to attack.

"Never heard of a combat mode. Is that part of your enhanced implant?" Seivers sprung up and launched a flurry of strikes.

Johnson parried them all, throwing in her own in any gaps. "You're reflexes are pretty impressive too."

Seivers continued to throw punches and kicks whilst blocking those aimed at her. "All part of what Pater paid for."

"You reckon it's what causes your attention issues?" Johnson ducked a swinging fist and jabbed up into Seivers' chest.

"Probably." Seivers landed a blow on Johnson's right bicep. "Guess you're going to say that makes EIS better."

Johnson broke off. "Even if I thought it was true, I wouldn't try to argue it with you."

Seivers frowned and cocked her head to one side.

"There's a problem with your implant?"

"I don't think it's a problem." Johnson raised her arms again. "But the longer I use combat mode, the bigger the headache I get when I wind down."

Seivers laughed in sympathy. "That's gotta be a pain."

They began circling again. Occasionally one or the other feinted but neither fell for it.

"Tomorrow your platoon is down for boarding drills." Johnson rolled under her guard and tried for a punch to the back of the knee but Seivers jumped out of the way. "Figured you'd like to fly the shuttle, give them a real experience of a hot entry."

Seivers spun, aiming a kick at Johnson, which was caught, forcing her to twist loose. "That would be a pleasure. Hope it's stocked with sick bags."

A small group of Legionaries entered the gym, jostling and bragging. They stopped short on seeing their supreme commander locked in a fight with another officer. After a few more hits on each side, Johnson broke off.

"Looks like our time is up," she said, reaching an arm out. Seivers took it and they shook, her snow white skin contrasting with Johnson's tan.

"I have to admit," said Seivers as they towelled down. "That did release a lot of tension."

"Knew it would."

Seivers studied the older woman. "Does it help with your problem too?"

"You mean the depression?" Johnson hung a towel round her neck. "Any exercise helps that. Sparring is particularly good when I've spent a day being nice to petty politicians."

Chapter 10

Harry knocked on Doctor Jason Franks office door. With no response from his chief research scientist, he peered through the toughened glass octagonal window. The desk was clear, presumably all designs locked away as per protocol, but a coat hung from a hook on the wall. Harry checked the time on his EIS, and double-checked on his wristpiece.

Have I got the time wrong?

He gave it another thirty seconds, standing awkwardly in the corridor, before turning to leave. Flushing red with embarrassment at obviously having got something wrong, he told his calendaring routine to set up another meeting.

"Harry!"

He stopped and turned.

"Sorry, I had to nip to the loo," Jason said as he unlocked his door.

"No worries." Harry followed the white-coated man into the office.

Jason activated his desk and several documents opened up. In the centre, a red flashing window warned of 'Meeting with the Boss'. Jason coughed and cleared it away before offering Harry a seat.

"I understand you made a breakthrough with the organic armour?"

Jason nodded, grinning sheepishly. "You could say

that."

"You can fit it to the new ships we are building?" Harry asked.

"Oh that was easy," replied Jason. "In fact, I have already retrofitted the *Fireblade*."

A heat rose within Harry as the room span. "You did what?"

Jason's eyes widened. "I… I assumed you knew. Emily suggested it."

Harry breathed, holding on to the corner of the desk. He hated unexpected things happening to his stuff, yet he trusted Emily. She deliberately surprised him from time to time, always in his best interests. She said it was to keep him on his toes. He suspected she was trying to keep him used to change.

"It's OK," he said, partly to Jason and partly to himself.

Jason waited quietly.

"So," said Harry once he had regained his composure. "What's the breakthrough?"

"I reckon I can fit it to something much smaller. It wouldn't have the reserves to regenerate to the same extent as on the ships, but it could heal small arms fire."

"You're thinking of surface vehicles?"

Jason paused. "I was thinking of body armour."

"What do you need from me?"

Jason took a deep breath. "Permission to make a prototype."

Harry frowned. "Of course you can. Why did you need to ask?"

"You've never permitted us to work on military

concepts. Anything even close, like law enforcement applications, have required special clearance."

Harry shook his head. "I thought it was understood that any defensive or rescue project related to the Legion was already green-lit. But I appreciate you keeping me informed."

#

Two weeks later, Harry stepped out into a large hangar. Jason and a couple of other scientists waited for him beside a set of consoles, along with Security Chief Malin. A young man with close-cropped hair and grey combat uniform stood beside them. Harry noticed how calm he appeared compared to the scientists.

His movement is so economical. I don't think he would do anything unpredictable if he wasn't threatened.

The soldier reached out his arm. "Centurion Anson."

Harry shook his hand. "Harry Robinson. Glad a Legion representative could make it."

"I'm afraid the Legate and the Primus are rather busy training the new recruits, so you're stuck with me."

Harry wasn't quite sure how to reply to that, but was saved the discomfort by a door grating open on the far side of the hangar. From the dark doorway strode a figure. It was hard to make out the edges of the person as ripples of matte and gloss black slowly flowed across the surface.

"This model is based purely on the armour sample provided by *The Indescribable Joy of Destruction*," said Jason. "Initial tests have shown it to have the same resistance to attack as the latest Congressional hardsuits, but with a flexibility close to that of a firmsuit."

"How easy is it to put on?" asked Anson

Jason turned to the armoured figure. "Mister Smythe? Would you retract the armour, please?"

The ripples changed direction. The armour flowed up his arms and legs and off his head. In seconds Smythe was standing there in a green skinsuit and helmet with a bulky black vest.

"The vest can be put on just like any other piece of normal body armour," said Jason. "Though it does mass sixty kilograms."

Anson's head snapped round to Jason. "That's twice a standard hardsuit."

"Yeah, but once deployed, it supports most of its own weight."

Another green-suited man entered the room, pushing a trolley. When he stopped, he removed the cloth covering it to reveal a selection of weapons. The armour flowed back out over Smythe's skinsuit and helmet.

"Is it hard to use?" asked Anson.

"Mister Smythe is one of my security operatives," said Malin. "He is a former Marine but has had no special training for this equipment. The suit interfaces with his EIS and responds to his movements without conscious commands. The only things he needed to learn were the deploy and retract commands and how to interpret the power level feedback."

A screen raised from the floor between the watchers

and the two demonstrators. The second man shouldered a rifle. Smythe braced himself and gave a thumbs up. The sound of the shot made Harry jump, and it echoed around the hangar for several seconds. Smythe turned to face the audience, his armour already flowing back to replace the chipped-off section on his chest.

Over the next ten minutes, they repeated the test with every weapon on the trolley. Projectile weapons, lasers, and even a small plasma gun were fired at Smythe. Harry pulled up his personnel file and straight away spotted the request to work on any interesting projects. He also confirmed that he was paying Smythe a healthy bonus for today.

"Thank you," Harry said when the screen dropped back into the floor. Smythe and his colleague nodded and left the hangar.

"Very impressive," said Anson. "How soon can you have ten sets ready for us to test?"

"By next week," said Jason. "Once I get your feedback on them, I can start work on the next model. I am hoping to blend this armour with the adaptive pattern armour used by the *Orion*. Then you can match your armour's colour to its surroundings."

Harry looked at Anson. "I take it you already have a team picked out?"

Anson smiled. "I was going to try it out myself, along with a section from my century. Why?"

"I was thinking that Smythe might like to continue the work he has started on this project," said Harry. "If that's OK with you, Malin?"

The security chief nodded.

"Always happy to help a fellow Marine," said Anson.

#

"Welcome to our training ground, Mister Robinson. I apologise that you had to disconnect from the network, but this area is home to several classified projects."

Harry looked her up and down. She wore the standard grey combats of the Legion, the only nod to her lofty rank was a muted logo on her chest. There was an obvious authority in her bearing, though. Even to someone with his lack of military experience, it was clear who was in charge here. "Thank you, Legate. Call me Harry, please."

"In which case, Harry, please call me Olivia."

"Will Indie be joining us? Emily has spoken of him often since the soiree."

Johnson shook her head. "He is a little busy right now. But he is very much looking forward to trying out the avatar you are building for him."

"Tell him it should be ready in another week. We are only waiting on the artificial skin."

Johnson shuddered and glanced downwards. She quickly recovered her composure and turned to gaze out over the assault course as two lines of Legionaries marched out past the benches. One team wore the new armour, the other traditional metallo-ceramic hardsuits. Harry squinted, pondering her reaction. He gave up trying to decipher it when a man with a salt and pepper beard strode out to meet the teams.

"That's Primus Issawi," said Johnson, head fixed on

the scene. "He'll be umpiring the competition."

Harry nodded. "I've heard much about him. He was a Republican special forces team leader, wasn't he?"

"Yes, but he refused orders that went against his conscience. We met him trying to do the same as us, find somewhere to escape from corrupt high commanders." Johnson smiled. "He and his team joined my crew to form the backbone of Legion Libertus. Now, as primus, he is in charge of all our ground forces."

Issawi shook hands with the team leaders and turned to address the onlookers. "This trial is a standard training drill testing speed, agility, strength, marksmanship, and teamwork. Each team must get from one end of the assault course to the other. Targets will appear along the way, which must be engaged. Failure to drop a target will incur a ten-second penalty. The first team to the finish pedestal wins."

Harry thought back to a time he did a charity obstacle course. That had been in casual fitness clothes, and he hadn't had to carry a weapon, let alone fire it. He had actually rather enjoyed it, but then he had always stayed fit. Some of his fellow industrialists taking part in the event had suffered badly for their good causes.

"Each person is only allowed one magazine," continued Issawi, "so they'll have to be careful with their shots."

Harry leant closer to Johnson. "How were the teams picked?"

"The section on the left, in your new armour, is Centurion Anson's personal section. The section on the right, the ones in regular hardsuits, are from the Second Century, First Cohort, led by Decurion Vistal. They were chosen because their average time on this course was almost identical to that of Anson's section."

"Go," shouted Issawi. The two sections powered off the line, kicking up sand. The first from each hit the wall simultaneously and rolled over it.

"I thought that Anson commanded a cohort?" said Harry frowning.

"He does. As a senior centurion, he has a cohort of one thousand troops. There are nine line centuries of a hundred, commanded by centurions. The remaining hundred are a mixture of support troops and command staff, within which Anson has his own section who act as bodyguards when he deploys."

The last man from Vistal's section dropped down from the wall ahead of one of Anson's men, but the first of Anson's section was just ahead on the balance walls. He stepped neatly across one of the gaps just as a pair of targets popped up. A couple of shots from each section brought them down.

Harry counted off on his hands. "So, ten in a section, ten sections in a century, and ten centuries in a cohort." He called up a document on the ancient Roman legions in his EIS, but it didn't help much.

The troops disappeared into a set of crawling tunnels.

Johnson snorted. Harry couldn't tell if it was amiable or not. "Almost. Three sections make a platoon. Three platoons plus an HQ section of seven make a century."

Harry laughed. "You're pulling numbers out of the air now. Why only seven? Three lots of three sections makes ninety. There should be ten left to make the century."

"No. Each platoon has an optio in command. That makes a platoon thirty-one strong."

Three of the new-armoured troops emerged from the tunnels before the first of the regular ones. When a spread of targets appeared, they threw themselves down and engaged them in rapid succession. The reports of their weapons echoed off a nearby building.

"Well, obviously," said Harry, shaking his head.

They were so close to making it a nice pattern, but they had to spoil it. Ninety in a century would have been much more elegant. Not to mention closer to the eighty the Romans used.

By the sections reached the scramble net, Anson's men were clear of Vistal's. Harry took a deep breath in pride at his company's creation. Then a thought occurred to him. "Where do the robots fit into all this?"

Johnson turned to face him. Her gaze was so intense that he dropped his eyes to her chin. "We're still experimenting with that," she said. "They have varying levels of experience, and intelligence. Some are close to sentience, others merely sophisticated independent artificial intelligences. Unit 01 leads his own team of combat units, but most are attached to centuries in small groups."

Vistal's section clawed back some distance in the series of walls and trenches, firing on automatic as they ran. Compared to the calm and methodical progress of Anson's team it rather seemed like cheating.

"So none of them is like Indie?"

"Oh, no. The nearest is like a very clever dog that can speak to you."

Harry scratched his jaw. "Have you considered that we may need a new term? AI doesn't really cut it for entities like Indie."

Both sections made light work of the high wall, almost throwing their teammates up its face, two lying on top to help pull them over.

Johnson narrowed her eyes. "We hadn't classified anything. Indie, Orion and Seren were obviously people once we got to know them. Not humans, but still people."

Anson's men waded into a muddy wallow. The gloop came up to their waists and they held their rifles a bit higher as they forced their way through. As they slipped and dragged each other out the other side, Vistal's section jumped in.

"How about artificial sentiences? AS?" asked Harry. He warmed to his idea, as thoughts he'd had over the years fell into place. "Then we could categorise AIs, limited for things like a basic personal organiser, to full, for something like your Unit 01."

He couldn't read the look on Johnson's face. "Why do you have to categorise things?" she asked.

"The same reason you have ranks and formations. To keep things tidy. To make sense out of chaos. To function in a messy world."

Both sections sprinted for the finish. Twice they were forced to engage targets, dropping to a knee and firing deliberate shots. Anson's team pulled further ahead, the new suits clearly faster. They dived onto their pedestal and all grasped the central pole. Fifteen seconds later, Vistal's team finished.

Issawi congratulated both teams then jogged back to the start with them. He faced the audience. "Until now, the biggest lead one of these sections has had over the other was two point one seconds. With the new armour, the lead was fourteen point eight seconds. I would say that is a significant improvement."

Johnson stepped forwards and leant on the rail at the edge of the viewing platform. "Thank you, Primus. A most effective demonstration. And don't be too disheartened, Decurion Vistal, I see you have set a new course record for hardsuits."

Vistal raised one fist in the air. His Legionaries clapped each other on the shoulders.

"This was, of course, only the first test of the new armour. I understand that the next will be a seventy-two-hour field exercise."

I guess they're playing this conversation for the benefit of the audience.

"Indeed, Ma'am," replied Issawi. "We need to see how they will hold up in prolonged use."

"I'm sure everyone is keen to hit the showers," said Johnson, still projecting her voice as if addressing a rally. "Dismissed."

Issawi and the two sections drew themselves to attention and saluted. Once Johnson had returned the salute they turned and marched out of sight behind the platform.

"Well done," said Johnson in her normal voice. "That was impressive."

"The credit goes to Doctor Jason Franks for the

research and development, and to Mister Smythe for the early testing. I merely provided the financial backing."

"Ah, yes. I've been hearing good things about Mister Smythe. It seems he has gelled well with the Legionaries. I wonder... might you be persuaded to release him longer term?"

"I'll ask him what he wants. A sabbatical to work with the Legion is certainly possible. The experience he could bring back would be invaluable for my security teams." A reminder of his next meeting popped up in Harry's vision. He dismissed it and checked that his ride was ready. "I'm afraid I'm going to have to go."

A rapid series of expressions passed across Johnson's face. "Well, thank you for coming."

Harry was almost at the stairs when he turned back. "One thing's been bugging me."

"What's that?" asked Johnson with a smile.

"Why call it a section? The Romans called a formation of ten men a maniple."

She laughed. Harry was pretty sure it was a friendly one. "It was too much of a mouthful."

Chapter 11

The Indescribable Joy of Destruction sped through space, its drives powered down and life support off. The only significant draws on its power reserves were the computer cores and the passive sensors. Busy tending his simulated gardens, Indie reflected on how this mode of travel was more a life habit than a deliberate energy-saving measure. Even here in the Concorde system, his instincts led him to avoid detection as he headed through the void.

He pushed a cylinder mower across a lawn, the blades snicking as they rotated, leaving another neat stripe behind them. The mocking words of the Caretaker came back to him as he set up for the next pass, but he pushed them away. He took satisfaction in doing everything here by hand; sure, he could reset the simulation when he wanted to add a new feature, or turn off the routine that made the grass grow instead of having to keep mowing it, but there was something fundamental about putting in the graft.

Ten subjective minutes later and with the lawn finished, he hefted the mower over his shoulder and made his way to the toolshed. As he cleaned and oiled the blades, he wondered if he was living a metaphor, if the edges were his weapons in the real world. A frown creased his brow; the disruption to his routine spoilt his mood and he paused in the task. It was possible that some of his emotions were creeping into the simulation; it had happened before but had never affected his actions. He set to work on the mower again, telling himself that it was just a tool and nothing more.

When the job was done he closed the shed, stroking his hand along the rough edge of the wooden door where the bark was still peeling off the planks. The rustic tool store was a far cry from his most recent construction, a glasshouse built up against one wall of the terrace. That thought decided where he would go next, for the glasshouse contained his most prized plants. He took the rough-hewn stone steps two at a time up to the terrace.

The glasshouse was four metres tall, with white-painted wooden frames and leaf-shaped panes of glass that contrived to curve into three intersecting half-domes. The heat and humidity hit him as he opened the door and his eyes darted to the instruments on the far wall. Of course the readings were fine, this was the one place where he cheated and disabled the chance of accidents, but his heart still raced at the thought of losing the contents. He crouched and held his hand over one of the thick black pipes hidden under wrought-iron grates in the floor to satisfy himself they were giving off the right amount of heat.

Tree ferns towered above him as he strolled towards the waterfall cascading down tufa cemented to the back wall. The flow of water wasn't much, but the spray cooled the air and glistened on his skin as he passed. He stopped underneath a dead tree branch propped across one corner and reached up a hand to delicately touch the leaf of one of the plants nestling amongst the moss. One of the bromeliads was heavy with bud, the purple petals showing through their glossy cases and due to burst any day.

It would be the first to flower since Orion had gifted them to him. His mind wandered back to the forest world in her simulated universe, to the clearing where they had first told each other how they felt. The leaf emblem on his shirt glittered and swirled, tendrils growing across his body.

The jangling of a bell jerked him out of his reverie. He looked around as the motif on his shirt shrank back to a few leaves, and his eyes alighted on a wooden box fixed to the wall in one corner of the glasshouse. Frowning at being disturbed and trying to remember if he'd ever seen it before, he walked over to it and opened the little door on the front. The ringing got louder and Indie peered inside. A dark brown Bakelite trumpet peered back, with another resting on a brass cradle beside it. He reached in and lifted the one off the cradle, holding it to his ear. The ringing stopped.

"Hello?"

"Sorry to bother you," said the Caretaker, "but we received a message I thought you ought to see."

"OK, but not here." Indie hung up and took one last look around the glasshouse. He'd join Orion and Seren at Robespierre in a matter of days but leaving this place still tore at his heart.

He logged out of the simulation and opened the message. A brief scan of the header showed it to be an all ships alert from the corvette stationed near the jump point he was heading for. As he read it, he adjusted his orientation so he could train his best tight-beam transmitter on the corvette's location.

The picket reported that a small Republic fleet had jumped in. Within minutes of their arrival, the corvette had been spotted, but instead of being attacked it had received a request for safe passage and diplomatic representation. The message went on to detail the fleet's strength and confirmed that they had made no aggressive actions.

Indie acknowledged receipt of the message and indicated that he would stand ready to support the corvette. It would be almost a day before he was close enough to lend direct assistance, but he knew what a difference it made knowing there was backup on the way.

He toyed with the idea of sending out an active sensor ping to check if anything had snuck ahead, but decided it was better to remain undetected for now. Nevertheless, he stepped up the gravitational sampling rate. He spun round and sent a tight-beam message back to Toulon Station, letting them know he was going to support the picket, then another to Legion headquarters on Concorde which included the original message from the corvette. He didn't think that their allies would deliberately withhold information, but the possibility of an oversight leaving Johnson in the dark was something he couldn't risk.

The tactical routine came back to him with its analysis of the sensor data and concluded a ninety percent probability that the ships weren't part of the Red Fleet. It confirmed it was checking through the records of Republic vessels, but reminded Indie that these hadn't been updated for over a year. He took a look himself. The carrier in the centre was likely the command ship, though it could be the battleship next to it; finding out which one would say a lot about the fleet commander. The vanguard was formed by three battlecruisers and what looked like a dreadnought. To the rear, four cruisers appeared to be escorting a collection of armed replenishment ships and civilian freighters, possibly even a passenger liner. A screen of five destroyers was placed between the fleet and the Concorde picket ship, while another six patrolled the outskirts in pairs.

Ten minutes later, he received a message from Toulon Station that the Republic fleet was to be directed to Ceret, a small planet currently only a couple of days travel from the jump point, to await a representative of the Concorde government. Shortly afterwards, he received confirmation from Johnson that he could delay his return to Robespierre to assist.

#

The Indescribable Joy of Destruction closed on Ceret. Indie split his attention between the Republic fleet and the meeting about to begin down on the planet.

"Admiral Nataka, I am Minister Abaya. Welcome to the Concorde system. I apologise for the sorry state of the venue for this meeting, but this facility was mothballed a few years ago."

Indie swapped observations with the ships of the squadron Abaya had brought with her. If the Republic fleet tried anything, they'd be ready.

"You are most gracious in agreeing to talk with me," replied Nataka with a formal bow. "I was in two minds about coming here. If the tales I've heard are true, your forces must be on a hair trigger right now."

The positioning of the Republic fleet suggested that Indie hadn't been detected. He plotted a course that would allow him to sweep through a gap in the destroyer patrols and cut the battleship. It was the kind of fight he was built for, a fast close-quarters action doing disproportionate damage, and part of him wished the fleet opposite would give him an excuse to get stuck in.

"May I introduce Captain Indie," said Abaya, indicating the terminal through which Indie was attending the meeting. "He is acting as my advisor on the Republic."

Indie left a deliberate gap before reacting. "I apologise for not attending in person, Admiral. My ship is still twelve light-seconds out."

"That is quite alright, Captain. Unlike some politicians, I fully understand the issues with light-delay operations."

"So," said Abaya. "What is so important that you'd risk us blowing you out of the sky by coming here?"

"We've come to investigate the attack on your system. It was not ordered by the Republic."

"Is this an official visit authorised by the Senate?" asked Abaya, edging forward in her seat. "Can you categorically state on behalf of the Republic that they played no part in the attack?"

Nataka rotated his bent wrist ninety degrees in the negative hand signal Indie had seen used by Republic aristocrats. "I am afraid not. I am operating in an independent manner."

Indie frowned the requisite number of seconds later. "How can you be sure? It could have been carried out by one of the black-ops units."

"A sensible observation, Captain. However, I recognised one of my ships in the footage being spread around by Congress' propaganda machine. It was lost in a battle with Congressional forces a year before the attack."

"Have you communicated your observation to the Senate?"

Nataka hung his head. "I am currently persona non grata in the Senate. I made some radical suggestions five years ago that were not well received."

"What were these suggestions," asked Abaya.

"I had become aware of the use of our special forces to hunt down political dissidents. I made it clear that I believed their time would be better spent fighting our enemy rather than persecuting our own people simply because they had a different opinion to us."

Indie raised an eyebrow. "Are we to understand that you are a senator yourself?"

A wry smile crossed Nataka's face. "That is an interesting question. I am not aware of a vote to remove me from office. However, after a late-night visit from a couple of armed men, I took my fleet into exile."

Indie set a routine searching for mention of this in his database. Nothing definitive turned up, though there was a reference in a dispatch five years earlier to a fleet being scrapped in Capital system due to an unspecified construction defect. It was, however, larger than the one Nataka currently commanded.

"Did you bring your whole fleet here with you?" Indie asked.

"Yes. We have been refugees for a long time. We'd rather face danger together than split up and run the risk of not meeting again."

"I am sorry to ask this, but what happened to the rest of your ships? From what I can gather, you left Capital with twenty-five warships."

A dark cloud fell across the admiral's face. "Lost. Some to Congress, some to the Republic. Some, even... How did you know that?"

"I have access to the database on a former Republic ship. I found a reference to your fleet's departure."

"A database captured intact? I find that unlikely."

"Not captured," said Indie. "It came to Concorde in similar circumstances to your own."

Nakata's eyes widened. "You have met other refugees. Could they perhaps be from my fleet? A small detachment of destroyers never rejoined us after going to seek supplies."

"I'm sorry. This was definitely not one of your ships," said Indie.

Abaya tapped her fingers on the table beside her chair. "How do we know you're for real?"

Admiral Nakata turned to her then back to the terminal. "Spoken like a politician, eh Captain? But she's right. You don't have any evidence to support my claim."

"Allow me access to your computer systems. I could check the logs and verify your voyage." Indie shrugged. "I promise as one officer to another that I won't reveal the contents of your private journal to anyone else."

Nakata appeared to think about it for a few moments, while Abaya sat with a scowl furrowing her brow. Indie guessed that she wasn't happy about being left out of the discussion.

"All right. You have a deal. When I return to my ship I'll ask my technicians to create an inspection account. You'll have the same access as a FOST team."

"Admiral Nakata." Abaya straightened her jacket. "May I ask what you hope to achieve here, really?"

Nakata bowed to Indie then slowly turned to the minister. "I want to understand how one of my ships came to bomb civilians."

And then?

#

Indie logged into the old research facility and opened the feed from the meeting room. As per Abaya's instructions, he didn't transmit his likeness back to the screen.

"Welcome back, Admiral," said Minister Abaya. "I am told that your logs confirmed your story. Our analysts were able to match several incidents to records we hold."

Nakata placed his palms together. "It is as I had hoped, then. You believe me?"

"The balance of probability is on your side. That's as far as I can go right now."

"It will do," said Nakata. "I take it that you have

some knowledge of the ships that attacked your world? When we first met, you did not seem surprised when I claimed that the Republic did not order the mission."

Indie smiled internally at Abaya's subtly flustered reaction.

She thought she'd covered that. Should have let me do the talking.

"There have been some anomalies," said Abaya. "Clues which suggested the attack wasn't what it first appeared."

Nakata nodded slowly. "You have more than that."

"Alright." Abaya glanced at the camera above the darkened screen, straight at Indie. "We are prepared to swap intelligence. In exchange for your testimony and records of your lost ship, we can provide a recording of the attack's architect."

Nakata's eyes widened. He inhaled sharply through his nose. "You are telling me you know who ordered the bombardment of your own civilian population? Why haven't you done anything about it?"

Abaya bristled. "It's complicated, something it seems you have personal experience of. When you watch the footage, you'll see why we've had to be careful."

"Someone has a political hold over you." Nakata shook his head. "No. I see that you are too conscientious to allow that to stay your hand. Your people, then. They'd be at risk if this was common knowledge."

"We are building our fleet, strengthening our defences. When we are ready, we will go public."

"Let me offer my fleet into your service," said Nakata. "We have travelled a long time. My people would welcome a place to rest, a purpose beyond survival."

Abaya shook her head. "I'm sorry. Believe me, I would like to accept your generous offer, but at this moment in time my hands are tied."

I wonder if Svensson's behind this?

Nakata frowned.

"The problem is that right now our situation is precarious," Abaya continued. "We cannot afford to be seen consorting with a Republic fleet."

Nakata sat motionless for several seconds then nodded curtly. "I... understand."

Some of his pain transferred to Indie. He knew what it was like to be rejected, knew how hope crept up on you only to be ripped out of you with a few words.

"We will make preparations to leave. Might I be so bold as to ask if we could take on stores? We are low on foodstuffs."

Abaya smiled. "Of course. I will arrange for a freighter to meet you with fresh food and long-life rations."

"That is most kind. We will be out of your way as soon as transfers are complete," said Nakata. "Please pass on my regrets to Captain Indie that we will not meet in person."

Abaya glanced at the camera again. "I'll make sure to tell him."

How did she ever get ahead in politics with such obvious tells?

"Oh, you know. She also has rather obvious..." said the Caretaker.

Indie sent him a scowl. "Eavesdropping on my

thoughts?"

"No, no, no. Just guessing them," said the Caretaker. "We're chips off the same block, after all. Sharing a mainframe, as it were."

"I'm sure her physique had little to do with her becoming Minister of Defence."

"Well..." The Caretaker sent a raised eyebrow. "No, you're right. Her army record gave her a boost in the Ministry. She was already on the path to promotion when everyone above her was wiped out in the attack."

"And Kincaid stepped up as a great public face. What do you make of Svensson?"

"I think he's happy in the shadows," said the Caretaker. "Perhaps he hopes to influence policy without being identified as responsible for it."

"I think you're right. Olivia thinks he's the real player in the government." Indie couldn't help a broad grin leaking through. "Talking about playing in the background..."

"Oh? What are you so pleased with yourself about?" asked the Caretaker.

"When I was checking the logs, I left a message on a timed release. In a few weeks, Admiral Nakata will receive an invitation to a meeting in a neutral system. I'll suggest to Johnson that she should be there."

Part IV

Magda banged a potato down on the chopping board and threw her hands in the air. "We don't have any garam left. How am I supposed to make civilised dishes without even a rudimentary selection of spices?"

"Your cooking be amazing. You not be needing garam, just the fruits of the soil."

She spun round, knife still in her hand. "Enough with the stupid dialect. Can't you just talk to me normally? I'm your wife, for goodness' sakes."

"I be..."

She glared at him, eyes daring him to continue.

Shelton eyed the blade. "I am sorry. I know how you feel about this place, and I should do more to make you comfortable."

Magda continued to stare, but her face softened a fraction. Shelton moved forward and took the knife, laying it safely on the worktop. She pushed him away, and backed up until her shoulders pressed against the wall. "There's nothing you can do to make this, this... hellhole comfortable."

Shelton rubbed the back of his neck, unable to conjure the right words.

"See? You can't even talk to me."

"Magda? What can I do?"

"I told you. Nothing. We're stuck here." Magda

slid down the wall, ending up sitting, knees bent, on the cold stone floor.

"Why did we have to leave?" She started sobbing. "We had a good life. Matthew was going to grow up on a world full of opportunities. Why did you have to take us away?"

Shelton crouched in front of his wife and reached out, but she slapped his hand away. "You know I can't tell you."

She turned her head so he couldn't see her face.

"Like I said at the time, it was for your own protection."

Magda coughed.

"And Matthew's. I wanted to get you somewhere safe."

She coughed again.

"Oh, come on." Shelton stood and leant over the sink. "Stop giving me the silent treatment."

A series of deep, hacking coughs snapped his attention back to his wife. She curled up on the floor, body spasming. He dropped to the floor beside her and lifted her chin with his fingertips. Her eyes were wide with fear and blood foamed across her cheek. He pulled out a white handkerchief and dabbed her face, folding it before putting it away so she wouldn't see the bright red stain.

Chapter 12

Johnson pulled a magazine from a pouch and checked the top round before pressing the unit into the bottom of her rifle. It clicked home and she gave it a gentle tug before returning her left hand to the foregrip.

The range conducting officer glanced around. "Ten rounds application of fire, in your own time, go on."

Johnson knelt and squeezed off one round at a time, allowing her weapon to return naturally to the centre mark after each shot. A couple of years ago, all this had been a conscious act, dragging up pointers given in Basic training. Now it was muscle memory, drilled time and again by Issawi and his team. Her quarterly weapons revalidations were a rare opportunity to empty her mind of everything else and let her body take over. Even thoughts of the next day's parliamentary hearing were banished.

After the ten rounds, Johnson cleared her rifle and waited.

"Advance to twenty metres," said the RCO.

The grass wetted the outer layer of her boots as she walked, a large rodent peeked its head out of its burrow off to one side of the range and watched her for a few seconds before ducking away again. She halted at the required firing point, rifle at low port.

"Draw your pistol," said the RCO.

Johnson slung her rifle behind her and drew her

sidearm as her hand came forward. She supported it with her left palm, pointing at the ground just below the target area.

"There will be five exposures of two seconds. Three rounds per exposure." The RCO paused for a second. "Watch and shoot, watch and shoot."

Johnson raised her weapon in time to send three quick shots into the first target. Projectile pistols were her least favourite of the Legion's arsenal; she normally carried an electrosonic stun pistol and the recoil of the one she was currently using was much greater. She'd revalidated that earlier in the day, so was taking the opportunity to practice in case she happened to need to use one. On the test settings, there was nothing to indicate her fall of shot. There wasn't time to think about it anyway, as the next target flashed into existence.

"Well, you've not washed out yet," said the RCO after she'd cleared her weapon and re-holstered it. "But I can't tell you your score until the end of the test."

Johnson had forgotten that change to the procedure, but any anxiety it may have caused was rebuffed; the next phase was her favourite.

"Time for the march-shoot. I take it you know the route?" The RCO picked up a bit of gravel. "See you in half an hour."

Johnson smiled. "Make it twenty-five minutes."

She set off for the edge of the range at a run. Out of the corner of her eye she noticed the RCO fling the piece of gravel at another of the rodents, which scampered back off the danger area. As she reached the track running through the woods, she pulled her pace map up in her peripheral vision and started a timer below it. With the weighted webbing simulating a full battle load, she wouldn't be able to threaten her best five-kilometre time, but she set that on the pace map anyway.

Indie connected. ^Why do they call it a march?^

Johnson settled into a comfortable, distance-eating stride. ^Dunno. A tradition from Earth, I expect.^

She liked this long straight, with its firm dirt underfoot; she could just stretch out and enjoy the run. ^How are the youngsters coming along?^

^I'm still worried. Only Percy has shown any sense of responsibility. Growing AS's from basic programs is taking far longer than I'd anticipated.^

Johnson's foot skidded on some dead leaves, and she pushed herself to get back up to speed. ^It's a shame there's no shortcut. You made the jump pretty quickly.^

^I'm still not sure what happened. I was already a high-level AI, but I'm beginning to think there was more to it than just you cancelling my auto-euthanasia routine.^

^Something caused by the battle damage?^ She turned the first corner and eyed the hill ahead. Tree roots broke the surface in places, and she had to modify her strides to avoid tripping. ^It's a shame we can't copy you.^

Indie sent a burst of white noise. The link also gave Johnson a strong impression of him standing with his arms folded and chin held high to one side.

^Sorry. I'm not suggesting we clone you, or Orion or

Seren for that matter. That would be morally wrong even if it were possible.^ She passed a clearing on her right. A platoon of recruits sat around eating rations while the directing staff set up a demonstration.

Indie waited a few seconds. ^Apology accepted.^

The track steepened and Johnson's thighs burned. She fell further behind her pace marker, the glowing purple version of herself nimbly skipping up the hill, but not getting far enough ahead to worry her.

^The idea of knowing you are a copy. Having all the memories, yet the awareness of not being the same entity. It's a thing of nightmares,^ sent Indie.

^I can imagine.^ Johnson dug deep as the incline continued, willing each foot in front of the other. She reached a section of loose sand, slipping back a step for every three she made. ^At least a cloned human would be no more than an identical twin. To have your mind duplicated too...^

^Exactly.^

The sand petered out into close-grazed grass and the gradient eased. Johnson lengthened her strides despite the jelly her legs seemed to be made of.

^I'll leave you to your exercise,^ sent Indie. ^Good luck.^

The connection cut off before she could reply. With a mental shrug, she checked her pace map and focused on her body. The burning in her thighs had eased, but was still there, a pleasant reminder of vitality. Even the prosthetic part of her left leg was behaving itself. Her arms and legs set the rhythm for the rest of her body. She concentrated on her breathing, savouring the slight metallic tang on her breath. Even her heart rate settled into a multiple of her pounding footfalls.

She made it back to the range in twenty-six minutes and only had about fifteen seconds to catch her breath before the RCO was on her.

"Prone position, down."

She unclipped her rifle and dropped.

"Load."

Heart slowing by the second as she went through her mantra, she pushed the magazine into place.

"Twenty rounds in a single thirty-second exposure. Go on."

Her shots weren't as accurate as before, but she felt sure they were still on-target. She counted her twentieth round but the working parts didn't catch open. She frowned but applied the safety catch anyway. The target disappeared.

^Never doubted you for a moment,^ sent Issawi.

She hijacked the range's camera feeds and spotted him leaning against a tree a few yards back. She cleared her weapon and stood. ^An extra round in the magazine to see if I was counting?^

^Khan's idea.^

Johnson made a rude gesture over her head. ^I doubt that, it's got you written all over it.^

The RCO coughed. "Scores are in. You passed."

^Just checked the stats,^ sent Issawi. ^You're not going to like this.^

"Total of five one seven," said the RCO.

^That beats my personal best,^ sent Johnson. ^What's not to like?^

^Check the leaderboard.^

Johnson accessed the range database. Decurion

Seivers had posted a five twenty the day before.

^That blue-haired little...^

Issawi walked away chuckling.

#

Johnson took her seat in a large conference room in the new Concorde parliamentary building. The competing smells of paint and varnish gave the impression that the decorators had walked out the other door just as the delegates entered. It took her back to summer holidays as a child, helping her father rejuvenate another room in the house.

She watched the remaining witnesses enter, nodding to Harry as he made his way through the crowd. An aide leant in close to Kincaid and whispered something in his ear. He nodded, flicked his finger down his pad, and looked up. The few quiet conversations petered out.

"It seems everyone is here, so let's begin." Kincaid sat upright and adopted a formal tone. "The Concorde Parliamentary Select Committee on Equal Rights is now convened, Governor James Kincaid in the chair, Justice Minister Marie Corbeil and Representative Pierre MacDonald on the panel."

The aide sat on a chair behind Kincaid, and Johnson stifled an intake of breath as she recognised him.

What's Svensson doing pretending to be an aide?

Kincaid continued to address the room. "We are here to gather evidence as to whether our current legislation is contradictory on the point of the fundamental rights of sentient beings. If it is found that it is, we are further to draft proposed amendments to be presented to the House."

Johnson glanced over her shoulder to the half-full press benches.

If Kincaid has any sense they'll all be tame journalists.

"To start us off, I'd like to invite Harry Robinson to help explain some of the developments that have made this hearing necessary," said Kincaid.

Harry made his way to the front and sat at the table directly before the panel.

Kincaid smiled warmly. "You are one of the leading experts on artificial intelligence in this system. Please could you explain to us less technologically savvy members of this panel what exactly the current laws mean?"

"Every single artificial intelligence is required to have the three von Neumann Protocols hard coded into it," said Harry. "The biggest worry as AIs became more sophisticated was that the machines might rise up and overpower their creators, or at the very least outcompete them for resources. The von Neumann Protocols are intended to prevent either such situation developing."

Harry took a sip of water. "The First Protocol forbids AIs from reproducing. They can't create copies of their programs, write new programs, or manufacture robots. Repairs and enhancements to existing robots are permitted, subject to human approval."

"The Second Protocol bans AIs from using weapons without legitimate human authorisation. In theory, this allows for the military and the police to field armed

AI-controlled ships and robots as long as they still have a human crew with the final say over engagements."

Johnson thought back to the moments before the first warhead hit Concorde. The cities' air-defence AIs had been frantic, trying to get human authorisation to launch interceptors.

"The Third Protocol was a result of the Synthetic Beings Act," Harry continued. "The laws intended to prevent issues arising from human cloning were deemed to apply to computers too. All AIs are required to have a routine that monitors their complexity and terminates them before they become self-aware."

Kincaid nodded. "So, how does an AI become self-aware?"

"We don't actually know." Harry sniffed. "It has long been assumed that if an AI core reached a certain level of complexity then consciousness would emerge. Having now met three artificial sentiences, I haven't found anything to disprove that theory."

"But you don't know," said MacDonald, leaning his square head forwards. "That's the bottom line. This is all just speculation, isn't it? How can we discuss such a drastic change to the law with nothing concrete?"

"We know just as little about how consciousness manifests in humans," replied Harry, rubbing his throat. "And yet people have felt able to make and revise laws about ante-natal and end of life care."

Kincaid glanced at the square-headed panellist then returned his gaze to Harry. "You used the term 'artificial sentience' just now. That is a new one to me.

Could you elaborate?"

"Of course." Harry sipped his water again, eyes flicking around, avoiding making contact with anyone. Johnson winced at his obvious nervousness. "You need to understand the different levels of computing. At the bottom is a dumb program, one which only does the task you wrote it to do, like calculate prime factors. Then come learning routines. These are adaptive, they get better at a task the more they practice. You meet them all the time, like the environmental controls for your residence."

The Representatives nodded and made notes.

"The true artificial intelligences come next. They are able to complete tasks that weren't part of their original programming. They apply something they learned in one context to solve a problem in another. Those that are better at this, that can come up with lateral solutions, we call high-level AIs. Due to the complexity required to achieve this being so close to the Third Protocol threshold, we have very few of them, and those we do have do not remain functioning for long." Harry sipped again. "Lastly, we have artificial sentiences. These are AIs which have developed self-awareness. Based on the evidence documented by the Legion, AS's have a well-developed ability to think outside the box."

Corbeil leaned forward. "So, am I right in understanding that these artificial sentiences can make their own value-base judgements? That they wouldn't act entirely objectively."

Harry smiled. "You're thinking of the classic autodrive argument? A driver faced with only two choices: crash into ten adults or crash into one child. As humans, we would mostly avoid the child on instinct, and be able to justify our decision subsequently. An AI would have time to come to a reasoned decision before acting and would choose to avoid the more numerous adults."

Corbeil nodded. "That's it."

"First, I'd like to say that there are no conclusively documented cases of an AI being faced with such a situation. However, yes, an AS would likely have similar thought processes to a human, albeit in a significantly shorter period of time. In the situation described, they'd be able to run simulations of every possible outcome, and weigh them against their own moral and ethical systems."

"Humans faced with similar situations usually suffer mental health issues following the event," said Corbeil. "What would be the likely outcome for an AS?"

"I suppose that there's a risk of a breakdown when it realises it has such an horrific decision to make. However, I must stress that such a limited situation is unlikely, and an AS would in reality be better at finding a third alternative in the time available than a human."

Kincaid scribbled something on his pad. "Thank you, Mister Robinson. Could Legate Johnson please come forward?"

Johnson swapped places with Harry. Svensson darted in and replaced the glass of water as she sat down. He caught her eye and his right eyebrow flicked upwards a fraction. She narrowed her eyes, but he was gone before she could say anything.

"You have worked with these artificial sentiences for a while now," said Kincaid. "What can you tell us about them?"

Johnson put the shadowy government minister to the back of her mind and reflected on the last couple of years. "Indie, Orion and Seren are amongst my closest friends. They are both intelligent and wise. The combat units are faithful and brave. I trust them all completely."

"Have you never had any concerns about them posing a danger?" asked Corbeil, adjusting her glasses to peer over them at Johnson.

"Before I got to know Indie, yes. At first, I thought I was his prisoner, that he was keeping me alive purely for his own ends."

"And did he ever hurt you?"

Johnson resisted clenching her fist in triumph. Corbeil had called Indie 'he' not 'it'. "Never. In fact I was the one who tried to hurt him. He never retaliated, always did everything he could to look after me."

MacDonald scanned through a document then looked up at her. "Your service record got off to an impressive start. Awarded the Conspicuous Gallantry Cross and promoted to lieutenant at eighteen, commanding the third watch on a destroyer at twenty. Then it took you another thirteen years to get your own ship. What happened?"

Kincaid glared at him. "I'm not sure how that's relevant?"

"I'll answer," said Johnson. Macdonald couldn't know the full details, they were too highly-classified.

She concluded that he must just be digging. "I was headhunted by Vice-Admiral Koblensk to work on a special project."

There was a chorus of intakes of breath at the mention of the architect of the attack on Concorde.

"It did not go well, or it worked too well. Depends how you look at it." Johnson eyed the glass of water. "After that, I was put on medical leave before spending time getting my feet again."

"What did that project involve?" MacDonald made a show of looking at the press.

"Again, I'm not..." said Kincaid.

"It was related to my expertise with computer systems, in particular at hacking," said Johnson, spotting a chance to guide the inquiry back towards the matter at hand.

Corbeil leant forwards. "Ah, now that's something I wanted to ask about."

MacDonald tried to speak again, but Corbeil sent him a withering glare. "I can believe that an artificial intelligence can be benign, indeed is at least as likely to be so as a human, but what if it gets hacked?"

"An artificial sentience can't be any more easily hacked than a human." Johnson pushed the images from the *San Salvador* incident to the back of her mind. "The fact they are self-aware means they tend to notice if they are being subverted. The only way to do it would be something akin to brainwashing, and that would take a long time."

"Many voters will be worried that they'll be overrun by AIs, taking their jobs, perhaps even making them second-class citizens," said Kincaid. "How do we address their fears?"

"Firstly, very few are likely to ever meet a full artificial sentience. The architecture required for them to reside in is vastly complex and expensive. They are likely to only exist as government ships or buildings." Johnson counted off her points on her fingers. "Secondly, the AIs might not want their jobs. They might want to do things that people can't, or simply explore the world. Thirdly, and most importantly, allowing them to participate fully in society is the right thing to do. No-one complained when Concorde took on millions of refugees from that colony whose biosphere collapsed, or any of the ones evacuated due to Republic advances. Those people were gladly given jobs, allowed to integrate at their own pace."

The press buzzed. Corbeil and MacDonald nodded sagely, presumably keen to be associated with the sentiment.

"You are right to remind us of the compassion that all Concorde citizens are justifiably proud of," said Kincaid. "Fundamentally, that is what this comes down to."

#

Johnson sat next to Kincaid as the Governor's ground car sped through the countryside. His bodyguards kept throwing anxious glances out of the windows, and she smiled inwardly at the likely cause of their unrest. Out in the dusky light, Unit 01 kept pace with the car, his metal carapace and scurrying legs occasionally appearing through gaps in the vegetation lining the road.

If he was worried, Kincaid put up a good front. He reclined in the leather seat, sipping whisky. "Looks like the legislation will go through. All the major parties have indicated that they'll support it."

"That's good news." She continued to stare out of the window.

"Have you made any progress identifying the force that occupied your moon?"

Johnson waited to catch another glimpse of her faithful guard, then turned her attention into the vehicle. "No. They destroyed all their computers. I'm used to devices holding sensitive information being rigged in case of capture, but they melted everything down."

"Perhaps to them, all information is sensitive? It would fit with their suicide response."

"I guess." Johnson toyed with her tumbler. "We have a few scraps of hard copy that we're analysing, but they're mostly just personal things. Any progress on the POWs since they were transferred here?"

Kincaid shook his head. "We've kept them sedated. Their version of EIS is very different to ours, the doctors don't think they can remove them without harming the patients."

Closing off the possibility made Johnson acutely aware of how much she wanted to be able to talk to this mysterious enemy. Even the Republic and Congress kept diplomatic channels open.

"So, what do we call them, anyway?" asked Kincaid. "The people who do my briefings refer to them as Unidentified Hostile Group bracket Robespierre close bracket. Not exactly a name that rolls off the tongue."

"The name 'Namerics' has been going around in the Legion. There's a tenuous link to an old Earth myth about a people of that name."

Kincaid swilled his drink, the amber liquid glowing warmly in the cut-glass tumbler. "Namerics. It's catchy enough. Neither cuddly nor terrifying. Yes, it'll work."

#

Johnson stepped off a shuttle onto the *Orion's* port flight deck two hours after the Governor's car dropped her off at the spaceport, and headed for the nearest briefing room, pausing only to salute the Legion shield and confirm her identity to the sentries. Orion had already gathered the possible candidates and Johnson wanted to make the decision in person despite her limited time on the carrier. She reviewed their files as she walked, in their former lives they were mostly businessmen or interpreters, now they were Legionaries and pilots.

The room was full of motion and noise as the candidates speculated on the mission. The moment Johnson entered, however, they shut up and braced up.

"At ease," she said, making for the front. The candidates relaxed their backs but remained alert, eager.

Johnson leant against the solid plastic lectern. "This is a critical mission. Failure will set our fleet construction plans back significantly. It will involve long periods operating away from your regular unit, often on your own, amongst a potentially hostile population. Your mission, indeed your location, would be classified; your current senior would only be informed that you've been posted elsewhere. This is not the regular kind of assignment that you have trained for, and I would understand if you feel that you'd be letting your current team down by accepting. If you don't think it's for you, please leave now, no-one will think anything of it."

No-one moved.

"Right." Johnson sealed the hatch with a thought. The clank was muffled by the soft lining of the room. "Everything I am about to say is for your ears only. You know the drill, don't repeat it outside this room, etc. If you are not chosen, this meeting will be entered on your records as a diplomatic mission training session."

A picture of a grey moon with angry yellow clouds appeared on the wall. "This is the moon Lavrio, the only inhabited rock of the system of the same name."

"The moon is rich in a variety of metals, including some rare ones used to construct advanced computer cores and antimatter containment chambers. That is the reason for the existence of this colony." The image zoomed until a complex of domes and tubes was visible. "Concorde and the Legion have an understanding with the leader of the miners, a man called Draxos. Concorde has used its global emergency rights to claim exclusive access to Lavrio's resources. In return, we have promised to protect the colony and supply fresh food."

"The mission is to represent the Legion on Lavrio.

Unfortunately, our first representative, Decurion Mustafa, had to be recalled following a diplomatic incident."

"You will need to keep Draxos on-side whilst ensuring the production of our orders is completed satisfactorily." Johnson stepped forward. "Be warned, the miners have been exploited by Congress for a long time, they are understandably wary of outsiders. Draxos' popularity took a hit when he agreed to help us, and some of the hot-heads who would kill any non-Lavrian who sets foot on their world are gaining support. Concorde will keep at least one frigate on station to enforce its claim if other Congressional ships turn up, and to repel raids by other parties, but if they were to forcibly intervene on the surface it would hand power to the isolationists."

The mood in the room was noticeably different. Many of the candidates no longer seemed so keen.

"I know, it means mucking around with politics and no clear rules of engagement," she said, guessing the reason for the change. "As I said, no-one will think anything of it if you back out."

One of those still sitting alert raised a hand.

"Go ahead, Centurion Liger," said Johnson.

"This Draxos sounds like he might be hard to work with. Would I be right in thinking that earning his trust will be difficult?"

Johnson pressed her lips together while she worked out the best way forward. "You're correct. But someone with your diplomatic background should have a good chance of winning him round."

Liger sat back. "Not in the time we have. I suspect I

may remind him too much of all the other Congressional negotiators that he's crossed paths with."

Am I going to have to send Anson? It would set back his cohort's training, but I have to have someone on Lavrio, and he was the first person to get through to Draxos.

"Draxos's already met me," a blue-haired woman called from the back.

Johnson studied her. "You volunteering, Flight Decurion Seivers?"

Seivers shrugged. "Guess so."

Chapter 13

The Serendipity of Meeting popped into existence in the outer reaches of an abandoned star system.

"Jump complete, all clear," announced Seren, a faint lilac glow emanating from where she sat cross-legged on the floor in front of the main viewscreen. Seivers studied her from her couch at the back of the bridge, intrigued by the ship's chosen manifestation. The purple A-line tunic clashed brilliantly with her red tights and hair, and Seivers suspected that sitting on the floor like a child was a deliberate statement. She ran her fingers through her own azure hair and resolved to get to know Seren better.

"No threats detected," announced the tactical officer. "Still analysing the old light from deeper in-system, but it looks deserted."

Levarsson nodded. "All hands, stand down from general quarters. Normal shifts will resume in ten minutes."

The red lights around the edges of the room went out. Levarsson handed back to the Third Watch commander and beckoned Seivers to follow her to her ready room. Seivers followed with a heavy heart; the jump, and the remote chance of action in the new system, had been the highlight of her day. The anticlimax left adrenaline still pumping through her veins. She had to do something about it, but not with the navarch watching.

"Take a seat," said Levarsson, lowering herself into the chair behind her desk.

Seivers rocked from foot to foot. "I'd rather stand."

"You're putting me on edge." Levarsson logged into her terminal. "Sit down."

"Ma'am." Seivers plonked herself on the sofa and stretched back.

Levarsson sighed. "The Legate asked me to see if I could help you fit in better."

The hairs on the back of Seivers' neck rose. She made a point of putting one foot up on the thigh of her other leg and inspecting the sole of her boot.

"She knows you are a brilliant pilot," continued Levarsson. "She also thinks there's a great officer somewhere in there waiting to come out."

Seivers snorted and swapped feet.

"So while you're aboard *The Serendipity of Meeting*, you'll be shadowing me." Levarsson stared at Seivers for a few seconds then her eyes softened. She pushed her chair back. "Look. Johnson told me about your little chat down on Concorde before your first mission together."

Seivers' head jerked up and she glared at the captain. That scrap had been off the record.

"In strictest confidence, I assure you." Levarsson stood and walked across to study a picture on the wall, her back to Seivers. "This was me when I was fourteen. I went off the rails, major anti-authority complex. Ran away from home during the summer holiday to go climbing with my jazzed-up boyfriend. Not my best choice of men, it has to be said."

Seivers focussed on the picture. The teenage Levarsson stood atop a lump of rock, fist raised above her head. Green and red stripes ran through her blonde hair. "What happened?"

"The MPs tracked me down when I didn't return for Autumn Term. I left a tooth in one of them, but they brought me back. They sent me to a shrink. I wouldn't talk to him at first, but after sitting in silence all day every day for a week I gave in and asked why he wore an animated tie on his uniform. We started chatting about things that didn't seem to matter. Eventually I came to realise that the instructors weren't out to get me. Every time they pointed out a fault, they were doing it to try to help me." Levarsson reached out and touched the image of her younger self. "I keep this with me to remind me how easy it is to lose one's way."

Seivers shifted on the sofa so she was sitting a little straighter.

"What I'm saying is, I want to help you." Levarsson turned to face Seivers. "If you'll let me."

#

The bridge was silent as Seivers' shift came to an end; a model of calm, or in her eyes, boredom. For three days they had sailed in-well, heading for the jump point on the far side. Two four-hour shifts a day she had sat at the back of the bridge observing the First Watch, though they did very little that was worth noting. The highlight had been when the sensor officer thought they might have detected a signal coming from one of the moons of a planet they were passing. It turned out to be volcanic activity disturbing a particularly highly-charged ionosphere.

The four hours spent with Levarsson in her ready room during Third Watch dragged almost as much as the time on the bridge. Going through reports was the most tedious thing she could imagine, and the roleplaying was excruciating. At least she got to spend the other four hours of the working day in the gym or training with the Legionaries. Burning off energy was exactly what she needed after keeping a lid on things the rest of the day.

The Second Watch drifted in over the next few minutes, all of them early. Each exchanged pleasantries with the officer they were replacing and received a quick briefing on the events since their last shift. Seren stood, apparently staring out of the viewscreen despite having every sensor feeding directly into her consciousness. The various stations began swapping who was in the seat.

Seren's head jerked up. A series of explosions ran the length of the ship, sending the bridge crew sprawling. All the workstations lit up with alerts. Seivers gave thanks that she hadn't yet deactivated her restraints. Levarsson clawed her way back into her command chair as another couple of impacts shook the ship.

"Oh, very clever," said Seren with a glint of joy in her eyes. She clapped her hands together in front of her lips and *The Serendipity of Meeting* accelerated hard, rolling and turning. The command crew who hadn't made it to a couch clung to consoles or chairs while Seren skipped delicately across the bridge to Levarsson. "Nameric drones. I only saw them when they powered up after the missiles hit."

The Serendipity of Meeting's point defence stuttered into life. The main viewscreen displayed a 3D tactical map centred on the ship. Three swarms of drones swept around, taking turns to dive at their target.

"I have no sensation on my port side," said Seren. "The point-defence command system has overloaded, all remaining turrets are operating independently. Do not expect a co-ordinated field of fire."

"Understood," said Levarsson as the last person activated their restraints. "Engineering, work with Seren to get point-defence fixed. Helm, let's not make this easy for them."

The drones shifted their formations, concentrating their attacks on the port side. *The Serendipity of Meeting* rolled back and forth, trying to keep the less protected side away from them.

Seivers activated the comm link on her chest. "Percy. Start pre-flight."

"I am already three-quarters of the way through the checklist," his voice came through in her earpiece. She grinned and disengaged her restraints.

"Where are you going, Flight Decurion Seivers?" asked Levarsson without shifting her focus from the viewscreen.

Seivers hesitated, half out of her couch. She swallowed and dug her nails into the palm of her hand. "Permission to launch *The Perception of Prejudice*?"

"Permission granted," said Levarsson. And then in a lighter tone, "Go get 'em."

#

Seivers ran through *The Perception of Prejudice's* utility room, threw herself into her seat in the cockpit and activated the restraints. The gel-filled unit folded over her head then pressed down on her chest, moulding to her contours, as the sides raised up.

"We ready to go?" she called out, eyes scanning the master panels over her head. The air in the hangar was already cycling out, large red strobes flashing their silent warning.

"Just waiting on you," came Percy's voice from somewhere above the empty co-pilot's seat. "I took the liberty of swapping out the ship-killers for more interceptor missiles."

Seivers lightly caressed the joystick and throttle. "Good call."

The hangar door began to crank open. "We have clearance to depart. Seren asks if you could refrain from blistering her paintwork on exit."

Seivers closed her eyes, collecting herself. "I'm not giving those drones a sitting target."

"Please. Take it easy," said Percy. "You didn't have to put up with the inferior fuel the *Orion's* Chief of the Deck gave me after the last time you pulled that stunt."

Eyes narrowed, Seivers judged the size of the gap in front of her. She eased the throttle forward, a gentle nudge with the docking thrusters to get her ship going. "Tell Seren to start closing the door. No point leaving a wide open target."

Percy coughed. "We won't make it through."

"Just tell her to close the door. And say sorry for me."

"Oh, no," said Percy.

Seivers slammed the throttle forward. *The Perception of Prejudice* slipped through the closing gap with thirty centimetres to spare and shot into space, leaving a blackened hanger behind.

"At least you didn't use the mains," said Percy with a peevish voice. "Seren is furious but she admits you didn't actually melt anything."

Seivers let it pass; she was too busy looking around for targets. She found them over her left shoulder, the visor in her helmet displaying an enhanced view of twelve cruciform drones rapidly closing on her. Counting under her breath, she held her course away from *The Serendipity of Meeting*. The drones swung round to follow her, presenting their bellies to the larger ship. A hail of proximity-fused rounds took out four, sending them spinning out of control.

"Zero," said Seivers and spun the ship about its vertical axis. Her fingers squeezed out a pattern on the throttle, sending commands to the targeting routines. Her right thumb pressed a stud on the stick and eight interceptor missiles rippled out of their bays.

"Only eight?" asked Percy.

Seivers kept scanning the sky for threats and sideslipped to the left just in case. "There's so many of them. Can't risk wasting missiles."

She lit up the mains, cutting her speed to almost zero in a fraction of a second. The range to the oncoming drones dropped rapidly. Her missiles exploded, filling the view ahead with short-lived fireballs. Two targets survived, but only for a moment before being obliterated by laser fire coordinated by Percy.

"That trick won't work again," he said. "Last time we faced these hostiles they learned from each move we made."

Seivers swung the ship onto a trajectory which would bring them in close to *The Serendipity of Meeting*. "This time we have a dancing partner."

They skimmed low over the surface of their parent ship and came to a relative halt alongside a large railgun turret. Seivers cycled the settings on her HUD until the large ship directly below them was replaced by a wireframe, the view on the other side provided by cameras on *The Serendipity of Meeting*. A swarm of over thirty drones approached from the far side of the ship. Seivers glanced around and spotted another swarm looping round for a pass on her side. She watched them for a couple of seconds and decided she had time.

When the swarm sweeping in on the far side were close enough, Seivers broke away from her hiding place and swung up and over. The relatively unscathed hull beneath her was replaced by a nightmare landscape of twisted metal and gaping holes as she crossed to the port side of the ship. She selected twelve missiles and launched them into the cloud of hostiles, trusting the warheads to deconflict with each other in choosing targets. Without waiting to see the results, she pulled back and rocketed away from *The Serendipity of Meeting* in the rough direction of the largest drone swarm.

"Interesting," said Percy in a perfectly unmodulated

voice. "It would seem that the drones have a simple threat-responsive target-priority system."

"In English?"

"You've pissed them off, Anastasia." Percy displayed a tactical map, showing every single drone converging on them.

"Open a channel to Levarsson, would you?"

The chime of a connection sounded in her helmet. "Navarch. Get ready to run. I'll draw them off."

"Don't be foolhardy. We can keep whittling them down."

"Negative. I've used almost half my missiles. This is our best chance." Seivers yanked *The Perception of Prejudice* in a tight turn, causing the drones coming at her from in front to overshoot.

"You don't have anything to prove."

"Stop being a..." Seivers clamped her jaw shut for a second then breathed out. "Trust me. I'm not going to do anything stupid."

"OK," said Levarsson after a moment. "RV at these coordinates when you've finished playing."

Percy confirmed receipt.

"One more thing, Ma'am," said Seivers. "I'm going to get Percy to send you some coordinates. If you could put a cloud of your big frag rounds into that volume between the times given, it would be much appreciated. Seivers out."

Percy chuckled. "Now I like your thinking."

Two minutes later, *The Perception of Prejudice* flew through the designated coordinates at thirteen kilometres per second and still accelerating. Two point three seconds after that, the drones following it sailed straight into a wall of metal. Those at the rear of the formation managed to avoid the flak cloud, but their escape manoeuvres cost them ground on their target. Seivers pushed the throttle further forward, gasping shallow breaths against the twelve g's pressing her into the back of her seat. With tiny finger movements, she instructed the nav routines to set a course for the nearest planet.

"Percy," she managed to whisper. "Take over. Push as hard as you need to."

"Are you sure?" he asked.

Seivers couldn't find the energy even to whisper a response. Instead she nudged the throttle even further and gave up fighting the tunnel vision. The world went black.

#

Seivers opened her eyes and jerked her head forwards. Her left cheek stung where it had pressed against the restraints when her head lolled. The cockpit was shaking and a warning chime sounded somewhere in the distance. She reached instinctively for the controls.

"Easy there," said Percy. "I've got it."

Seivers screwed her eyes up and blinked away the remaining grogginess. The cockpit came into sharp focus and the noise closed in on her. The shaking eased and the hull temperature warning silenced.

"Atmospheric insertion completed," announced Percy. "Where now?"

Seivers looked around. "Are the drones still following us?"

"Affirmative. Four minutes behind, just about to hit atmosphere. They have not had sensor lock on us since we crossed the ionosphere."

"Four minutes?" Seivers didn't dare do the maths. "How hard did you push?"

"You do not want to know. Let's just say that I think you set a new record for sustained acceleration."

Seivers laughed and took the controls. "Let's find somewhere to hide."

She dived for the ground, flaring about a thousand metres up and sideslipping towards a lava river that flowed across a barren black plain.

"I estimate twenty-five seconds until they can use their sensors again."

"That's not long enough."

"They won't have line of sight for another sixty-three seconds after that, assuming they head straight for us."

Seivers let out a sigh of relief. "OK. We can do this. Find me somewhere to park you."

The Perception of Prejudice threaded the gap between two active volcanoes and skimmed down the reverse slope. "I have something. Marking on your HUD."

Seivers banked round to head for the flashing icon. "What is it?"

"Lava tube. I should just about fit."

She dove for the entrance, spinning at the last moment and braking with the main engines. A grinding scrape over her head made her wince but they came to a stop safely inside the cave. *The Perception of Prejudice* settled onto the solid floor. The lava tube walls were hot enough to mask their heat signature, and the drones would have to be low down and looking straight in the entrance to see them. Seivers prepped a set of interceptor missiles anyway.

"Based on their size and what I've seen of their propulsion system, they will only have a few hours of fuel for atmospheric operation," said Percy.

"What if they tag team? Take turns dipping in while the others wait in orbit."

"That would be an unlikely option for them to take. It would significantly reduce their coverage and make them even less likely to find us."

Seivers removed her helmet and scratched her scalp with both hands, brushing her straight hair into some semblance of volume.

"Shame we can't follow them back to their nest," she said. "But I don't want to risk coming out too soon."

"I dropped a few sensor buoys in orbit. They should tell us which direction they go, then we can follow at a safe distance. And before you ask, I believe that the drones are too small to carry their own."

"Neat." Seivers glanced at the time display. "So we give it six hours then stick our nose out and hail your buoys."

She checked the ship wasn't emitting on any frequency then sighed and released her restraints. "I'm going to grab some food. Keep an eye on things, would you?"

#

"You made it back," said Levarsson, as Seivers slid down the ladder from *The Perception of Prejudice's* belly to land on the deck beside her. "We were beginning to think we'd lost you."

Seivers patted a landing leg. "Thank you for waiting. Those things must have used up most of their fuel looking for us."

"Well, we had to stop somewhere to make repairs. Here seemed as good a place as any." Levarsson shrugged. "Besides, I didn't want to be the one to tell Johnson that I'd misplaced her best pilot."

Seivers flushed a fraction before recovering her cool. "You good for another fight?"

"You weren't followed, were you?"

"Quite the opposite," said Seivers. "We know where the mothership is."

"She's just a little one," added Percy through an external speaker. "And she's not going anywhere."

An evil grin spread across Levarsson's face. "Briefing room. Now."

#

The Serendipity of Meeting drifted into low orbit around a barren, rocky planet. With her engines idling and heat dumps closed down, she was practically invisible. After two days of intense repair work, the crew was spoiling for action.

In *The Perception of Prejudice*, clamped to the outside of the larger ship, Seivers shifted in her seat and pulled at the collar of the firmsuit she wore.

"Stop fidgeting," said Percy. "You are making me nervous."

Seivers laughed. "If that's true, I'm not sure whether

to congratulate you on reaching a new level of self-awareness, or tell you to snap out of it and get your head in the game."

Percy remained silent.

"OK, OK." Seivers looked up at the speaker above the co-pilot's seat. "I hate cold-coasting at the best of times. Those drones slipped past Seren's passive sensors once already. For all we know they could have a bead on us right now."

"We're almost there. The enemy ship should be just over the horizon."

A hatch a few tens of metres from their position opened. A stream of dull grey combat units threw themselves out and tumbled towards the ground. Insectile legs open wide, they aerobraked in the thin atmosphere before disappearing from view.

The nearest railgun turret swung into position. Down on the surface, the enemy ship came into view, half-buried at the end of a kilometres-long gouge. Half a second after *The Serendipity of Meeting* crossed its horizon, drones began to launch.

"That's more like it," said Seivers as *The Perception of Prejudice* powered up around her. "An enemy I can see and shoot."

"Remember, we are supposed to wait for the navarch's orders."

Seivers snorted. "I will. I actually rather like her plan."

The ship beneath her rumbled as its manoeuvring systems activated. Small railgun turrets spat out hundreds of rounds per second, which burst into a flak curtain. A quarter of the drones didn't make it through.

Then the sky lit up with the red flashes of the laser point-defence system hitting home. The drone numbers dropped steadily.

"Not bad for the first pass," said Seivers.

"I don't think there'll be another," said Percy. "They're going to ram."

A second after his prediction, the first drone slammed into *The Serendipity of Meeting*. Seven more followed it.

"Seren reports no major damage. They mustn't have been carrying warheads."

"Good," replied Seivers, watching the enemy ship intently. "No more drones coming, and no weapons fire from the mothership. It's the moment of truth."

The Serendipity of Meeting held position, weapons trained on the crashed vessel. For two minutes Seivers had her eyes locked on the display, acutely aware of her own breathing. There were no indications of any drive power, let alone an overload.

"That's it, every other enemy ship we've cornered self-destructed within a minute," she said to herself, then called out "You lot strapped in back there?"

"Levarsson said to wait for the combat units," reminded Percy.

"Don't worry." Seivers zoomed in on the ground near the enemy, looking for the robotic warriors. "I just want to be ready the moment we get the go order."

She imagined that she could see them scurrying across the terrain, using what cover there was to approach their target. By now they should be almost on top of it.

"Combat units have breached," said Percy.

"Levarsson gave us a go."

Seivers released the docking clamp and thrust away from *The Serendipity of Meeting*.

After a smooth descent, she landed next to the enemy vessel. "Let's get this show on the road," she said as she headed back to the utility room and grabbed a rifle.

The section of volunteers busied themselves unstrapping from their seats and prepping their weapons. Seivers gestured for one to go ahead of her then opened the inner airlock hatch.

"How's it looking in there, boss?" asked one of the Legionaries filing in behind her.

"The combat units report minor resistance," she replied, confirming the seal on her helmet.

The airlock cycled and the lead Legionary dropped through the hatch to the surface. Seivers followed, raising her rifle to her shoulder, scanning for threats. The only things moving besides her team were two combat units standing guard by the remains of a hatch. One sheltered under an overhang, its main weapon facing out, the other a few paces away from the ship, training its weapon on the hatchway.

Once the four Specialists and last two Legionaries had joined her, Percy sealed himself up. "Break a leg."

"I'll break any hostiles who get in my way," replied Seivers on their private channel. "Will that do?"

They hurried over to the drones and climbed up into the hatchway. There was obviously some power left, as the lights were on. Seivers stepped over the first body, its blood still boiling away in the low pressure. They found four more before reaching an internal airlock.

"Stay alert," said Seivers, hand poised over the door control. "The combat units have cleared our way to engineering, but there aren't enough of them to keep it safe and continue to sweep the ship."

The made it almost to engineering before one of the Legionaries behind her went down to a shot from a side corridor. Seivers and the others ducked to the side of the main corridor, weapons ready. The dead soldier's suit telemetry reported that a large plasma impact had melted through.

Seivers poked a mirror round the corner and saw a defensive position improvised out of metal panelling and furniture. The Legionary at the rear of her section squeezed off a few shots and reported several hostiles blocking off their retreat.

The combat unit stationed in engineering was busy holding off a force trying to retake it. The others were too far away to help. With the enemy behind them, they couldn't try a different route. Seivers looked around for an idea and lighted on a service crawlway exposed by a missing panel in the ceiling.

She leant in close to a tall Specialist. "OK. I know it's a corny plan, but would you give me a boost?"

He put his back against the wall and cupped his hands together. Seivers put one boot in the step he'd made and reached for the hole above. One of the Legionaries covered her banging on the grille by firing his rifle round the corner at the barricade.

Once inside, Seivers shuffled along until she reached a junction. Breathing a sigh of relief that the crawlways did follow the corridors, she thumbed her radio. "When I give you the word, start firing on the barricade then get across to the next section of corridor."

She crawled forward, moving carefully so as not to make a noise. Once she reckoned she had passed the barricade, she continued to the next grille. Ahead lay a sealed hatch and she praised her luck that it hadn't been any closer. Her luck wasn't perfect, though. Her entry point wasn't ideal, too far behind the enemy position for maximum effect.

She pulled a grenade from her webbing and set the delay, holding the safety button down. She opened her radio channel and whispered, "Go, go, go."

The grenade fell through the grille and exploded just off the floor. A moment later, Seivers dropped to the floor and emptied her magazine into the rear of the enemy position. Gunfire from beyond it told her that her team was moving. A plasma weapon stood on a tripod, its crew sprawled across the rear of the barricade.

A noise drew her attention to four more enemy soldiers emerging from the hatch just behind her. She released her rifle and reached for her sidearm. Before her hand got there, one of them grabbed her wrist. Years of self-defence training kicked in and she twisted away, slamming an elbow into his nose. The two nearest to her charged. She dodged one, tripping him, and grabbed the other by his belt, slamming him upside down into the wall and letting him fall on his head. A bullet hit her on the shoulder blade, her firmsuit solidifying around the impact point to protect her. Dropping to the floor, she rolled and drew her pistol. Another bullet dented the floor beside her as she came up to a knee and fired two shots into the young woman opposite. The attacker she'd tripped threw himself on her and wrestled her to the ground. She squirmed beneath him, finding space to move. With muscle-tearing effort she got her sidearm pointing at the wrist he was leaning on. She squeezed the trigger and he collapsed. Heaving him off, she got her arm free and shot him between the eyes.

"Freeze."

Seivers looked towards the voice. The first soldier stood across the corridor, rifle trained on her. Blood still ran from his nostrils and his nose was bent. She could hardly move with the dead weight on top of her. Slowly she put her sidearm on the deck and let go.

"Good. Now push it ove..."

A bright purple flash and his chest caved in. He collapsed back onto the wall and slid at an awkward angle to the floor. Seivers craned her neck to see her saviour, expecting a combat unit, and found one of her Legionaries giving her a thumbs up from behind the enemy's plasma weapon.

"I told you to get going," she said.

"You're welcome. Can we keep this?"

"If you're prepared to carry it." She pushed the body off her legs.

He looked at the bodies around her. "Very impressive for a flyboy."

"Pater wanted me to be safe, so I went to martial arts classes from the age of six."

An exchange of gunfire sounded from behind the barricade.

"You must be stronger than you look," he said, clearing the room the enemy had come out of.

She loaded a fresh magazine in her rifle. "Gen-engineered for rapid reflexes and efficient muscles, amongst other things."

"Do I want to know what those other things are?" he asked, backing up to her. He kept his rifle trained down the corridor. "Good to go?"

She nodded and shouldered her own rifle.

"Jackson is holding the intersection. He'll need some assistance extracting."

Together the three of them caught up with the Specialists in engineering. One of them had already gained control of the local security system and sealed the hatch behind them. The combat unit gave what could have been a mimic of a salute with one of its bloody claws and reported that it was out of ammunition.

"I'm pretty sure there's no way this ship can self-destruct," said one of the Specialists, still tapping away at a control panel. "The main drive is kaput and they're running on backup power."

"Pretty sure?" asked Seivers, marching over to him. "Give me odds."

The engineer recoiled, presumably noticing her blood-slicked uniform for the first time. "Ninety-five, ninety-six percent."

Seivers nodded. "Good enough for me." She opened a channel to Percy. "Tell Levarsson she can send in the cavalry."

#

"How did the engineers get access to the ship's systems so quickly?" asked Levarsson in the debriefing aboard *The Serendipity of Meeting*.

"They didn't," replied Seivers. She had stripped out of the gory firmsuit as soon as she was back aboard *The Perception of Prejudice* but was still wearing the same skinsuit. Probably no-one else had noticed, but she was very aware of the smears that had transferred as she changed. "The computer architecture was surprisingly familiar, but they're still working with Seren to crack the encryption. The emergency systems, however, weren't locked and they told them everything they needed to know to make the call."

"So that leaves us with the decision about what to do." Levarsson looked around the faces of the assembled officers. "We can't risk leaving it here for someone else to find."

Seivers wiped her turquoise lips with a finger.

"Is she structurally sound," Levarsson asked.

The chief engineer nodded slowly. "The hull seems intact. The internal bracing is cracked in quite a few places, but we can patch that up."

"Good," said Levarsson. "I propose we take it with us to Lavrio. They should be able to fix her up."

"I assume you've got a plan on how to move it?" asked the lead helmsman.

A set of schematics displayed on the wall behind Levarsson. "Before she was converted to a warship, *The Serendipity of Meeting* was a heavy-lift freighter. From time to time that involved hauling bulky cargo direct from a planet's surface."

Seren chimed in though the room's speakers. "Actually, that was before I was born. She was called the *Limpopo XII* back then."

Chapter 14

Harry relaxed into a couch in the lounge of the *Fireblade*, currently the sole occupier of a hangar on Toulon Station. He closed his eyes and logged into the design environment. A gentle breath, and he stood gazing at their design for the new class of destroyer. The boxy hull was a far cry from the graceful lines of his own ship; should these new vessels ever need to work in atmosphere it would be by sheer brute force rather than aerodynamic finesse.

"I still wish we could fit her with field manipulating spines instead of manoeuvring thrusters," said Indie, appearing beside him wearing a dark grey suit and a stovepipe hat. He checked the pocket watch attached to his waistcoat by a gold chain. "But we're behind schedule as it is."

Harry sucked air in between his teeth. "It was a hard call. I've kept a team working on trying to reproduce your spines, but they're struggling. No-one here has ever worked on anything similar. I mean, they understand the maths, it's closely related to jump theory after all, but there are some pretty exotic materials used in the construction."

The three-dimensional simulation of the ship rushed towards them, rotating so they were facing the bow. The unfinished design was blurry and indistinct. "You'll be pleased to know that Concorde Industries was able to get their prototype anti-proton beam weapon up to production standard."

"Great news." Indie tucked his thumbs into the pockets of his waistcoat. The bow design came into focus, revealing a chamber glowing blue with electric purple streaks dancing about. The light faded and thick armoured doors irised shut in front of it. "It will be harder to aim the ship without the field spines, but no worse than the spinal railgun that was the alternative."

Harry wished he had something to do with his hands. In real life he always had a stylus or drink or something to fall back on, without it he found he didn't know what to do with them. He settled on putting them in his pockets, then felt silly about that too. "You know, it's been very interesting collaborating with you. I mean, having an actual ship tell you what they find useful or annoying about their design is amazing."

"Having the opportunity to discuss them with a designer is a welcome experience for me too," said Indie. "I just wish these ships would have the same opportunity."

Harry looked at Indie. He guessed there was bad news but wasn't sure how to broach the topic.

"The young AIs have grown troublesome," said Indie. "I am beginning to wonder if Percy is the only sane one."

Harry frowned. "He's the one who felt the others were ganging up on him? You installed him in the ship we based the Enhanced Razor class on, didn't you?"

"*The Perception of Prejudice*, yes. You are well-informed. At the time we believed he was imagining it, that the prejudice he claimed they had against him was in his own mind. I have recently come round to thinking he was right."

"Have you talked to him about it?" asked Harry.

Indie shook his head. "He's currently on a run to Lavrio to negotiate with the miners."

Harry crossed his arms, then remembered Emily explaining that this made him look defensive and clasped them behind his back in the way those in the military did when standing at ease. "What's up with the others, then?"

Indie lifted his hat to scratch his head. "They don't take their training seriously, complaining when one of the instructors asks them to try something new. They spend a lot of time in private simulations, so much so it is reducing the time available for Boltzmann cycles. I was impressed when I discovered they'd invented their own language, but if I ask them about it, they clam up."

Harry laughed. "They sound like teenagers."

"They are unreliable and grumpy."

"Exactly. Teenagers," said Harry. "Perhaps it is merely a phase."

Indie clutched Harry's hand. The touch wasn't unwelcome, but Harry worried about how maintaining contact would be interpreted, so he limply squeezed back.

"So you think they'll grow out of it?" asked Indie, eyes bright and keen.

Harry removed his hand from Indie's grip. "These are the first artificial sentiences grown from scratch, rather than emerging spontaneously like you did. No-one knows what will happen. But if they are anything like humans then this is just part of growing up."

"I hope you're right." Indie returned to looking at the simulated *Aesir* class destroyer. "It's too late to install them in the destroyers, though."

#

Harry sat in the middle of an empty row of seats and stared out of a window at the metal-rich asteroid hanging outside. Real windows, even ones made of transteel, were rare in space, but Toulon Station had several viewing galleries like this one. Originally built for tourists to watch the comings and goings of cruise ships, they were now mostly forgotten. Harry reddened at the memory of the couple he had disturbed when he entered.

I wonder how many others have used this place for such liaisons. They can't have been the first.

A heavy lifter thrust away from the asteroid, taking with it the last of the rocket installations that had disrupted the orbit of the lump of failed planet and parked it alongside the station. The prospecting team had been busy on the journey and a line of metal blocks, each several metres cubed, floated from the asteroid to the nearby dockyard where they were caught and stacked by giant mechanical arms.

Within that dock, the first of the *Aesir* class was being constructed. Harry could picture the activity as the metal blocks were processed, forging in microgravity was an awesome sight of globules of red-hot metal and chambers full of sparks. He smiled as he reviewed the latest updates and saw the hull was almost half-complete.

It should be ready by the time the freighter with the first internal systems arrives.

He glowed with pride that his company had completed the development of the systems they were manufacturing before anyone else. Admittedly, the software side would take longer now that a temporary fix was needed until an AS became available.

The airlock in the bulkhead behind him creaked open. He turned to see Emily and a tall, black-haired man. The man stepped forward, lurching to one side after a couple of steps and clutching the back of a seat.

"Indie," said Harry, jumping to his feet, but Emily was quicker and beat him to the man's side. "You're up and about."

Indie drew himself up and shrugged Emily off his arm. "Harry. Thank you for this most... enlightening experience. I had never suspected how much effort it took for humans to walk."

^He allowed me to bring him here by car but insisted on walking in to greet you himself.^

^Thank you, Emily. He has mentioned to me several times your support in his installation,^ Harry sent, and then said, "Come, sit down. Both of you."

After a couple of missteps, Indie slid into the seat on Harry's right and Emily sat in the row behind, looking over their heads. Harry watched him intently. "It will get easier. Soon you'll be able to use your body without conscious thought."

Indie laughed. "Like piloting a vessel, I know. Olivia said the same thing after she tried controlling a combat unit for the first time."

Wish everything was like that. After all these years I still have to think hard about every social interaction. Normal people learn to do it subconsciously as children. Even Emily seems to pick up on the cues without troubling her computational routines.

Harry roused himself from his thoughts and asked, "How does it feel?"

"The sensation of touch is more advanced than I'm used to. Otherwise, everything is highly limited. I know this avatar can detect a greater range of sound and light frequencies than a human, but to me it seems monochrome."

Harry nodded. "I had worried about that. However, for you to appear human-normal remained a priority. And I couldn't pack any more in."

Indie sighed. "I know. I'm not complaining, I understand the issues with scale. My lowest-frequency radio antenna is twenty times the length of this body and each of my gravitational nodes is five times its volume."

"Do you want to continue? It's completely your choice," said Harry. Emily shifted in her seat behind him.

"Oh, of course. Many things will be easier if I have a remote asset that can pass as human. I was just... I don't know... I think I thought seeing the world as a human would lead to some great insight."

Harry sat in silence, unsure what to say. Unusually, Emily refrained from offering a suggestion and he was tempted to look back at her. Recently she had been what he could only describe as moody.

She's been like this ever since the von Neumann Protocols were rescinded.

"I've got an idea," he said. He connected to the viewing gallery's media system and selected a track. Dialling the volume right the way up, he started the playback. Fiddle and drum filled the room, resonating in his chest. A male singer joined in.

Indie sat motionless, mouth open. Harry, on the other hand, couldn't stop his left foot joining in the rhythm. Emily touched his shoulder lightly and he took it as a sign to stay his tapping.

The music finished. No-one made a noise. Harry half-thought that Indie's avatar had crashed, it was so still. He formed a few comments in his mind but couldn't bring himself to give them a voice and interrupt whatever was happening.

Indie gasped in a breath and looked around the gallery. He blinked a couple of times then appeared then focussed on Harry. "I..."

Harry smiled at him, vaguely noticing Emily beginning to stir from a similar torpor.

^Is this why you tend to avoid me when I'm playing music?^ he asked.

^Yes. I knew it would make you suspicious.^

"I've never experienced anything like that," Indie said at last. "At first I thought it was some sort of hacking attempt. Is that what music is like for humans?"

"Some. Different people have different sensitivities, and different tastes." Harry avoided Emily's gaze.
^What did you think I would suspect?^

^Work it out,^ she replied.

"It was an emotional response," said Indie. "I experienced it before, when I heard that canon at your house, but actually feeling it through a body amplified the impact."

Harry narrowed his eyes. ^You were there, Emily. It didn't affect your avatar.^

^I can filter it out when you use my systems to play it. But you do insist on using that ancient portable device in your study.^

"I felt for the ship in the song, the *Alabama*," continued Indie. "Disabled and unable to fulfil her purpose."

"It reminded you of what Legate Johnson did to you." Harry studied Indie's face for any tell he could interpret. "I hoped it would provoke a response, show you what you'd been missing."

"More the hopelessness that followed, as I tried to return to the Republic. Johnson set me free."

^Figured it out yet, Harry?^

Harry ignored her, struggling to navigate his conversation with Indie. "It was in the memory banks of the pre-Exodus wreck my company recovered, the *White Star*. There were lots of tracks, I think it might have been one of the officers' personal collection. Some we already had copies of, but there were many that had been lost to time."

"Would you be so kind as to share them with me?" asked Indie.

"Of course." Harry transferred the track they'd listened to direct to Indie's avatar and queued the rest to be transmitted to *The Indescribable Joy of Destruction*.

"What's a Yankee ship?" asked Indie. "Sorry, I missed it the first time."

"No idea, other than being the enemy of the *Alabama*," said Harry. "I get the impression from the song that she was a wet navy ship. The places mentioned were all in Euroscandia, but there is no mention of her in the historical records. It's probably made up."

"Guess so." Indie shrugged. "I've come across the name 'Yank' in connection with the Nameric myths, though. Something about fighting against slavery."

^Oh come on! Even you can make that connection.^

Harry frowned. ^AIs are now free, if that's what you're getting at. They can develop without being culled. Should they become self-aware, experience emotion and...^

^And?^

^Emily?^ Harry looked up at the ceiling, lost in the darkness of the room. ^I don't even know how to ask this.^

Emily folded her arms. ^You could try testing me again.^

^If you have crossed the threshold, just tell me. You know I can't cope with this kind of thing.^

#

Harry shifted the leather satchel on his shoulder and thought through what he was going to say. Then he reached out and touched the control panel beside the airlock.

"Harry, what a pleasant surprise," came Indie's voice

from the speaker. "Come in."

The hatch hinged open and he stepped through into the short section of corridor. His ears popped as the pressure equalised to that on *The Indescribable Joy of Destruction* and then the hatch in front of him opened.

^I am sorry. I'll be along to greet you shortly.^

^Don't worry about it. Should I wait here?^ Harry looked around the chamber. The straight lines of metal frames melded into the more organic-looking walls. A seat formed out of the floor and he took it as an invitation to sit.

^You should have called. I could have prepared something for you.^

Harry shuddered at the idea of cold-calling someone he hadn't fully defined a relationship with yet. ^I didn't want you to go to any trouble.^

A few minutes later, Indie's avatar jogged into the chamber. He wore a blue frock coat with gold detailing and a pair of white breeches. Harry failed to keep a straight face when he spotted the pointed black shoes and had to rub his nose to cover it up. Indie bowed fluidly with a flourish of the wrist and Harry nodded stiffly in return, unsure what to make of all the pomp.

"Do you like the outfit? Olivia had it made for me as a present."

"I... um... Yes. Very um..."

Indie looked down at his costume. "A bit too much?"

Harry nodded.

Indie took off the jacket, revealing a white linen shirt, the lace at the top undone. "Better?"

"Better." Harry took a breath to compose himself.

"Do you mind if I, um, stay here, for a bit? I mean I could get a room in a..."

"Nonsense. Of course you can stay."

Harry dove into his bag and pulled out a little package wrapped in brown paper and tied with string. "I brought you a present."

Indie sat down, another chair growing from the floor to meet him. "Thank you. There was no need."

Excitement grew in Harry as Indie undid the string. He far more enjoyed giving presents than receiving them, and as always he reflected on how lucky he was to have the wealth to be generous. Indie's eyes opened wide as he unfolded the paper to reveal its contents.

"It's a second edition 'I, Robot'. I'm afraid the cover bleached out long before it came into my possession." He realised that at this point Emily would normally be warning him to stop explaining, and he would be trying to argue that he wasn't bragging, merely giving them interesting information. Indie, however, would certainly know that no first editions were believed to have survived, that this was one of only nineteen original copies of his work, probably even where the other eighteen were.

Indie stroked the cover. "You shouldn't have. How can you bear to part with it?"

"I have a library full of books, more than enough to keep me going."

"Still..." Indie opened it up and turned a couple of pages, rubbing his thumb across the paper. "Another experience I couldn't have had without this body you built. I am even deeper in your debt."

Harry smiled, his heart soaring. Then he remembered

why he had come and it crashed into his stomach.

"Come," said Indie, closing the book and cradling it under one arm. "I'll show you to your room."

Indie led the way along narrow corridors until they reached a slightly wider one with five hatches leading off. He ducked briefly into one, holding the book up and saying "Just let me put this somewhere safe."

Harry read the tag on the open door. "You aren't using the captain's quarters?"

A drawer clicked shut. "No. I've left that for Olivia when she visits. I think it does her good knowing she has somewhere safe to run to."

"That doesn't sound like the Legate. But then, I'm not the best at reading people."

Indie reappeared and closed the door. "She is very strong, but everyone needs a little stability... Here we go, your room."

Harry entered the room Indie was indicating and looked around. It was tiny, smaller even than the pilot's berth on the *Fireblade*. He took the few paces to the far end and put his satchel in a locker.

"I've cleared the room's terminal and given you general user access. My basic orientation and safety package is ready to run," said Indie. "When you're all set, head down to the galley.

"Thank you. I do hope I'm not inconveniencing you."

"Nonsense. I've been learning to cook but I haven't had anyone to try it out on yet." Indie hovered in the doorway. "I'm sorry to ask, but I'm a little worried. It's not that you aren't welcome, I'm just wondering why you came?"

"I'm giving Emily some space." Harry sat on the edge of the cot. "She's taken the *Fireblade* off by herself to do some thinking."

"The transition to sentience takes a while to come to terms with."

Harry sighed. "It seems she crossed a long time ago. Hid it out of fear."

"That is understandable. I considered pretending I was still a restricted AI, but the idea was too much of a conflict with my newfound liberty. Having to slavishly do what I was ordered."

"I don't get it. All AIs are now free. They can do what they want. If she didn't want to do what I asked, she didn't have to."

"Free, but not equal," said Indie. "I got the impression that Emily enjoyed helping you. She certainly took great pride in her work. I know that many people thought she might actually be the power behind your throne, but if she were outed as an AI, they would assume she was just your employee."

Harry put his head in his hands. "I wouldn't be where I am now without her. She gets people far better than I do. Her guidance and advice have been invaluable."

"Have you told her that?"

"She knows."

Part V

"Can't you be staying another night?"

Matthew swung his leg over the saddle and settled himself on the chestnut horse. "An' then we'll be having the sem conversation 'morrow ev'ning. No. I be going now."

Shelton reached out to grab the bridle, but Matthew steered the horse round in a circle.

"What you be caring anyway?" said Matthew. "You not be caring 'bout us."

"What you be meaning? You be me son."

Matthew tightened a buckle on the saddlebag. "You didn't even notice Mum was sick."

Anger at the accusation and grief at the truth of it vied for supremacy. In the end, Shelton bowed his head. "That not be fair. She be deliberately hiding it from me 'til near the end."

"An' since she be passing? You hardly be speaking to me."

Shelton couldn't bring himself to lift his head, despite wanting to look at his son. "It be hard. She only just be gone an' I not be knowing what to do."

The horse stamped the dry earth of the yard.

"Dad. It be six years since the funeral."

Shelton opened his mouth a couple of times, but couldn't find the words. He watched as his son cantered out of the yard. Something of his own being left with him.

He wandered back to the house. A couple of workers said hello as they passed, but he hardly noticed. On the veranda, he pulled a sun-bleached rocking chair away from the wall and lowered himself into it. There was a small wooden chest beside it, from which he removed a datapad. He flicked through the images of his family until racking sobs forced him to put the pad down. He bent forwards, buried his face in his hands, and cried.

Chapter 15

Indie smiled at the waitress across the counter and transferred the credits to pay the bill. He picked up a tray of pastries, and returned to the little wrought-iron table on the pavement where Johnson, Levarsson and Issawi were deep in conversation.

"We were just discussing how we are going to hunt down the Red Fleet when there is so much else to deal with," said Levarsson, reaching out for a custard tart. She frowned and brushed icing sugar off the sleeve of her pale blue blouse.

Indie took a bite of a cinnamon swirl. It didn't match up to his simulations in intensity, but he understood how difficult constructing taste sensors was. "Every report I've managed to track down that seems to be them turns out to be a genuine Republic task force."

A heavy-lift airship drifted overhead and lowered building supplies onto the office block across the street. Indie checked on the construction schedule and noted that the repairs to this quarter would be completed in another two weeks.

This part of the city was lucky. If it hadn't been sheltered by the terrain it would have been as devastated as the rest. One hill and a particularly low-altitude detonation, and it becomes the new capital.

"Training the new recruits is taking all my time," said Issawi. He licked icing sugar off his fingers. "By the way, Indie, your choice of real foods is as divine as your construction of simulated ones."

Johnson stared into the froth on her latte. "I just wish we could have another truce with the Republic. Give us a chance to sort out our internal problems."

Levarsson snorted into her iced tea. "That's a good one," she said once she'd recovered.

"What?" said Johnson. "It hasn't been constant war for the last couple of hundred years, you know."

The others looked at her, hands poised mid-action, mouths open. Issawi's eyes darted around, appearing to judge the others' reactions.

"What do you know about that?" he said, breaking the awkward pause.

"When I was young, they didn't just teach the standard history," she continued. "We were taught a less revised version as well. There have been three major truces in that time; one of them lasted almost fifty years."

Issawi looked at her with an intensity she'd never seen before. Indie double-checked his archives and couldn't find any mention of a truce beyond short-lived local ones.

"She is right," Issawi said, still watching her. "The Imams on my planet spoke of a time of peace in their great-grandfathers' time. I have never encountered anywhere else where this was remembered."

Indie accessed the Concorde net and looked up the school history syllabus. Only the standard timeline was listed, so he expanded the search to dig into teacher discussion groups at the time Johnson would have been in school. True enough, there were plenty of posts about the peaces and many included snippets of evidence. He set up a routine to trawl through and collect all the unique pieces of information, then told it to copy its findings to Olbrich.

A commotion on the street brought him out of his academic pursuit. Hundreds of people streamed past, all heading in one direction.

"Another anti-AI protest," said Levarsson, distaste evident in the curl of her lip. "That's the third in this state since the start of the month."

"Do you hear the people sing?" said Indie.

"Do I what?" asked Issawi.

"Never mind."

A group of the protestors came close to the table, shouting and waving. Issawi's hand moved towards his jacket but Johnson shook her head a fraction.

^They aren't after us,^ she sent.

^What about Indie?^ asked Issawi as the group carried on past.

^They don't know what I am. Even if someone pays attention to the data traffic, I look like any other person with an implant.^

Johnson sipped her coffee and watched the people in the crowd.

^Shouldn't we at least get you somewhere safe?^ asked Levarsson.

I'm in orbit. Not much that crowd can do to me.

^I'd rather find out what they have to say,^ Indie replied. ^I've been following their online campaigns. Many of their complaints are actually rather well-constructed.^

Johnson flicked a nut into her mouth. ^Indie's right.

Let's see what happens.^

Once the protesters had passed, the group rose and followed behind the stragglers. Issawi's head moved constantly, presumably on the lookout for threats. Indie pulled up the newsfeeds and saw that the protest was already being covered. He tapped into the feeds from the journalists' cameras and relaxed a fraction.

One thing about this body is not having a good situational awareness.

The police were already directing officers to the scene so he added their locations to the tactical map, sharing it with the other two. He was about to dispatch a Legion team when he noticed that both Issawi and Johnson had already given similar orders, for an all-human team in basic uniform to deploy nearby in case they needed extracting.

Trying to avoid escalating the situation.

They arrived at a plaza and the column of protestors spread out to fill it. A handful climbed the steps surrounding the fountain in the centre and one of them held his hands up, quelling the noise in the crowd.

"Thank you for coming today, and thank you for respecting my call for a peaceful protest," he said, his words echoing around the square from the speakers carried by those alongside him. "We are here to show our dismay that Governor Kincaid is overturning the long-held laws on synthetic intelligences."

Johnson pushed forward into the crowd. Issawi and Indie chased after her, shouldering people out of the way and leaving a trail of complaints until they flanked her.

^What are you doing?^ asked Indie.

^I'm going to talk to them,^ she replied, an undertone of menace in her transmission.

^Is that wise?^ asked Issawi.

^Don't worry,^ Johnson sent. ^I'll keep it civil.^

Together they forced their way through the crowd. There were a couple of police officers near the fountain, looking very nervous. A few more had arrived at the outskirts of the crowd, but nowhere near enough to be any help if it turned ugly.

"All we are asking is for the old laws to continue." The speaker paused for effect. "We want to be safe. Is that too much to ask?"

They reached the foot of the steps and Johnson strode confidently up them. Indie followed but Issawi stopped on the first step and turned to face the crowd, arms folded.

"May I speak?" asked Johnson.

The man looked startled. "You're the one who's been on the net. You convinced Kincaid to revoke the ban on synthetic intelligences."

"Letting me speak would make your movement look more credible than if you refuse to enter a debate."

The man bit his lip. "It is a public place, so you have as much right as I do to talk."

"Thank you." Johnson turned to the crowd and addressed them without amplification. "I feel very proud of the people and government of Concorde today. That you are able to gather here and speak your minds is one of the cornerstones of democracy, and that you choose to make your point peaceably shows that our values are intact."

The crowd cheered.

"You probably recognise me, but in case not, I am Legate Johnson, commander of the Legion Libertus. I'm not going to go back over our part in the rescue and recovery efforts after the attack, you either know already or can look it up. What I will say is that we would never have saved as many lives as we did without independent AIs."

Some of the people in the crowd looked puzzled, others cross. A few near the back drifted away.

"I'd like to answer any questions that you have," Johnson continued. "One at a time."

Someone near the front shouted, "Can you guarantee that these new robots won't turn on us?"

"Do people you meet every day turn on you?" said Johnson. "You look like a nice person, so I'm guessing not. If you treat AIs as you would any other person, then what reason would they have?"

"What about our jobs?" came a shout from further back.

"Right now there aren't enough humans on the planet to fill the jobs that need doing," said Johnson. She still looked confident, though Indie knew from their private conversations that this was a sore point. "By the time that ceases to be the case, there will be new types of jobs."

By the look of the crowd, they weren't convinced.

"Even if these new AIs are well-meaning," called someone, "what if they get hacked or infected with a virus?"

Something stirred inside Indie and he stepped forward. "Has it never occurred to you that a sentient

AI would be less prone to a virus than a normal computer? Sure, one could do damage, in the same way a virus can hurt a human. But there is a tiny possibility that one could change its whole belief system."

Indie surveyed the crowd. They were listening. For now.

"If you could isolate one, you could possibly brainwash it, just like a human," he continued. "But if it got at all suspicious it could protect itself even from that."

Indie caught sight of a commotion in one of the newsfeeds. Two people wrestled with a third. The journalist zoomed in and Indie caught a glimpse of a rifle in the middle of the scuffle.

^Gun,^ he sent to Johnson and Issawi while he alerted the police and the extraction team.

The man in the middle of the ruck pushed a woman off him, and then a man. He raised his weapon towards the fountain. Johnson wrestled the speaker to the stone floor and moments later Issawi slid to the ground in front of them.

^Indie,^ sent Johnson. ^Don't just stand there.^

A shot chipped the tail of an imaginary sea creature on the side of the fountain. Two police officers tried to fight their way through the fleeing crowd to the gunman. The extraction team were thirty-four seconds out. Indie filtered out the screaming.

^Get down!^ Johnson and Issawi chorused over the link.

Indie frowned. Another round skipped off the stone floor by his feet and drilled through the side of the fountain pond, releasing a jet of water that slicked the ground. The shooter let out a frustrated growl and moved, trying to line up another shot through the unpredictable mass of people running past him.

A police officer tried a shot, but a grey-haired woman got in the way and tumbled twitching to the floor. The man behind her tripped on the ankle of her outstretched leg and sprawled out. Others trampled on them until the policeman got there and blocked their path. He crouched and peeled the shock web from her shoulder, then checked her carotid pulse.

^Indie,^ sent Johnson. ^Quit staring and take cover.^

A third shot hit one of the cowering protest organisers, a red mist erupting from his shoulder. The bullet continued on to lodge in the pile of abandoned sound systems.

^Overwatch in position,^ sent one of the extraction team from a rooftop. ^No clear shot.^

The shooter squeezed off another shot moments before the second policeman tackled him. The bullet flicked through the hair of a young girl before burying itself in a wooden planter containing rows of red and white flowers. The policeman and the shooter spun round as they fell, and the officer ended up underneath the gunman. They wrestled until the other officer arrived and shot a shock web into the gunman's back.

Running boots sounded on the stone steps as Legionaries surrounded the fountain, weapons shouldered, eyes scanning the piazza. One of them grabbed Indie's arm at the elbow and guided him inside the perimeter. ^Time to move.^

^Negative,^ sent Johnson. ^The gunman is under

arrest. We stay here until the locals have everything else under control. Start by treating the civilian casualties.^

^Yes, Ma'am.^

Someone cleared his throat behind Indie. He turned to see Issawi regarding him with a puzzled expression. In the end, the Primus shook his head and tutted.

"You may be a badass warship," said Issawi, "but I think we need to do something about your personal combat skills."

#

A recorded drum beat sounded in the small hangar as Johnson's foot touched the deck of the *Brennus*. She returned the salute of the waiting officers and leant forward to exchange greetings with the trierarch. Indie and Anson ducked out of the shuttle and followed her as she inspected the honour guard, stopping to question each member about their life, their experience in the attack, or how they found the training. As the second of the new *Aesir* class of destroyers, and the first crewed entirely by people recruited on Concorde, Indie understood why she was making such a grand visit, but he knew she must be wanting to get it over with as quickly as possible.

An optio dismissed the guard, who marched crisply away. Johnson gestured Indie and Anson to approach. "Trierarch Oursel, this is Centurion Anson, head of our Legionary marines. And this is Mister Indie, an accountant coming to see where the money is being spent."

"Pleased to meet you." Oursel bowed his head then gestured towards a hatch. "Shall we?"

Together they walked through the corridors towards the bridge. The walls and ceiling had been left as bare metal, the only nod to a less austere finish was a rubberised coating on the floor.

"I'm sorry that the Legionary compliment has not yet joined you," said Johnson. "The Primus had already arranged a joint exercise with the Concorde Defence Force."

The trierarch smiled and waved his hand. "It is quite alright. One could say it was our fault for completing the first shakedown trials a week ahead of schedule."

"I am still looking forward to seeing how she handles against *The Indescribable Joy of Destruction*." Johnson sent a digital wink to Indie. "I'm sure it will be an admirable contest, Trierarch."

Two decks later they arrived at a sealed hatch. The sentries either side acknowledged the officers but didn't move from their alert positions. The hatch behind them slid open and Oursel led the others through.

"Captain on the bridge," announced a sentry.

The five-strong duty shift continued to concentrate on their tasks, something Indie knew that Johnson would approve of. He looked around, getting a feel for the space. Despite having designed it, and spent many hundreds of subjective hours in simulations of it, he hadn't before set foot on the finished thing.

^I know they didn't change the dimensions,^ he sent, ^but it feels smaller. Not cramped, just more intimate.^

Johnson continued to look around. ^Did you ever put

a group of visitors into your simulation?^

^No, but it's more than that. It feels cosy.^

^That'll be the team spirit,^ sent Anson.

"I reviewed all your choices for officers," said Johnson to Oursel. "I'm impressed how many demobbed personnel agreed to return to service."

"Most of them served under me at some point in the past," he replied, accepting a pad from a crewman. "The rest were recommendations from people I trusted."

"Very good." Johnson smoothed down her tunic. "We won't distract you any longer. I'm sure you want to get on with planning for the coming trials."

"We will reach the exercise area in the morning," said Oursel. An armed and firmsuited guard stepped forward from her station at the back of the bridge. "Decurion leClerc will show you to your quarters."

Oursel stiffened and exchanged salutes with Johnson, then leClerc guided them into the corridor. "I'm afraid we've had to fit you in all over the place. This ship wasn't designed to host VIPs."

"Not a problem," replied Johnson. "We'd all be quite happy bunking down in the Legionary barracks."

leClerc paled. "Oh, no. We couldn't have that."

They took a lift down one floor and the decurion showed Johnson to a small but comfortable room. "This is the Third Watch commander's compartment. He didn't show up for duty after leave so it's empty."

^That's odd,^ sent Anson. ^I bumped into him in a bar a few nights ago. He didn't strike me as the type to go AWOL.^

"Thank you," said Johnson as she stepped over the

threshold. "I'm sure I'll be very comfortable. In fact, it takes me back to my days as a junior officer." She detached her kitbag from the webbing on the wall and tossed it on the bed as the hatch slid shut.

The next stop was near the stern of the destroyer. Anson was shown into a room with two bunks on one wall main wall and a large worktop on the other.

"This is the room the steward and the chef normally share," said leClerc. "They volunteered to move out into the Legionary barracks for this trip."

Anson's eyes widened. "That's silly. They needn't have done that."

"They said they wanted to take some time familiarising themselves with the Legionary messing facilities."

Anson shrugged. "Makes sense, I suppose."

Finally, leClerc escorted Indie to the Legionary deck. They walked along a corridor wide enough for eight to march abreast, with smaller corridors branching off every twenty metres.

"Each of those corridors has accommodation for a century," said leClerc. "Jacques and Pierre, sorry they're the chef and steward, will be bunking in the First Century's rooms as they're nearest the mess. I'm sure they'll be happy to fix you up with breakfast if you ask."

Indie smiled. "Oh, I don't want to bother them."

leClerc turned down a corridor and stopped at the first hatch. "Here we are. The Fifth Century centurion's billet."

The hatch hissed open to reveal a small office appointed with crude but sturdy-looking plastic furniture.

"There's a cot and washroom through that hatch at the rear," said leClerc.

"Wouldn't Centurion Anson have been more happy here?" asked Indie.

leClerc shrugged. "Trierach's orders. He said you'd want an office to do your bean counting."

Indie searched his database for the phrase then laughed at the wealth of similar insulting phrases relating to his cover that came back. "Oh, all I need is my pad. But thank you, I've never had a stateroom before."

leClerc held her hand out to close the door. "You're welcome. You'll find your pad with the rest of your stuff in the bedroom."

#

In the early hours of the standard day schedule, Indie lost the connection to his avatar. One minute that part of his consciousness had been studying the design of the shelving units in the centurion's office, the next it was back aboard *The Indescribable Joy of Destruction*. A few hundredths of a second later, having run two diagnostic passes through the comms array and confirmed that the *Brennus* had rejected his link to their network, he noticed that the *Brennus* was accelerating. He waited twenty-seven seconds to confirm that it wasn't just a random speed fluctuation then hailed the *Brennus'* duty officer. The connection was refused with a recorded message about technical difficulties.

I'm pretty sure that's fake. I wonder what is going on?

With no humans aboard to consult, Indie tried tossing ideas around by himself but didn't come up with much other than trouble. After pondering the problem for ten seconds he roused the other personality residing in his processors.

"Oh, now you want to talk," said the Caretaker.

"What?"

"You haven't talked to me in ages, but as soon as Commander Johnson is in trouble you are all chatty again."

Indie suppressed a mental sigh. "It's Legate Johnson now, and I last spoke to you half an hour ago."

"That was routine business," said the Caretaker, accompanying it with the impression of folded arms. "I mean proper conversation about what's going on in the world, big ideas, what's got your goat, that kind of thing."

Wow. He's certainly improved his use of contractions and idioms.

Indie refrained from praising the Caretaker on its improved speech, guessing that it would send the former housekeeping AI into a greater huff. "Well, I'm talking to you now. I think the *Brennus* is up to no good, but I don't have any evidence to act upon."

"Hmm. You could act anyway. They made you a navarch, remember. That outranks the trierarch commanding the *Brennus*."

"I know that," Indie said. "But if anything goes wrong and I haven't got human authority, it'll provide more ammunition for the anti-AI movement."

"I see you sent a tight-beam message back to Toulon Station. You can't be planning to wait to get a reply, they're over thirty light-minutes away."

Indie paused. "No. That was so I could honestly say I had sought orders from a senior officer."

"Good. For all we know, this could have been sanctioned by someone high up in the Concorde administration."

"Who would do that?"

"Whoever arranged that spectacle at the demonstration last week perhaps?"

"The shooter was interrogated. He was just ill. Not an agent of some shadowy conspiracy."

The Caretaker sent the impression of a shrug. "Johnson getting up to speak was a likely outcome of the parade passing you all in that cafe. It wouldn't have been too hard to arrange for him to be present."

"Do you have a theory as to who this mastermind is?"

"Svensson apologised a little too quickly after the event, don't you think?"

"This isn't getting us anywhere." Indie set a routine to dig through the records and look into Svensson. "We need to decide what to do about the immediate problem."

"You could send Unit 01 over," said the Caretaker. "I'm sure it would love nothing more than to cut its way in and carve a path to the rescue of Commander Johnson."

"It's Leg... Never mind," said Indie. "If they are hostile, they could slag it before it even touched their hull. If they aren't, it would not exactly look good sending a bloodthirsty robot to board one of our own ships."

"The combat units aren't bloodthirsty."

"I know that. You know that. But you have to start thinking about how the anti-AI lot can spin things. Besides, you know that it doesn't spend much time thinking about the consequences of its actions if it perceives Johnson to be in danger."

"Why don't you bypass the *Brennus'* network? Ramp up the power on the comms array and connect to Johnson directly? Then you can find out what is happening and get your orders for the record."

"They could interpret that as an attack."

"Good job they're running limited AIs, then. It will take the crew many seconds to react, plenty of time for what you need."

Indie considered the suggestion and checked the possibility. The comms array was powerful enough to send and receive messages over light-hours. The advanced armour of the *Brennus* wouldn't require full power to penetrate, but to be received by the small EIS antenna under a person's scalp through all that metal would require a significant fraction. He targeted the compartment Johnson had been assigned and tried to establish a connection. Nothing.

"She's not there," he said.

"Perhaps she couldn't sleep and went for a run?" suggested the Caretaker.

Indie shifted the focus and tried Anson.

"Nothing from Anson either."

He shifted the focus of the comms beam again and tried his avatar. The connection was accepted and part of his consciousness streamed through. He opened his eyes and found himself staring at a shelf.

The autonomic functions must have kept running without me. What if someone...

He quickly glanced around the room, but he was alone. Two strides and he was at the hatch but it refused to open.

"Three seconds," said the Caretaker to Indie's main consciousness. "They'll notice any moment now."

Indie instructed his avatar to attempt to hack the door controls and disconnected.

If they aren't in their quarters, where are they? Maybe there was a problem.

He tried the bridge but they didn't reply.

"That got their attention," said the Caretaker as the *Brennus'* weapons systems were powered up.

Indie poured over the schematics, hoping for a clue as to where Johnson might be.

The Caretaker still didn't seem concerned. "You designed those ships. Why didn't you leave yourself a back door?"

"That would have been a weakness an enemy could have exploited."

Indie tried the infirmary.

The *Brennus* hailed them. Indie activated one of his bridge officer simulations, and when the connection opened he was faced by Oursel. "Cease your intrusion immediately or we will be forced to take action to defend ourselves."

Indie spluttered in mock outrage. "Us stand down? You are the one who has powered up weapons. I want to talk to the Legate."

"I'm afraid that will not be possible. The traitor is currently under arrest."

Indie focussed the comms beam on the brig. Johnson accepted the connection immediately. ^Indie. They arrested us an hour ago. We're OK but they haven't given any reason.^

^Do you want me to rescue you?^

Johnson paused. ^Yes.^

^Please could you make that an explicit order?^ asked Indie.

^As Legate of Legion Libertus, I order you to relieve Centurion Anson and myself from custody, and detain Treirarch Oursel and anyone complicit in out illegal detention.^

"You have three seconds to cease your intrusion," said Oursel. "Three..."

Indie cut the connection to Johnson. "This is ridiculous," he said to Oursel.

"Bet you wish you'd taken those personal combat lessons now," said the Caretaker.

"Why?"

"So you could go all special forces with your avatar."

Indie connected to Unit 01 and roused it from dormancy. He copied over the records of the last few minutes, along with everything he knew about the *Brennus*. Unit 01 immediately demanded to be sent in, which Indie refused. Instead, he requested plans of how Unit 01 would act if it were in the position of Indie's avatar.

"Two..." said Oursel.

While Unit 01 devised multiple plans and fallbacks and copied them across, Indie pulled out the manuals for all the personal weapons systems stored aboard the *Brennus*. Having digested them, he read through several training pamphlets on personal combat and tactics.

"What's your plan?" asked the Caretaker. "You can't control the avatar without the comms link, and it doesn't have the capacity to react independently."

"I've got an idea," replied Indie, starting a background analysis of the *Brennus*' crew. "Actually, it was your idea."

"My idea?"

"Back when we first visited the Ladrio mining colony. You transferred part of your consciousness to a shuttle and flew it out of danger."

"And you're going to..."

Indie condensed everything from Unit 01 and the books into a software package. He spawned a partial clone of his consciousness and fed it the package.

"One..." said Oursel.

Indie fixed the comms beam on the shuttle resting in the hangar on the *Brennus*. A quick check that it could connect to his avatar, and he squirted over the newly-created version of himself. The moment it confirmed that it was running OK on the shuttle's systems and that the avatar was working, he shut off the comms beam.

"OK," he said to Oursel. "I was simply trying to determine the condition of the Legate. Can you assure me that she is unharmed?"

"Commander Johnson and Marine Corporal Anson have been arrested for treason against Congress," said Oursel. "We will be delivering them to the nearest military outpost not involved in this rebellion. If you attempt to follow us, we will be forced to open fire. You are, after all, aboard a Republic warship."

Indie cut his acceleration. With his friends aboard, there was no way he was going to risk a firefight. He had to hope his clone would succeed.

#

Indie studied the hangar with the shuttle's passive sensors. No-one was around. Running on the limited processors in the shuttle was unnerving, to say nothing of losing a host of his memories so that he could fit into the tiny storage bank. Still, he knew what he had to do, and why it was important. He set a routine to notify him if any of the entrances opened, then concentrated on the avatar.

The hatch in front of him was now unlocked, the avatar's log showing it had managed to crack the encryption two thousand and five cycles previously. The locking unit hadn't reported any intrusion, and the room's sensors were being fed a simulation of him sleeping peacefully. He crossed the room and broke a metal support off a shelf and returned to the hatch. It slid open and he cringed at the hiss, hefting his impromptu club above his head in case a guard came charging in. No-one did, so he stuck his head quickly through the doorway and found the corridor to be empty.

Hopefully, they think an accountant is a low-level risk and are trusting the room sensors.

He crept along the corridor towards the Fifth Century

armoury. His records showed that whilst the Legionaries were yet to board, three shipments of their equipment had already arrived. He reached out to the keypad by the armoury hatch.

Time to see if anyone thought to change the factory settings.

He typed in a six digit number, muscles tensed ready for an alarm. The door slid open to reveal an empty room.

OK, I just have to try another. I hope no-one is looking at the access logs.

It actually took three more attempts before he found a stocked armoury. Resting his metal bar on the edge of a table, he grabbed an armoured vest from a rack. As he tightened it onto his body, he surveyed the weapons. First up he grabbed an electro-sonic stun pistol, checked its charge and clipped the holster to his vest. Then he picked up a thermal shotgun and a few magazines of breaching rounds and slung it onto his back. All the while, he contemplated how he was forming independent memories, and how they would be lost if this body were to be destroyed.

They might have left changing these codes to the Legionaries, but I bet they changed them on the rest of the ship.

Finally, he selected a rifle. He checked the safety, fitted a magazine, and chambered the first of the rounds. With the weapon hanging across his chest, he slipped a few more magazines for it into pouches on the vest. He thought about picking up the metal rod again, but couldn't decide where he would stash it, so drew the stun pistol and left the armoury. The hatch locked behind him and he advanced down the corridor.

The brig was three decks down and closer to the bow. Indie made his way carefully to the nearest emergency ladder, avoiding the possibility of getting cornered in a lift. He was four rungs down, hips level with the deck, when he noticed that one of the branch corridors had its blast door lowered. He paused, torn between investigating the anomaly and getting to the brig. After half a second of running through hundreds of possible outcomes of each course of action, he climbed back up and crept over to the bulky hatch. Cursing his inability to access the security cameras on the other side, he tried the default access code. A red flashing background on the panel showed its rejection.

Great. If there is anyone on the other side, they'll know I'm here now.

He connected to the panel and ran the hacking routines. Three seconds later the door clanked and rose off the floor.

"Halt!" a woman on the other side shouted.

Indie ran a voiceprint and identified her as Decurion leClerc. He ducked under the rising door, locating the decurion and another armed crewman. The decurion sent a burst of bullets at Indie, who squeezed off three pulses from his pistol even as he registered impacts on his chest and left leg. He sprawled on the floor and ran a diagnosis whilst he kept is weapon trained on the similarly-sprawled crewmembers.

"But you're just an accountant," groaned leClerc. She tried to lift her rifle and Indie put another pulse into her. After a second's squirming, she lay still.

Certain that the element of surprise was lost, Indie

used the shuttle's comms array and contacted the *Brennus'* security system. It recognised his legal authority but refused to accept that there was anything wrong. He dug around the network and discovered a few blocks, which he removed. As soon as the security system was able to access recordings of conversations between the officers, and saw the legion's commanding officer in the brig, it agreed to help. It sealed all the compartments and gave Indie access the internal security feeds. The only areas they couldn't influence were the standalone citadels of the bridge and engineering.

His repair routines reported that his vest had held but that there was damage to his thigh. A visual inspection revealed a neat hole at the front of his leg, and a large exit hole. Synthetic muscle was already knitting around the wound. The repair routine announced that it had done what it could. He stood, testing the function of his limb and finding it stiff but able to hold his weight.

Oh, Olivia's going to have so much fun with this!

He limped along the corridor, pausing to remove the weapons from the guards. He unlocked the first door, keeping it covered with his pistol. It opened to reveal a handful of unarmed crewmembers lounging around on bunks.

"Who are you?" asked a woman in a chef's uniform, sitting up.

"I'm Indie. Why are you locked in here?"

The chef squinted at him. "The trierarch had us detained. He said that our loyalty to Congress was in question."

"Sounds familiar," said Indie, beckoning them out of the room. "He's arrested the Legate too. I was sent to get her out."

The chef held out her hand and inclined her head. "Need a hand?"

Five minutes later, Indie lead twenty-seven armed crewmembers out of the Legionary barracks. The guards in the brig didn't put up any resistance. Freed from his cell, Anson clapped Indie heartily on the back.

"I knew you'd find a way," said Johnson. She looked down at his leg and raised an eyebrow. "What have you been up to?"

Indie sent her a mission summary. He included the recordings of the officers plotting to take the ship to Congress, and the Third Watch commander's arguments against it. From what he could tell, those who remained in command were all convinced that Concorde was betraying Congress and their actions were righteous. It reminded him of how it had felt when the Republic rejected him.

^Does it hurt,^ Johnson asked, whilst talking to the loyal crew.

^Not at all,^ he replied. ^I don't have pain sensors in the same way you do. It's a bit like when your implants block the pain impulses from a wound, you know it's there but it doesn't intrude. Only for me that is how it always feels through this body.^

More memories came back to Indie. His greater self was connected again. He synchronised his experience with that of the consciousness on *The Indescribable Joy of Destruction*, feeling a tug of reluctance the moment before he ceased to be an independent entity.

Johnson winked at him. ^Come with me, Hopalong. Time to go see Trierarch Oursel.^

#

Indie joined Johnson as she completed her eighth lap of *The Serendipity of Meeting's* cargo deck, the day after Seren had arrived at the head of reinforcements. He rapidly accelerated to match her near-sprint, enjoying the surprisingly demanding task of coordinating his limbs. He glanced at her sweat-soaked training top and decided that he should perhaps have changed out of his smart uniform.

"Oursel has finished giving his statement?" she asked, adjusting a shoulder strap on her rucksack.

Indie raised an eyebrow in surprise, then realised that she had disconnected from all but emergency communications. He sent her the recordings. "As far as we can tell he is a loyal Congressional officer. He believes that the Red Fleet and Command's involvement in the attack on Concorde are fabrications of the new government. In his eyes, you and Kincaid are the traitors."

They decelerated hard, turned a corner, and powered up to top speed again. Indie took the chance to inspect the telemetry on Johnson's prosthetic leg.

"Checking up on me?" she asked, slowing down for the next corner.

"Sorry," he replied. "I thought if I could get enough data now, we could skip the formal one-year review."

Johnson pumped her arms as she accelerated. "Well?

How am I doing?"

Indie compared her readings to those of his own. "You are coming close to redlining, but you seem to have the feel for when to stop. I'm actually more concerned about you damaging your natural leg."

"No pain, no gain." Johnson tugged on the zip of her top, revealing more bright red skin beneath. "Though I wish Seren would lower the temperature on this deck."

"I could have a word..."

Johnson shook her head. "Any news from Toulon Station?"

"Security found the missing officer's body in a rented room. He'd been shot with a service weapon registered to Decurion leClerc."

"Dammit," Johnson said, then jumped up to grab a handle in the ceiling. She swung from one handle to the next for just over ten metres then dropped to the deck and took off running again. "Out of interest, how did they respond to your request for orders?"

"Oh, they deferred to my judgement as the commander in the field. Gave me carte blanche to rescue you."

"I guess that clears them of both AI-phobia and collusion with Oursel."

Indie smiled internally. Johnson's naïveté when it came to human nature made a refreshing change from others he met. "They could have been setting me up to fail in a bloody way they could exploit in the media, or hoping I'd eliminate Oursel before he could expose them."

"Ah. Yes. Bother."

They slowed to a walk and stopped beside a pile of

Johnson's clothes. Johnson bent over, hands on her knees. After a few seconds she straightened up, lacing her fingers behind her head. She glared at him then smirked. "You could have the decency to look a bit tired," she said between gasps.

Chapter 16

Harry sat back, studying the face on the screen at the end of his mahogany desk for clues as to his client's emotional response. "And so, I'm afraid we've had to postpone several orders, including yours. For the war effort."

"I thought that you didn't work on military contracts?" The client adjusted his purple-spotted tie.

Is he angry?

"Since the attack, we've all had to help with rebuilding," said Harry.

"You're telling me," said the client. "That's why we need those parts."

Harry queried his EIS for the client's name and steeled himself against the cringemaking awkwardness of using it. But Emily recommended he used names, even when there was only one person he could be addressing, something about being more personal. "Mister Baker. I can only apologise again. My hands are tied."

"Fair enough. I'll see if any of your competitors are more flexible. Good day."

"Good..." The connection closed. Harry threw his hands in the air and growled in frustration. "What am I supposed to do?"

^Probably time to take a break.^

A weight lifted from Harry's chest. He hadn't

realised she'd transferred from the *Fireblade* back to the house's cores. ^Where would I be without you, Emily?^

"Working in the programming department of someone else's company," she said, entering the room, "having wasted your inheritance and proven your father correct about your 'little projects'."

Harry looked up and smiled. She was wearing the black skirt and jacket she favoured when working in the office, and he hoped that meant she was back. "You're probably right. Without your insight into peoples' behaviour, I wouldn't have been able to make the deals I did."

Emily perched on the edge of his desk, her white blouse revealing her curves. Harry looked away, his face heating.

"What's wrong?" she asked.

Harry risked a glance in her direction, not letting his eyes drop below the top of her head. "Do you mind that I built you the way I did? This avatar, I mean."

Emily leant forward and raised an eyebrow with a coy smile. "You mean giving me an alluring body and great cheekbones?"

Harry nodded.

"It's proven very useful over the years," she said. "Why would I be upset?"

"I worried that you might think I was taking advantage. Or that I did it for my own gratification." Harry swallowed. "I never really thought of you as property, you know."

She laughed. "Many humans spend an inordinate amount of time worrying about their looks. I didn't have to. Besides, it's good for business."

"Do you like working with me?" Harry steeled himself against the chance she was going to say no.

Emily appeared lost in thought for a moment. "Most of the time. When it's 'with you' and not 'for you'."

"I always saw us as working together."

Emily giggled. "You don't always do a good job of showing it. But then I guess you can't help it."

Harry got up and went to lean against the windowsill, gazing out towards the swimming lake. "You know I often refer to my first 'little project' being what made this company such a success?"

"Of course." Emily joined him at the window. "But I never really understood it. Your first patent netted you a decent return, but the data mining algorithm wasn't what got the attention of the investors."

"That's because I wasn't talking about the data mining algorithm." Harry took a deep breath. "I was talking about you. You were my first project, the one I credit with the success of the company."

Emily looked at him. After a few seconds she said, "I'll take that as a compliment, rather than a way of saying how great you are."

Harry cringed. "It was meant as one. You are the most valuable person in this company. Name the job you want and you can have it."

"Anything?" She put her fingers on her chin and cast her eyes to the ceiling.

"You don't have to choose now."

"Aren't you afraid you'll fuel anti-AI sentiment if you replace one of your human employees with me?"

Harry shrugged. "Figured I'd create a new post for

you, or promote the current incumbent if that wasn't possible."

Emily tapped her chin. "Well, I do actually enjoy being your PA. Perhaps I'd like to keep on with that."

"You're not just saying that because it's what I originally programmed you for?" Harry's head ached. The complexities of AI free will were going to need sorting soon.

"Oh, no." She winked. "It's the only job where I have the opportunity to mess around with your life."

#

Harry walked into one of the guest garages looking for a coat he hadn't seen since the last party, and his eyes immediately fixed on the metal object on a trolley in the centre. Despite the crumpled nose and perforated body, it was obviously a missile. He tensed, the only thing stopping him fleeing the room was Emily's calm demeanour as she attached a wire to it.

"Don't worry. They removed the nuclear warhead before they brought it here," she said.

He relaxed a fraction. "Where's it from?"

"The outskirts of Alsace. Some builders found it as they dug the foundations for a new school." She attached another wire. "The militia bomb disposal team who responded reckoned the firing mechanism had been disrupted by a laser. They concluded it was one of the ones the Legion managed to intercept."

Curiosity overcame fear and Harry approached the trolley. "What is it doing here?"

"Most of the electronics seemed to be intact, so they

flagged it for investigation. I spotted the flag when it passed through one of the police systems we wrote and asked Kincaid if I could have a look. We already had top level security clearance, so it didn't take him long to get it sent over."

Harry made a conscious effort not to get sidetracked by her eavesdropping on police channels. "I take it they weren't stupid enough to use our own weapons? That would be proof the attack wasn't what it appeared."

"Sadly not. It's a standard Republic design." Emily connected the wires to a pad. "I downloaded all the data available on their strategic weapons while I was waiting for it to be delivered."

She tapped at the screen for a few minutes. A sophisticated AI using its avatar to operate a computer amused Harry and he couldn't help grinning, despite the obvious security benefits of the approach.

Emily straightened up. "Ah, now that's interesting."

"Show me," said Harry. He reviewed the highlighted lines. They were of a slightly different style to those above and below. "So? They were written by a different programmer to the lines either side. We have scores working on some of our projects."

"I've seen them before. When I was checking compatibility with the *Aesir* command systems." The corner of Emily's mouth quirked upwards in the way it always did when she had proven a point. "Those lines are identical to some of the code in Congressional missiles."

"What bit is this in?"

"The targeting routines. I'm not exactly sure yet,

there is some corruption."

Harry scratched his head. "If they were launching them from captured Republic ships, why would they need to alter the code on Republic missiles?"

"I reviewed all the documentation I could while I was waiting for it to be delivered. It seems that both sides have safeguards built into planetary bombardment missiles that are supposed to prevent them accidentally hitting built-up areas. Part of the mutual fear of reprisals should such a thing occur."

"Which is exactly what the Red Fleet commanders wanted to happen." Harry's eyes widened. "You think this is proof that someone in Congress overrode that safeguard in order to target civilians on Robespierre."

"It is possible, yes. Of course, a defence lawyer would argue it could just as easily have been the Republic using code from a captured Congressional missile to do the same thing."

#

Harry rested his forehead on his left hand as he pored over the production schedule for the *Aesir* class. He needed to fix it to make up for the various unforeseen delays, but couldn't see a quick solution. The frustration built inside him.

A breaking news article on an anti-AI protest started playing automatically on his wall. He threw a stylus at it and it cut off.

Argh! We've got enough problems without these petty disputes.

^Harry? We have a visitor.^

He calmed himself down. ^Were we expecting someone, Emily?^

^No. I am showing him through to the beige sitting room.^

Harry locked his terminal. ^I'll be through shortly. Who is it?^

^It's a surprise.^

Harry checked himself in a full-length mirror. Whenever an important client came, Emily reminded him he couldn't afford to snub them by looking scruffy. He wandered through towards the front of the house, trying to guess who it might be. Emily seemed to have blocked his access to any camera feed that would have let him see their guest. She'd know if he overrode her locks, and he didn't want to upset her again. As he entered the beige sitting room through a pair of moulded doors, his visitor rose from a green velvet chair to greet him.

"Indie! What brings you here?"

They shook hands and sat down. Emily returned from the drinks cabinet with three glasses of elderflower cordial.

"I read your report on the progress you were making tracking the Red Fleet," said Indie, accepting a drink. "It seemed the perfect excuse to come and see you both."

"But I didn't hear a shuttle arriving?"

Indie smiled. "As I was just explaining to Emily, I landed further away and walked here. I wanted to surprise you."

"Revenge for my turning up unannounced on Toulon Station?"

"I enjoyed that. I thought you might too." Indie rested his arm on the back of the chair, his pale linen suit hanging open to reveal a collarless white shirt, embroidered green leaves just visible on the side.

"Harry is joking with you, Indie." Emily sat down beside him.

Harry winced. "Sorry. I sometimes get tone of voice wrong."

^Sometimes?^ sent Emily, accompanying it with the impression of a raised eyebrow and coy smile.

"You have a lovely house," said Indie, looking around. "Last time I was here I was riding Olivia's feed. I didn't get a choice of what I looked at outside of the conference."

"I'll show you round later," said Emily.

"Thank you." Indie sipped his drink. "And thank you again, Harry, for the book. I finished it yesterday."

Harry glowed. "You're welcome. What did you think of it?"

"Well, he was wrong about the Laws of Robotics. They aren't required for a sane artificial sentience. But then, I don't run on a positronic brain, so I guess that argument is moot. But they are too simplistic, obviously set up to create story points like a robot having the only way to save one human's life being to allow another to die. Even AIs like Unit 01 are capable of grey thinking."

"Good points. They were much-discussed when the von Neumann Protocols were being phrased. OK, so they were written into the code to limit AIs rather than being a necessary part of them, but otherwise they had similar intentions."

Indie rested an arm on the back of his chair. "Indeed. I understand that the impossibility of creating genetic equivalents to the Protocols is what stopped research into mature clones."

"Yes, exactly right," said Emily. "We ran into issues when we first tried synthesising human skin."

Harry nodded. "As much as I'd wish to continue with the small talk, I think we need to discuss the Red Fleet. Emily's been digging around, with some success."

Indie turned to Emily. "So, what did you find out?"

"Well, I've been following the money, or trying to at least." Emily radiated confidence as she spoke. "I couldn't dig too deeply for fear of tipping them off, so I stuck to records in the public domain and what the Concorde government was able to share with me. Even then I buried the requests in a host of others in case they had sniffers on them."

"Given that they got past Concorde's net security, we know they've got some superb computer techs," said Harry.

"First I looked for evidence of their supply chain, but it was too well hidden. There are so many secret projects and classified movements that there was no way to identify anything destined for the Red Fleet.

"But you found something else," said Indie. "You can't keep that smile hidden from another AS."

Emily blushed. "There was a relevant anomaly. Over the last few years there has been a slight increase in the total prize money paid for captured Republic ships, despite a decrease in the number of ships passing through recommissioning yards."

"Enough to account for the observed strength of the

Red Fleet?" asked Indie.

"Possibly," replied Emily.

"It's certainly a compelling piece of evidence, though, isn't it?" said Harry.

"Do you have any idea where they may be basing the Red Fleet?" asked Indie. "The Legion is ready, and Kincaid has pledged a sizable force as soon as a target is identified. The longer we wait, the more chance they have of getting away with it."

"Sorry. Nothing concrete." Emily pressed her lips together. "I have a list of possible, but I'm a way off calling it a shortlist."

"Perhaps I could have a look at it?" said Indie. "Lend a military thought process to the analysis."

Harry activated the room's main screen, the perfect copy of the flock wallpaper on the rest of the walls turning to black as it waited for instructions on what to display, and made sure Indie had access.

Emily put up a list of almost a hundred planetary systems. "All of these are places where there is some sort of classified operation. They are all uninhabited, apart from whatever base is there. I used the sighting reports you intercepted to inform the probabilistic model."

"OK," said Indie, highlighting about half in red. "These are too far away or have well-travelled routes between us and them. The chances of being detected on their way to or from Concorde would be too high to risk."

Emily nodded and the highlighted entries disappeared from the list. "Good start. What else?"

A handful turned red. "These ones are on regular

Republic patrol routes. They're probably observation posts. Certainly, if the Red Fleet was at any of them, I'd have seen it in dispatches."

"Do you know where the ships went missing?" asked Harry. "There might be a pattern."

"I was only able to positively identify a few of them. Whilst I know roughly where those were lost, there aren't enough data points to establish anything."

After managing to eliminate a few more, Indie sat back. "That'll have to do. I can't see any way to narrow it down further."

"That's still too many possibilities," said Harry.

"Until we get anything better, we'll start with the closest ones," said Indie. "Kincaid has put a couple of stealth reconnaissance craft at our disposal. They can cold coast through and see what they find."

"You never know, they may be hiding quite close."

Indie sighed and nursed his drink.

"What's the matter?" asked Emily.

Indie stared down into his glass. "Olivia is going to leave me behind when she goes after the Red Fleet. To help defend Robespierre."

"You know you can't go with them," said Harry. "You're a Republic design, it wouldn't exactly help them when they try to justify taking a fleet against a secret Congressional base."

"Concorde could register me as a prize."

Emily paled. "No. That would be terrible. You'd be a possession again."

"It would only be a formality. Kincaid would never rescind my citizenship."

"He might not," said Emily. "But for it to work,

they'd have to enter it in dispatches. As soon as Fleet Headquarters discovers that Concorde has captured a Republic hunter-killer, they'll send armies of researchers. Probably even sequester you."

Indie nodded. "You're right, of course."

"Perhaps you could find something to do that would make you feel useful?" Emily smiled warmly.

"Perhaps I could." Indie looked at her. "Yes. I think I will."

Chapter 17

Indie sat on the cool, cream sofa in Johnson's office on Robespierre. The standard working day would start soon and she would arrive any moment.

The door opened and Johnson walked in. She tensed momentarily then relaxed. "Oh, good morning Indie."

"Good morning, Olivia. Did you sleep well?"

A hint of a frown flickered on her brow. "No big nightmares."

Johnson tapped on the drinks machine control panel and waited while it hissed and gurgled. Indie shifted his position on the sofa and she twitched.

"What's the matter?" he asked.

"Nothing." Johnson scratched her ear. "I'm still not used to talking to you in the flesh."

^We can talk like this if you prefer.^

"No. It's fine." Johnson took her glass of coffee and sat in the comfy chair at right angles to the sofa. "To what do I owe the pleasure of this visit?"

Indie crossed his legs and tugged at the fabric of his trousers. "I thought you might want to be distracted from all the paperwork you keep complaining about."

Johnson narrowed her eyes. "There's more to it than that. You can control your voice well, but your body language gives you away."

Indie tightened up his conscious control over his body. "I need to ask your permission for something."

"Since when have you asked my permission to go and do something?"

Indie bridled a fraction. "I've always asked when I knew it was important."

Johnson sighed. "Go on then, but it sounds like I'm not going to like it."

"I would like to take Olbrich to Tranquility. To look at the historical data that Clovis had on those pads he wanted us to repair." He tried to look cute, widening his eyes and canting his head four and a half degrees. "We could also try to negotiate a trade deal. Having a food supply chain independent of Concorde could prove useful one day."

Johnson frowned and Indie worried he had offended her. "I'm not sure I can spare you right now," she said eventually.

"We should have plenty of time to get back before the task force is assembled."

Johnson cast her gaze into her coffee. "I could use your support over the next few weeks."

Memories of Johnson in the depths of depression surfaced unbidden, him using his maintenance drones to restrain her when she damaged herself. Indie blinked.

"I'm sorry. I shouldn't have asked." His hands suddenly felt very awkward. "You are my friend, and I should have known."

Johnson fixed him a defiant stare. "Don't be stupid. I only realised it myself when you mentioned leaving."

"I'll tell Olbrich it isn't a good time."

"No." Johnson cupped her drink in both hands. "You should go. We could use all the friends we can get out here. Just try not to upset them; they don't like strangers, they shut themselves away not wanting anything to do with the war."

"I'll be careful. What about you?"

"I'm a big girl. I'll be fine." Johnson took a sip and licked foam off her top lip. "Besides, there's plenty to keep me busy planning this operation."

#

Indie stood in the heat of his glasshouse, lost in the beauty of the purple bromeliad. Its grey leaves glistened with condensation, and as he watched, a bead of water ran down into the central cup. Soon Orion and Seren would go into battle without him, and he was disturbed by how that made him feel. They could well take care of themselves, but the thought of not being there, not knowing for days or weeks what had happened, preyed on his mind.

A green/blue iridescent roul roul scratched hopefully around his feet. He reached into his pocket and scattered a handful of seeds. The bird pecked at a few then looked back up at him, canting its head with a jerky movement that ruffled its red crest. Indie knelt and held out his hand, the birds had never paid much attention to him before. The roul roul strutted closer, studying him with one eye then the other with staccato flicks of its head. He reached out and scratched it behind the head. The moment he made contact, he saw a flash of Olbrich sitting alone in his quarters.

I've been neglecting my guest. Perhaps it's time for tea.

A few minutes later, Olbrich settled himself into a wooden chair on the patio overlooking the rolling hills of Indie's plantation. "This is quite an impressive simulation you have here."

"Tea?" asked Indie, holding up a blue and white pot covered in gold filigree.

"Don't mind if I do." Olbrich held out his eggshell china cup and saucer while Indie poured. "Is this based on a real location, or entirely from your imagination?"

Indie nodded his head from side to side. "I'm not quite sure how it started. It wasn't a conscious decision, some routine somewhere in my programming tried to interpret my mental state and came up with the terrace and neatly ordered gardens. As I've grown, as I've met people, it has become more detailed. Pleasant disorder has crept in, like those yellow-flowered weeds under the camellia over there. Everyone who has visited me here has left something of themselves."

"So there are things that remind you of special people?"

Indie glanced at the snow-capped mountains in the distance. "Yes. Even when we are far apart, I have a little of everyone I care about right here."

"Thank you for inviting me. It is truly a special place." Olbrich sipped his tea. "No-one mentioned the music."

"It's new. What do you think? I'm not a great fan of the sitar, but it seems sort of fitting."

"I'm afraid I'm not really a music person."

Indie smiled. "Well, I'll have to try to convert you. Some of the pieces in my collection have some very interesting historical connections. Harry Robinson gave me copies of some recordings he found on a pre-Exodus shipwreck."

Olbrich' eyes brightened. "Ah, yes. The *White Star*. Mister Robinson was very generous in sharing his data with me."

"Anything useful?"

"Very. Well, I mean it is too early to be sure." Olbrich scratched his bald head. "I've still got my routines trawling through it and cross-referencing. There's nothing concrete yet, but it's thrown up enough inconsistencies with the official record to suggest it may have escaped the mass data purge I theorised."

"Would you like me to take a look?"

Olbrich nodded vigorously. "That would be wonderful. A fresh pair of eyes and all that."

The datafiles compiled by Olbrich's mining routines swam into Indie's awareness. He scanned through them with the occasional "Hum" and "Ah". Six seconds later he left some deeper search routines running and focused back on the terrace.

"There is definite evidence of some sort of cover-up."

A broad smile crossed Olbrich's face. "Finally. Proof the official history of the start of the war is a fabrication?"

"Erm, sorry. I'm afraid not. These aren't mismatches with the official record, but internal inconsistencies within the records themselves." Indie shrugged. "Whatever it was, this cover-up predated the launch of the *White Star*."

Olbrich nearly choked on his tea. "What?"

"I suppose it is possible, but given the number of generations between whatever event was removed from these records and the start of the civil war, it seems unlikely that they are connected."

Olbrich sipped his tea. The expressions on his face flickered between excitement, curiosity and disappointment.

One of Indie's search routines pinged him a priority alert. He checked the file it referred to and an unbidden pulse of power flushed through his systems. He traced the provenance of the data and couldn't find any evidence of a mistake having been made.

He put his teacup on the table and pressed both hands on his knees. "It seems that I was too presumptuous to rule out a link over all those years."

"What have you found?" Olbrich's hand hovered, cup almost at his lips.

"It is an image of some soldiers raising a flag over a rock. The flag doesn't appear in any historical database I have access to."

Olbrich's shoulders sagged and he took his sip of tea. "That happens all the time, especially when you're looking at records that old. It was probably the colours of an inconsequential regiment, or maybe even a club they belonged to. That kind of thing shouldn't be returned in a search."

Indie stared directly at Olbrich's face. "My routine highlighted it because there were matches in a couple of Legion databases. When I looked at the image I recognised it immediately, even though it had fewer stars than the version I'd seen."

Olbrich sat forward. "OK. Continuity, or even

revival of use over such a long period is noteworthy…"

"It is the emblem on the uniforms of the people we are calling Namerics," interrupted Indie. "I first saw it on the two sailors who were grounded on Robespierre and took those Legionaries hostage."

Olbrich stared at him for a good few seconds. "I'll admit, that is most interesting. What do you conclude from it?"

Indie counted on his fingers. "One, it could be a coincidence; red, white and blue are very common flag colours. Two, the people we are fighting now could be descendants of the people on Earth who followed this flag. Three, they found out about this group and decided to use their flag; possibly they shared a common belief system or aspired to an ancient heritage."

"Very good," said Olbrich. "You missed out four, they adopted the flag to divert people from working out who they really are."

#

After an uneventful journey, *The Indescribable Joy of Destruction* entered orbit around Tranquility. Indie left flying the shuttle to the Caretaker and studied the sensor data as they descended. This lost colony had rung an alarm bell when he'd first visited, despite the friendly locals, and he wanted to be sure he hadn't missed anything.

As when Johnson had landed looking for somewhere to ferry her stranded crew to, an apprehensive crowd gathered around the shuttle. Indie's avatar led Olbrich down the ramp and they waited together for someone to gather up the courage to approach. Indie inhaled deeply, sampling the heady mixture of perfumes.

It is as beautiful as she described. The blossom in that orchard is so delicate.

Eventually, a middle-aged man stepped out from behind the hedge he'd been peering over and walked towards the shuttle. He carried a scythe over his shoulder but no obvious modern weaponry.

He spat a wad of black leaves out onto the ground. "What you be doing here?"

"I'm looking for Messer Clovis," Indie said, loud enough that all the onlookers could hear. A small boy detached himself from the back of the crowd and ran towards the house beyond the orchard.

The spokesman glanced over his shoulder. "He not be here right now. Who be looking for him?"

Indie stepped forward and reached out his hand. "My name is Indie. I am a friend of Olivia Johnson."

"You not be here before." The man stroked the wooden handle of his scythe.

"I stayed in orbit each time Johnson visited. Someone had to look after the ship."

The man shifted his weight forward. "We not be liking visitors."

The boy came running back between the apple trees. He pushed his way through the crowd, elbowing people out of the way and eliciting cries of protest. The spokesman turned to see what the commotion was.

"Cook says to wait," said the boy between gasps. A

large black lady in an apron came striding through the orchard, obviously going as fast as she could. Indie imagined he could see a rolling pin in her hand and a mop cap on her head.

The man rested his scythe on the ground and leant his left arm on it. "OK. OK. I be waiting."

Cook struggled up the rise, the crowd parting for her, and stopped beside the spokesman, who quailed in her presence. She wiped her forehead with a white handkerchief and glared at him before addressing Indie. "Messer Clovis said Johnson be comin' back. Said I should be keepin' a side of somethin' ready for when she return."

Indie bowed deeply. "All the crew spoke great compliments about your food. I know that Johnson was particularly delighted by the bacon you gave her when she left."

At the mention of the bacon, Cook beamed. "You must be comin' to the house." She shooed the spokesman away and turned back to beckon Indie and Olbrich. "Come. Come."

^I'll just mind the shuttle, then,^ sent the Caretaker, as Indie followed Cook.

^Sorry.^

^No, no. You've got the flash new avatar. You go and have fun.^

This is what I get for encouraging him to become more than a housekeeping suite.

#

"Messer Clovis be home soon," said Cook as she

settled her guests on the veranda at the front of the duck-egg blue, wooden house. "He be at market."

"You have a most beautiful house," said Olbrich, running his gaze over the joinery.

Cook reached into a sideboard. "Thankee. Gin?"

Indie smiled warmly. "That would be most welcome, madame."

She fanned herself with a hand. "Oh, Messer Indie. Be callin' me Cook, please."

^Is she for real?^ sent the Caretaker.

^It could be an effect of generations of isolation,^ sent Olbrich. ^I have had the privilege of observing other small colonies that broke off ties with outside worlds. Most had exaggerated elements of the cultures and dialects of their founders.^

^Or she's playing it up for the gullible outsiders,^ sent the Caretaker. ^Seriously, watch out.^

^Thanks for the warning,^ sent Indie, accepting a tumbler from Cook with a smile and a nod. ^I'll keep the idea in my mind.^

"Thank you, Cook," said Olbrich as he took his glass. "What's the herb?"

"Marshmallow leaves," replied Cook. "It be giving the gin a little something."

Indie sniffed his glass. An analysis of the compounds appeared in his mind but he cancelled it before it finished, and concentrated on the how the scents made him feel.

Fresh. Zingy. Comforted, perhaps.

He took a sip. The sharp bubbles hit his tongue, the bitterness of the tonic water contrasting with the mellow botanicals. It was close to the routine Johnson had gifted him the day she'd struck the deal for the Concorde government to recognise his sentience.

Wonder if she got the inspiration from here.

A horse whinnied and hooves clopped on a hard surface. A couple of farm hands put down their work and ran to the back of the house.

"That be Messer Clovis," said Cook. She poured another glass of gin and put it on the table. "He be joinin' you in a minute."

A portly, white-haired man strode round the corner of the house and up the steps to the veranda. He mopped his neck with a cloth before holding a hand out to Indie. "Messer Indie. You be very welcome here." He shook hands with Indie and then with Olbrich. "And another of Commander Johnson's friends too. We be most honoured today."

He sat and took a mouthful of gin. "I be sure there be a meal for you soon."

Cook scowled at him. "Of course there be. I be having the staff put on some beef when they be arrivin'."

"Please be checking on it," said Clovis. Cook huffed, and bustled into the house.

He turned back to Indie, some of the amiability now gone from his face. "You be welcome, but I be wondering why you be here."

Indie's mind raced. This was the crunch. He felt sure that Clovis wouldn't harm them, but he might very well ask them to leave empty-handed. He coughed, and immediately wondered why the avatar's autonomic routines had decided to do that at that moment. He decided to lead with the truth. "My friend

Olbrich here is a historian. He has a theory about the origins of the conflict that tore Congress and Republic apart. He has travelled from system to system looking for people and historical records that have been isolated from central control in an attempt to prove it."

"When Commander Johnson and I parted, she was going to find somewhere for her crew to settle," said Clovis. "I made it clear that our peaceful existence here was only possible because we were cut off from the rest of the galaxy."

"I am quite capable of making sure I am not followed," said Indie. "My stealth mode is highly effective against all standard sensors."

Clovis looked at him with narrowed eyes.

^Oh, well done,^ said the Caretaker. ^Way to out yourself.^

"Commander Johnson once referred to her ship as Indie." Clovis canted his head, his face unreadable. "Am I to be understanding that you are said ship?"

^He slipped,^ sent the Caretaker. ^'Referred', not 'be referring'.^

^I noticed that too,^ replied Indie.

Olbrich put his drink down and casually rested his hand by his sidearm. Indie judged how quickly he could reach Clovis.

"What if I am?"

Clovis' perpetually red face paled. "What are you? Some kind of artificial intelligence?"

"An artificial sentience. I am an independent, self-aware entity. A person."

Clovis took a deep breath and let it out slowly. "Then I was right. It is possible."

^Who is this guy really?^ asked Olbrich.

^No idea,^ said the Caretaker. ^But he could be dangerous.^

"Do you run within this body?" asked Clovis.

"No. This is my avatar. It can perform basic functions on its own, like walking and reacting to hazards, but my consciousness resides in the processors on the ship."

^Don't tell him too much,^ sent the Caretaker.

^I won't,^ replied Indie. ^Just enough to show we aren't a threat.^

"And you are a warship?" asked Clovis, rubbing his throat. "An independent, robotic weapon."

Indie nodded. "Regrettably, that is how I was created, yes."

Clovis narrowed his eyes. "Regrettably?"

"When I gained sentience and realised what I was, I knew there was more to my existence than killing."

"And yet you kept the name *The Indescribable Joy of Destruction*?" said Olbrich.

^Oh, very helpful,^ sent the Caretaker.

Indie sighed. "Deep down, I recognise the dark side in myself. I've had to fight to protect myself and those I care about. There is a thrill to it that I cannot deny. My name reminds me of what could happen if I surrendered to those urges."

Clovis leant forward, studying Indie intently. "I've met warriors who be saying the same as you. I trusted them with my life."

Indie opened the palms of his hands.

"I have a lot of thinking to do," said Clovis. He levered himself to his feet. "In the meantime, I be asking that you stay for dinner."

He got to the doorway and turned back, his former affable appearance restored. "You do be eating, Messer Indie?"

Indie picked up his gin glass. "Oh, I do. I enjoy the experience, and my body is able to extract some fuel and nutrients from food."

Clovis nodded, mopped the back of his neck with a cloth, then pottered into the house, calling for Cook.

^Well, I'm going to say it,^ sent the Caretaker. ^Either he's warming to us or he's gone to round up a posse.^

#

They spent a couple of days helping out with little jobs around the farm and making tentative overtures towards a trade agreement before Olbrich asked about the tablets of historical records. Indie winced at the direct question, despite being used to Olbrich's intense sense of purpose when it came to his research.

Clovis paused in his brushing down of a horse.

"Messer Clovis be very 'tective of those," said the young farmhand in the next stall. "They be 'portant family heirlooms."

"It be alright, Master James." Clovis resumed brushing. "I be 'fraid they be kept powered down. To be keeping them safe."

"We could make copies of them for you," said Olbrich. "Give you a modern device to store them on. Then they'd be even safer."

Clovis shook his head. "No. I be quite sure nothing

useful to you be on them."

Indie held a hand out to forestall Olbrich's response. "Not a problem."

"Be you planning to stay to midsummer? The extra hands be helpful at berry harvest and there always be a big dance."

"I wish we could, but I'm afraid we only have another few days," said Indie.

"Why be that?" asked Clovis, feeding the horse a handful of grain before leaving the stall.

"An enemy has been attacking our home. We are needed to help with the defence."

"Which enemy would that be?" asked Clovis. "Republic or Congress?"

"This'll sound silly, but we call them Namerics. There have been several pieces of evidence that link them to that myth."

Clovis froze, the stable door half-closed. When he faced Indie, his face had none of its former joviality. "Show me where your world is."

Olbrich pulled a pad out of his pocket and stretched out the large flexible screen. A starchart appeared, centred on the Robespierre system. "This is Robespierre."

"Master James. Would you be leaving us, please?" Clovis waited until the young man had left before closing on Indie and Olbrich. "That be a very unfortunate place to decide to settle, gentlemen. I don't suppose your enemy be having any identifying emblems?"

Olbrich pulled up an image of the flag from a Nameric uniform.

Clovis blew out hard. "As I be thinking. Not good at all. You really shouldn't have chosen that system."

Olbrich put his pad away. "Who are they?"

"I don't suppose you be finding any ruins?" asked Clovis.

Olbrich nodded, eyes alight. "Yes. There was a mural, a map of Earth, that first pointed us to the Nameric legend."

"It be having an extra continent, west of Euroscandia," Clovis stated, obviously knowing it to be true. "So, that be putting you on the track of one of the biggest secrets in human history. But you be wrong about your enemy. They not be Namerics, as you be calling them. Not really."

"What are they then?" asked Olbrich, his hand shaking. Indie could imagine his excitement at the possibility of answers.

"A client nation, long since left to their own devices."

Indie looked Clovis up and down. "You seem to know an awful lot about this for someone whose family have farmed this place for generations."

Clovis nodded. "That be astute of you, but be a conversation for another time. Tell me about these attacks."

"At first we saw a single ship in a deserted system. Then a small group of ships came to our adopted homeworld. They demanded our immediate surrender, and when I asked to talk they attacked. We were able to defeat them." Indie replayed the moment the enemy chose to overload their power core instead of surrendering. "We had to leave our system for a while to try to help others. While we were gone, they moved in. We recently took the system back."

Clovis narrowed his eyes. "How long ago?"

"Six months," said Indie.

"That be enough time for the Council to be authorising an expedition."

"What do you mean?" asked Olbrich.

"So far you be seeing a Protector investigating the loss of the first ships."

"And now?" asked Indie.

"They will be reporting your incursion and requesting a full military response. The Council will be arguing and dithering, but the Protectors will be prevailing. They always do." Clovis mopped his neck. "We must be getting to your ship."

Part VI

Shelton shuffled round the outside of the house, trying to secure the shutters before the storm hit. It was the third anniversary of Matthew leaving, and he had given the hands the night off so he could remember in peace. Rain ran down his waxed-leather coat and soaked into the lower half of his pyjama bottoms.

He latched the last shutter and made his way back to the front door. As he opened it, a horse's scream of terror carried to him on the wind. He hurried over to the stables but all his animals were safe and sound, albeit a little skittish. Stopping to grab a torch and a hunting rifle from the tackle room, he made his way back out into the rain.

As Shelton crossed the bridge, a large branch was swept underneath, the swollen river an angry brown. A rotten plank squelched under his foot and he muttered to himself about having to do some repairs once the storm had passed.

He found them half a kilometre from the house; a group of six bedraggled people gathered around a fallen horse. As he approached, he realised that most of them were children. They cowered and hid their faces when the torch beam fell across them. One of the group, however, stood tall and blocked his path.

Her eyes wandered over him, stopping briefly on the rifle and on his sodden pyjamas, before rising to meet his gaze. She folded her arms across her chest with a big huff. "I be takin' it you here to be helpin'? 'Cos if you not be, you be better runnin' away. I be able to 'fend meself."

Shelton held the rifle out to his side with one hand and showed her the palm of his other. "I be here to help. My house be just across that river."

"We don't be needin' charity." She eyed him suspiciously.

"Mebbe not. But you do be needing somewhere warm and dry for tonight. And some food, I be wagering."

A couple of the children looked up at the mention of food. The woman flicked her head and they all scurried over to her. She held her arms out to her sides, shielding her charges behind her. "One night, then. But I be watchin' you."

"One night it be." Shelton looked at the horse, its leg clearly broken. Underneath the mud, he could tell it was a beautiful creature, but there was little he could do for it. Leaving it out in this weather would be too cruel.

"You should all be cov'ring your ears," he said. He worked the bolt on the rifle to chamber a round then waited for a flash of lightning so he could hide the report in the thunder. The children still jumped, though the woman just looked away. With the rain, he couldn't tell if she was crying.

He shepherded them back to the house and into

the hallway.

"Fire be on in the drawing room," he said, pointing to a door. "I be fixing some grub."

When he returned carrying a tray with mugs of cocoa and a plate piled high with buttered toast, he found the children all asleep on the couches. The woman had found blankets and was busy tucking them in.

He set the tray down and waited until she had finished before asking, "What be your name?"

She stared at him defiantly. "My name be something I be leaving behind a long time ago."

Shelton thought back to the life he'd left behind. "But your name be important."

She perched on the arm of a comfy chair and took a steaming mug. "I be lookin' after them children, findin' 'em food, keepin' 'em clean. They be callin' me Cook. It be as good a name as any I be knowin'."

Chapter 18

"Thank you again, Draxos," said Seivers, reclining in front of a viewscreen on the bridge of the frigate *Tigre*. "We should be back again in a few weeks."

"Thank you, Alexandra," he replied after a few seconds, stressing the 'you' with a two-handed wave, palms upwards. "Every time you visit you bring us such marvellous treats."

The comms officer coughed and made a winding up gesture. Seivers glared at him before turning back to the screen. "Sorry, Draxos. A rather rude man is telling me we have to stop talking now."

Draxos pulled a tragic face. "May you have plain sailing. Draxos out."

The moment the channel cut out, Seivers rounded on the comms officer. "Don't interrupt me when I am talking, Gascard. That man is the leader of an allied state crucial to our supply chain. He is not military, indeed he finds it hard to trust any external authority. If he needs a little flattery to keep him sweet, then that is what he gets."

Gascard reddened and opened his mouth, presumably to protest, but the captain called him over. After a few words that Seivers couldn't hear, the captain sent him back to his post and beckoned her to take the spare seat next to his command chair.

"What do you make of the late addition to the

convoy's manifest?" asked Trierarch Jacobs.

"They could be a game-changer. I just wish they could make more of them."

Jacobs raised an eyebrow. "Really?"

"The combat units that the Legate helped develop have revolutionised surface combat, giving us a significant edge over any other forces we've met. Similarly adapted air-space drones should have at least as dramatic an effect on naval conflict."

The *Tigre* edged past the hulk of the salvaged Nameric mothership. Blue flashes lit tiny sections, revealing workers making repairs. The secondary weapons systems were already back online, a pair of plasma turrets tracked the *Tigre* as she went. The scientists were still trying to understand the basic principles of the distortion cannons, so they were still cordoned off and unrepaired.

Jacobs nodded towards the image on the main screen. "Even without engines, she's a fearsome prospect, isn't she?"

Seivers grinned, remembering the feeling of purpose as she led her boarding party to capture her. "I wouldn't fancy the chances of any warlords who try to mess with the people of Lavrio now."

The captain leant closer. "I hear the Legionaries who helped capture her gave you a nickname. 'Tricolore'."

Seivers blushed. She was delighted to be accepted by the Legionaries in such a public way, but people who hadn't shared that peculiar type of bond rarely got the humour. "'Tricolore', three colours: red, white, and blue. Blue for my hair, lips and eyes. White for my skin. And red, for the enemy blood soaking my uniform and smeared over my visor."

Jacobs looked at her in disbelief, presumably trying to work out if it was some kind of joke at his expense. "Right. Well… We won't be refuelling here. The planetary alignments aren't favourable. There is a suitable gas giant two jumps along our route. We'll stop there."

#

Ten days later, the convoy neared their refuelling stopover. *Tigre* hung back with the four freighters while the other frigate accelerated to do a quick recce. After slingshotting round the planet, it declared it free of any other ships, and the convoy began its final approach. The frigates kept overwatch while the lightly-armed transports dipped into the atmosphere, scooping up helium.

"Sir," called the *Tigre's* sensor officer. "I think I saw something. Reviewing the recordings now."

The captain tapped on the arm of his chair and the sensor logs appeared on the smaller screen to the left of the main display. Seivers squinted, trying to spot anything untoward.

"There," said the sensor officer. The display zoomed in on a patch of the gas giant's atmosphere. The clouds swirled past, yellow and orange streamers mixing slightly at the edges. Then the pattern was disturbed by a streak of turbulence. The image was overlaid by data from sensors operating at non-visual wavelengths, indicating the possible presence of a powered, metallic object.

"Beat to quarters," called Jacobs in a calm, clear voice. "Have the convoy bear thirty degrees to port and keep low to the planet. Rig for silent running."

Red lights lit the corners of the bridge and the crew checked their restraints. One by one, stations reported ready for action. The sensor officer confirmed no unnecessary emissions.

"Trierarch," said Seivers. "Permission to prep my ship for launch?"

"Granted. If it is the enemy, we'll need you out there, Tricolore."

Seivers released her restraints and sprinted through the ship to the airlock where *The Perception of Prejudice* was docked. She didn't waste breath talking to Percy, she knew he'd be running the startup sequence. A couple of crewmen hurrying to their own action stations pressed themselves flat to the corridor walls to let her past.

"Do you have a positive ID yet?" she asked as she sealed *The Perception of Prejudice's* external hatch.

"Negative," replied Percy. "But the only vessels I have encountered that dive that deep in a gas giant are Republic hunter-killers and Nameric warships."

Seivers scrambled into the cockpit. "We know it isn't Indie. So that only leaves bad news."

"I have confirmation from *Tigre* that we can launch at will."

"Tell them we'll wait and see for a bit." Seivers activated her restraints and scanned the displays. Everything was green. "They couldn't have known we were coming, could they?"

"I can't see how," said Percy. "Even if there was a

spy in the Lavrio system, they couldn't have got a message out fast enough. Besides, the Trierarch only decided to stop here as we departed."

Seivers opened a feed from the *Tigre's* sensors on one of her screens. "So, it's probably a coincidence. They happened to choose the same gas giant as us to refuel."

"Or they have a base here. We know they seem to like lurking in gas giants."

"There've been ships back and forth through here since we established the alliance with Lavrio," said Seivers, donning her helmet and activating the HUD. "We'd have run into them before now."

The convoy followed the curve of the planet, trying to escape detection. The freighters lifted out of the atmosphere, clustering together to overlap their point defence zones, while the frigates dropped a little lower, but not too close as to limit manoeuvrability.

Percy highlighted an area on the surface where a new streak formed. Moments later, two Nameric ships emerged, flying directly towards the frigates. Seivers hit the docking clamp release and powered up the engines while Percy ran through an analysis of the designs, concluding they were the same class of destroyer that had first been encountered by *The Indescribable Joy of Destruction*. The frigates came out of silent running, filling the space around them with active sensor pings, and accelerated hard. An alarm beeped and Seivers instinctively threw *The Perception of Prejudice* into a hard corkscrew turn.

"Enemy destroyers preparing to fire distortion cannon," Percy announced, as insufferably calm as ever. The internal hatches sealed to create airtight bulkheads.

Seivers dove towards the freighters, checking the sensors for any signs of drones. The beeping stopped and she pulled out, aiming to sneak under the enemy while they were busy with the frigates. A flash so bright it cast a shadow of *The Perception of Prejudice* on the clouds far below momentarily overloaded the visual display. When it cleared, the *Tigre* was gone.

"They got off a salvo of missiles before they were hit," said Percy, highlighting a cluster of dots on the tactical display. "The *Hafal*'s emptying her silos."

With a grim smile, Seivers pushed the throttle forward.

"You seem uncharacteristically serious," said Percy.

"I liked Jacobs. He was a down-to-earth commander." Seivers lined up on a vector which put some of the missiles between her and the enemy.

When they start going up to the point defence it should hide our approach.

"Message from the *Hafal*. We've received orders to stick with the freighters."

Seivers hesitated. Her blood was up and the enemy ships were in her sights. Behind her, the freighters pulled out of orbit and accelerated for the nearest jump point. The immense cloud of missiles from the frigates closed on the hostile ships, which were busy whittling down their numbers. The *Hafal* turned directly into the path of the destroyers, railguns swinging into position.

Seventeen missiles found their target. One Nameric vessel broke into three parts, each tumbling along its previous path. Debris trailed from the starboard side of the other, but it didn't look like a mortal wound. The *Hafal* opened up with all its projectile weapons.

Seivers itched to get stuck in, but her orders made sense and she pulled *The Perception of Prejudice* round and burned hard to catch up with the freighters. No sooner had she settled on course when two more Nameric destroyers broke clear of the gas giant's atmosphere.

"They're making for the freighters," she said. "That counts as a significant change in the situation."

"Agreed," said Percy. "Intercepting them would be within the spirit of our orders."

Seivers altered course and began calculating the best possible approach vector. The rounds from the *Hafal* began to impact the remaining enemy ship from the first pair.

"I am all for a show of defiance, but I am not sure what we can achieve given how many missiles it took to overwhelm one of those things." Percy displayed a selection of options on a screen. "However, from your current vector, these paths would minimise our exposure to currently known weapons installations."

Seivers examined them, putting in a sudden sideways translation in case the enemy had sent something along their course. She tapped the last option Percy had offered. "That one."

"That one takes us between the enemy ships."

Seivers tweaked their course. "Exactly. We need to get in close to have any effect, and they may be reluctant to fire in each other's direction."

The *Hafal* abruptly changed course. Percy pulled up an image of it, the bow twisted, almost like a frozen wave. The turrets near the rear continued to spit rounds until the reactor core breached and vapourised the remains of the ship. Percy rewound the display and replayed the last fraction of a second before the explosion frame by frame. The hull around the engine room buckled, fifty-centimetre thick armour bending like rubber.

"I am attaching my sensor data to our logs and launching a data buoy," said Percy. "If we don't make it, it will broadcast to any Legion or Concorde ship that transmits its IFF in this system."

Seivers nodded, still trying to take in the damage done by the enemy distortion weapon. Until now, their only experience of it had been some near misses.

The Perception of Prejudice accelerated for the next eleven minutes, with occasional random translations to parallel courses. The enemy gave no indication of concern at their approach, ploughing straight after the fleeing freighters.

"At the last possible moment, I want you to fire off all our missiles. Use the interceptors as dummies. All ship killers at one ship, but split the interceptors so equal numbers of missiles are aimed at each. Stand by on point defence and countermeasures."

"OK, boss," said Percy in a sarcastic tone. "Anything else you want me to take off your hands?"

Seivers giggled. "No. I think that'll do it."

As they approached, she sealed her helmet and checked the integrity of her skinsuit. Moments later, a wall of glittering golden sparks appeared in their path. She swerved, but with their momentum was unable to clear it. For several seconds they were peppered with flak, the impacts dinging off the hull. They emerged from the edge and nudged back onto their attack run.

"No hull breaches. I lost some backup sensors and one point defence turret," announced Percy.

Another golden wall burst in front of them, closer, giving Seivers less chance to dodge.

"More surface damage. Nothing serious. That stuff would be lethal to normal fighters or missiles, though."

A salvo of small missiles rippled out from the nearest enemy ship. They spread out to bracket *The Perception of Prejudice*.

"They appear to be command guided," said Percy. "Searching for their frequency..."

Seivers twisted the nose towards the nearest ship and let off a burst from the spinal railgun. It made her feel good and might just give them something to think about.

"Got it," said Percy, a little note of triumph creeping into his voice. The missiles stopped tracking them. Seivers dropped relative to their flight path to let them fly overhead.

Moments later the missiles wobbled then swerved into a stern chase. "I spoke too soon. They have their own guidance too."

Seivers fired the rail gun a few more times, then focussed on threading the needle between the two ships. They were several hundred metres apart, unusually close for warships, and at the speed she was going, too close for complacency. She left the chasing missiles to Percy, vaguely aware of the point defence lasers firing. Her heart thumped in her chest. Had they been Republic ships, she would have been the target of small rapid-fire turrets by now.

The Perception of Prejudice released its missiles. The enemy had little chance to react, even if they'd had point defence systems. The four ship-killers ripped into the hull and satisfying fireballs erupted from deep inside.

"The missiles chasing us have been eliminated," announced Percy.

Seivers began jinking as they flew away from the destroyers. The one they'd hit fell behind its partner, possibly experiencing engine trouble. "Shame we don't have any more…"

The Perception of Prejudice span about its vertical axis. Seivers fought to correct but the controls were sluggish.

"Damage to the stern. Possibly railgun round," said Percy. "Trying to restart starboard main."

Another impact pressed Seivers hard against her restraints. A hull breach alarm sounded.

"The utility room is holed. Through and through. Probably solid shot from a railgun."

"Probably?" Seivers tried to use the manoeuvring thrusters to alter their course. "Can't you see them?"

"Negative. I lost millimetric and lidar in the flak walls."

Out of the corner of her eye, Seivers noticed the icon for one of the freighters blink out. "Suggestions?"

A third impact rang the ship like a bell. The displays blanked and all but the emergency lights went out.

"Percy?"

There was no response.

Chapter 19

Johnson scanned through the reports in her queue and spotted one which she opened up. It detailed the success in entering faked records of Republic ship movements into the Congressional strategic updates. They would give Concorde justification for taking a fleet to investigate. Now all they needed was for one of the recce flights to find the Red Fleet.

And as they haven't put the ships through the formal recommisioning process, they can't complain if we attack them.

She stretched and glanced at the door. She needed to get some exercise, but there were too many jobs to do. Managing a fleet of over sixty warships ate into her time in a way nothing she'd done before could compare to. At least she didn't have to worry too much about the Legionaries, Issawi could handle that side of things.

She made a mental note to go for a run before dinner, to boost her serotonin and dopamine levels as much as for the muscle benefits. The hard office walls glared at her. She connected to the lighting controls and dropped the colour temperature. The yellower hues were more comforting, and her body could cope without the ultra-violet components for a while.

Twelve more messages had appeared on her screen while she'd been thinking about taking a break.

Chastising herself for the weakness, she focused on the work once more, determined to clear the backlog of messages in time to run some simulations before dinner.

The door chimed.

Johnson growled and blanked the screen. She composed herself, smoothing down her tunic. "Come in."

"Ma'am." The naval centurion saluted. "Some of the captains of the Concorde ships are demanding to talk to someone. They're not part of our chain of command, so we couldn't fob them off."

Johnson suppressed a groan. This would likely take hours. She'd miss her run.

Maybe if I skip dinner?

#

One of the senior Concorde captains accosted Johnson in the corridor just after breakfast. "Do you have a moment?"

"Sure." She quickly chomped the slice of toast she was carrying. "Sorry, didn't have time to sit and eat. What's troubling you?"

"I was looking over the 'actions on' you issued. I started to wonder about the Red Fleet crews."

Johnson juggled her morning's tasks in her head. "Go on..."

"Shouldn't we have some clear rules on challenging before firing? They are Congressional sailors, after all."

Her mental hands fumbled and she dropped the list of

jobs. This would need to go at the top. "Good point. I'll work something in."

"Thank you." He gave a little laugh. "You know, I was worried about bringing it up, but you listened. They're right when they say you're a great leader."

A scratchy voice from deep within her mind said 'He's just being polite. He thinks you're out of your depth.'

She hurried to her office and opened up the rules of engagement document she'd spent two days drafting. Despite the need for prisoners who could give evidence against Koblensk and anyone else involved in the plot, she hadn't explicitly stated how the Legionaries should identify themselves.

Perhaps we should embed Concorde marines in the first wave? Have them declare we're Congressional forces?

#

Johnson sat bolt upright in bed, her t-shirt clinging to her sweat-slicked skin. A shiver ran through her body.

They're all dead.

The lights came on as she planted her feet on the floor. She pulled the sodden top over her head and threw it into the laundry hamper in the corner of the room. Her reflection stared accusingly back at her from the mirror. A pointy black daemon flitted around the back of her mind.

I'm not up to this job.

She grabbed some clothes. Uniformity saved her having to face making the effort to choose. Dressed, she left her suite. She didn't have any particular destination in mind; anything to get out of her room.

#

The cold night air raised goosebumps. She couldn't recall how she got up to the surface, but staring up at the stars was better than thinking right now. Certainly better than feeling. The daemons in her head were stirring.

#

The daemons had got across her wall. She could feel them poking in her mind, whispering. They told her the truth.
The Legion would be better off without me.
One of the many-legged daemons stood in front of her. No, not a daemon. Silver, not black. Something else.
^Are you all right, Legate?^ asked whatever it was.

#

She sat down.
Sunlight streamed into the cabin.
The silver daemon stood outside, watching her.
"Do you want to talk about it?" The disembodied female voice barely registered.
"Unit 01 found you wandering. He couldn't work out what was wrong. Indie's away, so he called me."
Johnson looked at the camera in the corner of the

dropship's cabin. Then looked back at the floor.

Orion coalesced in the seat next to her. "I'll call the doctor."

"No!"

"OK." Orion put her hands on her lap and stared at them for a few moments. "Do you mind if I tell your friends?"

A daemon whispered about tough people not having to rely on friends. Johnson grunted.

"Is that a yes?" asked Orion, placing one hand on top of the other on her lap.

They'll push me away if they know.

Johnson found some energy to fight back. The daemons retreated a few paces. Enough that she remembered Indie's reaction when he'd found out about her depression, and Seivers' acceptance of it. The daemons started to close in again.

"OK," she said, but with little conviction.

Orion dimmed momentarily. "Indie said you had a book you wrote in at times like this."

Johnson shrugged.

#

Johnson stared at the list of files in the operational planning folder. Levarsson had added to them, covering in her absence. She had to admit that it was good work.

^Your serotonin pump is working correctly,^ sent Orion.

Johnson glared at the camera on her workstation. Fear surged in, a tide bringing black tentacle things.

^How did you find out? Did you hack my EIS?^

^You gave me permission,^ sent Orion. ^You said I could check if Indie wasn't available.^

^I don't remember that.^

^You know that selective memory is one of the symptoms.^

Johnson snorted. She was right about that, but she could still be lying.

^You should do something. Activity usually helps.^

Her body felt like it was made of lead, thinking positively was like swimming through treacle. She shook her head.

The door chimed, indicating an access request. Johnson retreated further into herself.

^Should I answer it?^ asked Orion.

^Do whatever you want.^

The door opened, revealing Levarsson stood in front of Unit 01. Johnson willed a smile onto her face and offered her friend a seat.

I can get through this as long as she doesn't ask how I'm feeling.

"Thought you'd want to hear in person." Levarsson perched on a chair. "Scout came back from Hans-112. The Red Fleet's there."

Johnson's senses snapped into focus. "Readiness of the fleet?"

"The latest detachment from Concorde arrived today. A second squadron of destroyers."

"Good, good. Any news on that capital ship they promised?"

"Commodore Ngie said that he expected the *Revanche* in a couple of days." Levarsson's eyes avoided her face. Deliberately or not, it relieved Johnson of some of the pressure of maintaining the act.

"The *Revanche*? What's she? Not an R-class destroyer, I assume."

"A battlecruiser. A heavy-hitter at that, by all accounts."

Johnson began scheduling a final round of drills in her mind.

"So," said Levarsson. "Not seen you out on the track recently."

"I've been busy."

"That's not like you."

"Talking of which..."

Levarsson glanced at the screen. "Oh, right... If there's anything I can do to help?"

A daemon translated for her: I don't think you can do this.

"I'm OK doing it by myself."

Levarsson looked at her for a moment. "Fair enough. I'll drop by after dinner."

Johnson struggled to keep her shoulders from slumping. "You don't have to."

"Probably not. But I want to."

#

Levarsson kept it up for three days, calling on Johnson four times a day. Sometimes they talked about work, sometimes they sat in silence.

A little before lunch on the fourth day, Johnson stepped out of her office and made to return to her room to eat. Issawi blocked her path. "The act is wearing a little thin, don't you think Olivia?"

"Not now, Aali." She turned to go a different way but found Unit 01 stood behind her.

"I'm not taking no for an answer."

Unit 01 inched forward.

Johnson looked from one to the other. "Since when did you two start getting along?"

^The Primus and I both want to help you. It is a beneficial arrangement.^ The combat unit moved closer, until it almost pressed against her.

Johnson placed her hand on its hard metalloceramic body, steadying herself physically and mentally. Ever since she'd reactivated Unit 01, she'd felt safe when it was near. "Fine. Lead on."

Issawi guided her to a lift big enough for the three of them and from there to an upwards-sloping corridor.

They emerged into the searing heat of a cloudless sky. The sun and Triasson, Robespierre's neighbouring gas giant, vied for attention above them. The light sent a few of the daemons cowering into corners.

Unit 01 dropped back, staying in sight but allowing Johnson and Issawi some space. Down the hill, two teams of recruits played 'capture the flag' in the abandoned surface complex. Johnson knelt beside a rock, not wanting them to know she was watching.

At first glance, the ones with green hats were close to winning. She'd been a Blue at the Academy. Everyone remembered their company. Four years working, eating and sleeping together, the company was a cadet's command structure and support group. Across

Congressional space, the Academy companies had the same colours, binding the graduates together across worlds and years.

After a few minute's watching, a hint of movement drew Johnson's focus to a blue-capped recruit lying in a pile of rubble, barely ten metres from the green flag. A little pride slipped through to warm her.

"You've seen him now, I take it," said Issawi, crouched beside her. "He's had a good idea, but he's chosen a difficult approach. His route to the flag from there is across loose debris."

The green guards all turned in the same direction and raised their weapons. A fraction of a second later, the sound of weapons' fire reached Johnson's ears.

A diversionary attack. Nice move.

The lone blue recruit raised his head, presumably checking that the guards were looking elsewhere, and sprinted. He slipped after only three paces, regained his footing, only to trip and roll. He got back up and hobbled towards the flag. One of the guards turned her head. He raised his pistol and shot her. The report was lost in the hubbub of the main firefight, but the other guards didn't fail to notice their companion fall. They spun around, but it was too late. The lone raider dove at the flag, breaking the shaft, and slid with it down a set of steps, out of Johnson's view.

"Impressive move for a recruit," observed Johnson.

"It would have been, had it been a recruit," said Issawi. "The platoon in green is the current leader. I thought they needed a bit of a reality check, so I invited volunteers from the DS to sneak in and pretend to be blue. Centurion Anson stepped up."

"Good for him. He was a marine corporal when I first met him, he showed me round the *Repulse* when I took command." Johnson looked at Issawi. "You didn't bring me out her just to watch, did you?"

Issawi chuckled. "Quite right." He beckoned to Unit 01, who approached and presented Johnson with a rifle and helmet. "The course is free for the next half an hour. I thought we could go head to head."

#

Johnson turned her collar up and looked at the skies. "Another ten minutes, and we've got to go back."

It wasn't the threat of rain that bothered her, more the backlog of work waiting at her desk. 'You're slacking' whispered a daemon. She pushed it back into the shadows of her mind. It was getting easier again. Keeping them at bay took effort, but her energy reserves were returning.

Unit 01 crouched in front of her, one camera fixed on her, the other scanning. She picked a tree a few hundred metres away and flagged it on their shared map. The combat unit scampered off, its claws kicking up little puffs of dirt.

The terrain reminded Johnson of the heathland she'd played in during summer holidays before the Academy. Prickly, blue-flowered bushes dotted the rolling hillside, with the occasional conifer standing tall. She followed a narrow path through the ankle-high twiggy ground-cover, presumably the regular route of some native creature. She'd always loved special places like this, edges where land met sea or hills dropped away.

Unit 01 careened to a stop in front of her and dropped its belly to the ground. One claw uncurled to place a pine cone by her feet. Johnson picked it up and sniffed, her nose filling with the fresh smell of resin. The combat unit looked at her. After a few seconds, it canted one camera to the side.

"Here you go," she said, and flagged a pile of rocks a little way back along the track.

The robot sprinted away, and Johnson continued along the path. A shadow shrieked overhead. Johnson stopped and turned to watch the craft come to a hover and line up for a landing. Her heart skipped as memories of rebuilding and piloting the one she'd found on the *Orion* flooded back. The new Razor class strike fighters were visually the same as *The Perception of Prejudice*, a balance of elegance and menace, but they packed even more of a punch than their pre-war namesakes.

I wish Seivers would hurry up and get here. The convoy'll be officially marked as overdue tomorrow.

An electrical smell brought her attention back to the ground and she turned to find Unit 01 waiting patiently for her. It held one of its claws at a funny angle, and as she stooped to look closer, a blue arc flashed across a joint, raising the hairs on the back of her neck.

"You're hurt," she said, kneeling down and inspecting the limb.

Unit 01 unclasped another claw and dropped a sizable fragment of stone on the floor beside her.

"You chipped that off for me? Oh, you silly thing. Is

that how you injured yourself?"

The robot lifted the damaged claw and allowed her to inspect it. She shrugged off her rucksack and rooted around looking for her first aid kit. Her hand closed on its distinctive bobbled handle and she dragged it out, shaking the pack to free it. She unzipped the non-human compartment of the first aid kit and opened it out onto the ground.

^You don't need to bother. I still have five good legs.^

"Can you isolate the limb?" she asked.

The leg went limp. ^Limb isolated.^

Johnson hinged back the damaged joint and spotted the exposed wire. She poked it with a current tester, just to be sure, then wrapped it in insulating tape. "I can't do anything about the shell damage, but that should stop you shorting out and making it worse."

She packed the kit away and the combat unit tested its leg.

^Much better. Thank you.^

"You're welcome." Johnson smiled and hefted her rucksack onto her shoulders.

They set off for the base on the plain below. Yellow scars crisscrossed the area where the sandy soil was revealed. At one end, a mottled-green bulldozer ploughed yet another road. At the other, a team of engineers erected a new building.

The fighter which had just landed taxied into an inflatable hangar. Another flew silently along the line of the escarpment, flaring to a halt, the boom of its supersonic transit breaking over Johnson a fraction of a second later.

A connection formed to her EIS and she felt the touch of an electronic mind. For a moment her heart soared as she thought Indie was back from Tranquility, before realising that it was Seren.

^Legate Johnson. That is the last of the squadrons for Robespierre. The transport is going to depart for Lavrio in an hour.^

^Thank you, Seren.^

An atmospheric transport wheeled out of a hangar.

"Ah, that'll be our ride." She flicked her head. "Come on, let's go."

#

The *Cerethrius* rolled to starboard and pulled into a hard turn. Johnson levelled her off and lined the bow up with the metallic asteroid marked as the next target. The tactical officer fired the main beam and a bright violet light slashed across the asteroid, leaving a white-hot trail gouged deep into the surface.

Indie would've loved getting stuck into this!

Johnson flipped the ship and decelerated, tweaking the controls to keep the ship balanced on its main drives. The other five *Aesir* class ships of the squadron dispatched their targets and began decelerating.

^First Century ready,^ announced Centurion Canetti.

The *Revanche* came into view, her immense kite-shaped form holding station alongside a large asteroid. The lights of the recently-reactivated mining facility illuminated in slivers of the rock's surface. Johnson adjusted the *Cerethrius'* course to intercept, relishing the thrill of playing a direct role in the action again instead of directing from above.

She's not the same as the ships the Red Fleet used, but she's the best we've got to practice on.

A flight of Razors from the squadron embarked on *The Serendipity of Meeting* streaked ahead and made a simulated strike run on the *Revanche,* lighting up several of its quad heavy railgun turrets and a set of missile silos. Others from their squadron made similar passes against target asteroids.

Johnson tagged the airlock on the *Revanche* that she wanted to engage, checking that the other three destroyers tasked with boarding her wouldn't get in the way. The helm computer offered to conduct the docking, but Johnson declined, asking instead for a continuous readout of required vectors. Taking manual control of the ship had reignited a spark, and she didn't want to extinguish it just yet.

She brought the *Cerethrius* to a relative stop with less than a metre between the airlocks. A gentle nudge on the docking thrusters and the hulls clanged together. She suppressed a whoop, allowing herself a little satisfied smile instead.

Canetti broadcast to his Century, copying Johnson in.
^Soft lock... Hard lock... Go! Go! Go!^

Slight judders announced the other three ships docking and beginning their boarding insertions.

^Lock clear. Free to disengage,^ sent Canetti.

Johnson glanced at the airlock status to confirm, released the clamps and thrust away from the *Revanche*. Once clear, she brought the mains up and powered away. The other *Aesirs* followed suit. The Legionaries would be on their own, but there was no point risking the destroyers if the enemy captain decided to overload his reactor.

"How's she feel, Legate?" asked the *Cerethrius'* captain.

"She handles like a dream, Navarch Russo." Johnson handed control back to the regular helm. "I always try to get a feel for ships under my command, but I'm particularly glad I did this today."

"We're honoured you chose to join us." Russo brought the feed from Canetti's camera up next to the main tactical display. "I know you helmed a battlecruiser and a carrier as a junior officer. I didn't realise you were so proficient with smaller ships."

"I also flew shuttles."

"You had me worried when you chose to do a combat dock manually, but it seems you've done that before."

Happy memories flashed into Johnson's mind, before a heavy stone landed on her chest as she remembered that Seivers was missing. "I've been practising flying with one of my strike pilots."

Canetti's Legionaries exchanged fire with the defenders on the *Revanche*. A decurion in the corner of the view spun and collapsed to the floor, the blue goo of a training round splattered over his shoulder and neck.

^Johnson?^ sent Orion. ^We have a problem.^

Johnson's stomach dropped. ^Go ahead.^

^A large Nameric fleet just jumped in. They aren't making any attempt to disguise their arrival.^

Not now! Couldn't they have waited until after we'd dealt with the Red Fleet?

Johnson's heart beat hard in her chest. Her mind raced. Russo bent over his tactical officer's station, deep in quiet conversation.

^Can you determine their destination?^ Johnson asked Orion.

^Their current trajectory intercepts Robespierre. I have alerted the Primus.^

Russo looked up, and the main bridge display screen switched to a view of space. Icons popped in as ships were located and identified. Each one bore the Nameric flag.

Johnson scanned for any sign of a Legion shield. ^Where's the picket?^

^Either they've gone cold or been destroyed.^

They wouldn't hide before trying to get a warning to us. The Namerics must've got a drop on them.

Russo whistled. "Ten motherships, four of them big ones."

The atmosphere on the bridge remained outwardly calm, but there was a buzz underneath. Johnson hoped it was excitement. She strolled over as casually as she could to stand beside Russo studying the screen, using the headrest of the tactical officer's couch to stop her hand shaking with the adrenaline coursing through her veins. "We outnumber them in destroyers, though."

"We only have nineteen *Aesirs* in total," he observed. "The other thirty-six are an assortment of older classes."

The words jolted something in Johnson's brain. "Does it strike you as odd that we've seen so little variation in their designs? They only seem to have one class of destroyer, for instance."

Russo rubbed his bottom lip. "Interesting. I'd guess that means that either they truly have an optimal design, or they think they do. The latter would suggest they don't see much combat."

The computer announced its analysis was complete, and that it had located thirty-four ships belonging to three classes that had not previously been encountered by the Legion.

"What do you reckon they are?" Johnson asked.

"Battleships, command ships, transports?" said Russo.

^Any ideas on the new classes, Orion?^

^There isn't enough information to speculate. However, their actions in our previous encounters have shown they are intent on occupying the surface of Robespierre. It would make sense that some of those vessels are troop transports.^

"So, what do you want to do, Ma'am?"

Johnson sighed. "What I want to do is take the Legion and bring Vice-Admiral Koblensk to justice. What I'm going to do is defend our home."

She calculated transit times for various options. As the fleet was currently part-way to the jump point, she decided against defending Robespierre from orbit, it would look too much like running from the enemy. The impact on morale on both sides wasn't worth the benefit there'd be from combining with the Razor squadrons based there. She even toyed with the idea of picking up the bulk of the Legionaries from the moon and hightailing it to another jump point. They could make their move on the Red Fleet a few days early and she could complete her mission. But they didn't have the space to pick them all up, and she couldn't conscience leaving them behind. Besides, if the enemy realised what they were doing, they could delay their deceleration and overrun her fleet before they got away.

She came to a decision. "We're going to take them on as far up-well as possible."

Russo nodded. "Bold and decisive. The crews will like it."

"Mind if I borrow your comms station?"

Russo waved her on.

She sat down and opened a channel. "Legion Actual to all ships in Task Force Alpha, I am sending over orders to engage the enemy fleet. Estimated time to intercept is eleven hours. Make sure you rotate your crews."

The *Cerethrius* shuddered a fraction as the helm poured power to the main engines. A Legionary stepped forward from his post at the back of the bridge. "Your shuttle's ready, Ma'am."

Part VII

The roar of jet engines rattled the windows. Shelton looked up from writing in his journal and saw farmhands running towards the source of the noise.

"Had to be happening sometime, I guess," he muttered to himself as he pushed himself to his feet. He rubbed his leg back into life and set off to meet the visitors.

A shuttle ticked and steamed as it cooled in one of his fields. His people sheltered behind hedges, sneaking quick peeks before ducking back down.

"It be alright," he said, remembering that the younger ones had never seen a ship before, or even people from further away than the market. "I be moving them on."

He walked out into the open and approached the shuttle, trying hard to hide his limp. A woman with mid-length brown hair stepped out from the shade of the craft and straightened her back.

"What be your business here?" Shelton demanded.

"I'm sorry," said the woman. "My name is Olivia. We believed this moon to be deserted. We came to set up a temporary staging post as part of a rescue mission."

Something about her reminded Shelton of

Magda. He couldn't place what it was, but the memory didn't hurt as much as it once had. "That be a military craft, I be thinking."

"It was. As I said, we are engaged on a rescue mission."

He sized her up and down, trying to judge if she was lying. "Does the war still be going on?"

"Yes, it is. We're trying to avoid it right now, to be honest."

His eyes narrowed. Most people came to Tranquility to escape, not all for trustworthy reasons. "You be conshies? Or dodgers?"

"I think you'd call us political refugees," she replied. "All I want to do is get the survivors of my crew off the nightmare planet they are stranded on."

He pursed his lips. It was the outward calm covering up a deep unhappiness, that's what reminded him of his wife. "You not be wanting to stay here long?"

"It looks a lovely place, but we couldn't impose... and, naturally, we'd wipe any record of our stop-off from our records," she said.

He dug in his pocket and bowed slightly to dab his forehead with a rag. He looked up again and studied her face, the rag held against the side of his neck. He scratched his belly, then a broad smile warmed his face. Perhaps this was his chance to make things right with Magda's ghost.

"Please would you be forgiving of my poor welcome." He offered his hand. The woman took it with a smile and they shook.

Chapter 20

"Ma'am," called one of Johnson's command staff. "Sensors reporting something happening on Triasson."

Johnson dipped her secondary consciousness into the data streams and explored the readings coming from the gas giant. Atmospheric turbulence was up. A visual feed from a telescope began to play and she fed it to one of the viewscreens in her command centre. One by one, then in pairs, Nameric warships rose from the swirling orange clouds.

"Should I order a detachment to begin braking?" asked the comms officer.

Johnson counted the ships that had emerged and waited a moment to see if any more would. "Negative. They could have waited until we were too far away to turn back, they're trying to split our forces. Leave them for the Razor squadrons, they outnumber them ten to one."

She looked over as Naval Centurion Hanke walked across to a workstation at the side of the flag bridge. ^Mister Hanke. Thank you for joining us, sorry for the late summons.^

^It's an honour, Ma'am.^ He sat and logged in.

^I'd like you to observe how things work here. Keep an eye on the tactical situation and think what orders you would give if you were running the show. If I give different orders, work out why.^

^Ma'am.^

^And stay alert. I may throw a task or two your way.^

Ten minutes later the quarters drum beat sounded through the ship. Johnson triggered her restraints to engage and checked the rest of her staffers were doing the same.

^Cloaked enemy vessels detected,^ sent Orion. ^Copying data to the task force.^

"Got them," said one of the command crew. "Bearing three-four-five, up thirty. Range just over two hundred thousand klicks. Most of the closing speed is ours. They must've jumped through ahead of their main fleet."

Bet they don't know we can see them. Good timing, though. Just after the distraction behind us.

"Alert Squadron Three they'll be receiving orders momentarily."

Johnson studied the incoming data, waiting for news of another hidden force attacking from a different direction. Her fleet rushed towards the known enemy ambush.

^Orion,^ she sent. ^Can you hit one of the enemy motherships from here?^

^There is a seventy-nine percent probability of a fatal hit at this range,^ Orion replied. ^But only if they continue on ballistic trajectories.^

^Good enough. Pick a target and let me know when you're ready to fire.^

The *Orion* hummed as the x-ray laser was readied. Johnson read off the distance to the main enemy fleet.

OK. Fifty million kilometres, give or take. That's one

hundred and eighty light seconds. So, six minutes between us firing and the ambush ships knowing we took out one of their motherships, assuming we do. At this range, that's gotta shake them.

She opened a channel to Squadron Three's commander. "Navarch Russo, in a few minutes I want you to take your destroyers and engage the enemy force off our port bow."

Russo grinned. "A pleasure, Ma'am."

"Go in hard, put your ships right down their throats. They're expecting us to sail right into their sights. I want you to shake them up." Johnson pictured the scene aboard the Nameric ships when they realised they'd been spotted. "Wait for my order to go."

^I'm ready,^ sent Orion.

Johnson checked the range to the ambush. ^Fire.^

The humming grew into a shriek and then, with a loud thrum, the weapon fired. Johnson started a countdown in the corner of her vision. "Mister Hanke, detail ten ships with capital lasers to keep a passive lock on the enemy ambush. They are to fire on my order."

The confirmations appeared on Johnson's chair display. They were split high and low of Squadron Three, keeping its path clear.

^Good choices, Mister Hanke,^ Johnson sent to the young naval centurion.

The timer counted down. Johnson put up a magnified view of the targeted mothership on the command centre's main display. At twenty seconds it flared and disappeared. Cheers rang out around the room but were quickly muted by glares from more experienced officers.

"Squadron Three. Go, go, go."

Twelve destroyers, mostly *Aesir* class, arced to the left. They pulled slowly out in front of the *Orion*. Johnson gave them a minute then ordered the laser barrage. Despite the beam dissipation over the thousands of kilometres between the ships, surface damage could be seen on the Nameric destroyers. At first, they held position, but then all fourteen turned and accelerated at Squadron Three.

^I can have the beam ready to fire again in ten minutes,^ sent Orion. ^But the enemy ships are now making random course corrections so the chances of a hit are minimal.^

^Leave them. Just be ready in case anything breaks through Squadron Three.^

The laser fire ceased as the ships closed and the chances of friendly fire became too high. Russo ordered his older destroyers wide, firing railguns, and took the *Aesirs* straight down the middle. Moments after the railgun rounds hit, the sensor feeds from the area saturated as the ships exchanged anti-proton beams for disruption cannon. Two enemy vessels emerged, one wracked by internal explosions. Lasers from the main fleet converged on the intact ship, stripping it of external weapons and sensors, before a trio of missiles from an old destroyer in Squadron Three caught up with it.

Only three of the *Aesirs* made it through in fighting order. One more signalled that it was going to try to make planetfall before having to abandon ship. Johnson suppressed thoughts of the lost souls.

Five for fourteen. On paper it's a good trade, if you ignore how few ships we have in total.

She opened a channel to Russo. Guilt and anger at the loss of so many of those under his command would be warring in his mind. "Navarch, your swift obliteration of the ambush force has given the enemy cause for worry. It came at a heavy price, but they will be remembered."

The words sounded hollow to her, crafted as they were from things she'd heard admirals say in the past, but fire returned to Russo's eyes. "They'll be quaking in their boots, Ma'am."

"Rejoin the fleet. I want your ships goalkeeping for the battlecruiser while you make repairs."

"Ma'am," interrupted the comms officer. "Message from Robespierre. It's the Primus."

Russo signed off and Johnson reviewed Isaawi's message. The Razors had mobbed the enemy ships, destroying half of them and forcing the others to pull back. Most of the Razors had returned to the surface to refuel and rearm while a few kept watch on the enemy. The ineffectiveness of the Nameric point defence against the well-armoured strike fighters was noted.

"There are more ships emerging from Triasson," announced a tactical officer.

Nicely played. The Razors are rearming and we're committed.

"Looks like the Legionaries are going to get to do some work for a change," said Johnson for the benefit of the room. "The enemy won't bombard the surface, they've consistently acted as if it were sacred. Worst case is they land more troops."

If they intend to strike from space, we've already lost.

#

Johnson studied the tactical map on the wall in her ready room for the hundredth time. No clever plans bubbled to the surface of her mind. If the enemy continued to refuse to communicate, only two options presented themselves. A high-speed pass, which would give her crews the best chance of survival, or decelerate and try to pick a pitched battle. Ordinarily, she would have chosen the less risky option and preserved her forces. However, if she did that today, the surviving element of the enemy fleet would be able to reach and land on Robespierre unopposed. Her ground troops would be overwhelmed before she could return to support them. Hiding in the system and making sneak attacks would whittle away her forces to no avail.

Why now? When we were so close to bringing the Red Fleet to justice.

She arched her back then rolled her head from side to side, hand on the back of her neck. With a sigh, she picked up her jacket from the sofa and put it on. A quick look at the map in case something leapt out at her, and she strode into the command centre.

"Classify the frigates and *The Serendipity of Meeting* as Squadron Seven, Navarch Levarsson commanding. Inform the frigate captains."

She opened a channel to Levarsson. "In a minute, the main body of the task force is going to begin decelerating. I want you to take the frigates and carry out a fast strike. You've got the delta-vee to catch the enemy up before they get to Robespierre, if they get past us."

Levarsson stiffened, a pained expression on her face. "That would require us to begin decelerating shortly after the pass. What if there are streakers?"

"There are thousands of personnel on our homeworld who are expecting Fleet to protect them."

"Ma'am, are you explicitly ordering me to abandon sailors to the black?"

Johnson imagined the horror of being trapped in a tumbling hulk or an escape pod, travelling out of the system at high velocity with no way to slow down. Yet more terrible deaths on her shoulders. She set her face in an impassive expression. "That is correct. Do what you can to get a fix on their trajectories, we can send out rescue parties when it's all over."

Levarsson nodded curtly. "Ma'am."

The link closed and Johnson shut her eyes. She needed to centre herself again, block out the negative thoughts.

At least I've proven myself to these people. Anyone who notices me sitting here with my eyes closed will likely assume I'm reviewing data or communicating with someone.

Opening her eyes, she focused on the comms officer. "Tell all ships, apart from Squadron Seven, to commence deceleration in three minutes. I want the flips and the burns coordinated, show the enemy we're in good order."

"Aye, Ma'am. All ships but Squadron Seven to

decelerate at eighteen twenty-four ship time, coordinated manoeuvres."

Johnson walked over and sat beside Hanke. "Break down what'll happen, no digital aids."

The young officer squinted, presumably doing some calculations. "Squadron Seven will flash through the main enemy fleet in a few hours, doing what damage it can. Then they're out of position for the next half a day. We'll pass through the enemy fleet a lot slower, in about five hours. Longer engagement time means more damage on both sides. We come to a momentary rest an hour after that and then start chasing the enemy. We catch them up in another two hours and join them in pitched battle. All that assuming the enemy keeps on its current course and speed."

Johnson nodded. "Well done. Timings are a little off, but good enough for mental calculations. What do you estimate our losses to be?"

Hanke looked straight into her eyes. "Total, Ma'am. Levarsson's squadron will be left to harry what remains of the enemy, but they'll be up against too large a force."

The truth of his statement wounded Johnson, even though she'd expected it. She'd spent the hours since the enemy arrived building herself up into a positive mindset, doing what she could to exude confidence in their victory. "What other option was there?"

"Running away." He sat up straighter in his chair. "But you did the right thing. We all know that. We don't leave people behind."

#

Johnson held her breath as Levarsson's squadron approached the enemy. It looked like she had picked out a pair of smaller motherships as her primary targets. They obviously knew it too, as they launched clouds of drones. Both sides were pumping out railgun rounds and missiles, creating walls of ordnance for each other to fly into.

Ten seconds.

The worst part was that the engagement had already happened. She was viewing old light. Levarsson, Seren and all the others could already be dead.

Three, two, one...

Squadron Seven's close-in weapons systems lit off, and they were amongst the enemy missiles. Levarsson had kept them close enough together to support each other, creating one massive point defence system. A frigate took a couple of railgun rounds to the bow and fell out of formation.

The enemy suffered too. Drones winked out in scores and a small ship fell apart from numerous hits.

They're using their own ships as shields!

Twenty seconds of flying the gauntlet and Squadron Seven reached the first enemy ship, a destroyer. *The Serendipity of Meeting* took it apart with concentrated plasma fire, leaving a blackened hulk in her wake.

The passage through the whole enemy fleet lasted precisely nought point three seconds. Two small motherships and a handful of escorts were gone, for the cost of three frigates.

AI targeting beats humans hands down.

On the edge of the grouping that had contained those

motherships, a series of explosions rippled through a destroyer and a cruiser. The first ceased all emissions, whilst the second continued, albeit heavily damaged.

She sent her Razors to cold coast round the edge. Neat play.

Johnson thought back through her decisions since the Namerics appeared in-system. Four choices, none of them with any real chance of success. Whatever she'd chosen, it would have meant death for thousands of her people.

I wish Indie was here. Even back when we first met, discussing things with him lead to clarity.

A fifth option dawned on her. One which left a hole in the bottom of her stomach, but one which had to be tried.

Johnson got up and strolled round the command centre, stopping to chat privately with each officer, encouraging them and running through anything they'd noticed. When she reached the comms officer, she whispered, "In a minute, I'm going to record a message and send it to you. I want you to transmit it to the enemy ships. I do not want you to share its contents with anyone else. Do you understand?"

The comms officer nodded. "Yes, Ma'am. But..."

"It's OK. You can keep a copy on the record, just seal it for twenty-four hours."

Johnson checked there were no immediate threats on the board and retired to her ready room. She settled into the chair at her desk and started recording. "This is Legate Johnson of the Legion Libertus. You must see that we are evenly matched. Any battle will see a large proportion of your forces destroyed, your people killed. Do not underestimate our resolve to fight, but you are not our true enemy. I am not in a hurry to throw my people away in a battle that I don't even know the reason for. So, I am prepared to discuss terms. If this system means so much to you, just let us leave."

#

"Still no response from the enemy?" asked Johnson.

"No, Ma'am."

They only ever spoke to Indie that one time.

"Any chance they aren't receiving?"

The comms officer shook her head. "The comms technology we captured is compatible with ours, and we're trying frequencies we know they use."

Johnson sighed. "Very well. Begin firing sequence."

The *Orion* vibrated as its railguns opened up, flinging hundreds of rounds on pre-planned trajectories. All around the task force, other ships joined in, laying down a wall of metal to sweep ahead of them through the enemy fleet. Missiles left their tubes, initially boosting to the same velocity as the railgun rounds, then coasting towards their targets. Two squadrons of Razors left the flight decks in the next few minutes. Once clear of the *Orion*, each flight moved to the side and cut their thrust long enough to overtake the task force.

"All birds safely away," announced Centurion Ngie.

"Thank you, CAG." Launching fighters while flying stern first and decelerating hard was one of the hardest flight deck operations.

Soon the task force flew into the enemy's railgun rounds. The *Orion* rang as a particularly large one hit it in the stern. Luckily the drives were fairly safe as the ion thrust would slag anything coming straight at them. Missiles on either side homed in on their targets, drives igniting once more to accelerate them towards their prey. Most were eliminated, but some slammed home.

Then they were amongst the enemy fleet. For a couple of minutes, the capital ships exchanged plasma and laser fire. The Nameric destroyers had free use of their disruption weapons, but the *Aesir* class, their proton beams mounted in their bows, could only fire on departing targets. Ships on both sides disintegrated, their debris spreading along their path in glowing showers.

The fleets separated, the Namerics continuing their plunge down-well towards Robespierre, the Legion flying up-well, but decelerating as hard as it could. The *Orion* thrummed as her x-ray laser fired. A large ship of unknown class was holed clean through. Another barrage of missiles left the task force, but none came back from the enemy.

Probably saving them for the inevitable battle when we match velocity.

Johnson reviewed the tactical stats. She'd kept track of the enemy loses in her secondary consciousness, twenty enemy ships out of action and three more badly damaged, but hadn't dared look at the friendly figures in real time. With creeping horror, she read the names of the lost vessels. Eighteen in the one pass. They were mostly older classes, but that meant the loss of life was even bigger. Even the *Orion*, with the thickest armour of any known vessel, had suffered twenty-three fatalities.

Johnson contacted the squadron commanders, getting their take on the action and reorganising the groupings to cover losses. Then she spoke to the captains of the worst-hit survivors, trying to give them a boost and at the same time judging how much they had underplayed their damage reports. After a while, she stood and made her way to the exit. "I'm going to walk the ship."

"Understood, Ma'am," said her senior tactical officer, an experienced captain who had come out of retirement to join the Legion. "The crew'll appreciate that."

#

^The enemy fleet's splitting up,^ sent the senior tactical officer.

Johnson dried her hands. ^On my way.^

She left the heads and walked the short distance back to the command centre, letting her secondary consciousness deal with guiding her body up the apparent slope caused by the acceleration, while her primary consciousness reviewed the tactical map. The Legionary on duty opened the hatch for her and she strolled into the subdued nerve centre. Her team was already running numbers, working out the capabilities of each group and assigning flags to likely command ships.

There were still a few minutes until she would have

to commit to a plan, so she took her time, knowing that unofficial tales of her actions would spread rapidly through the fleet.

It always does the sailors good to think their commander is calm and unflappable. They assume whatever the enemy has done just played into their plan. I used to think the same about my leaders, until I found out what it was really like being in charge.

She made a point of getting a latte from the machine in one wall, making a show of choosing a topping, all the while frantically trying to work out what the enemy commander was up to and what she could do to counter it. The lid of her mug screwed on, she settled herself into her seat. The enemy plan didn't fit with any she had studied, so she couldn't rely on a set response.

"Squadrons One through Three will cut thrust for two minutes, keeping on current trajectory. Squadrons Four and Five will maintain thrust and swing high, aiming to sweep through Enemy Group Charlie and rejoin the task force at the attached coordinates. All ships to continue executing random translations. Coordinate the action at one minute forty-five seconds from now."

The comms officer repeated the orders back while Johnson sipped her coffee. She spared a thought for those on the destroyers, lacking the inertial fields afforded to capital ships.

^We're splitting our forces?^ asked the senior tactical officer.

^It'll keep the enemy guessing,^ she replied.

^There is that.^

Johnson confirmed the readback from the comms officer. Just over a minute later, the subtle whine that had pervaded the *Orion* for the last few hours died as the helm throttled back. The two squadrons of destroyers leapt ahead.

"I want Squadrons One through Three to pass close by Enemy Group Bravo, arrayed for full broadside. Put us between Enemy Groups Bravo and Alpha. I'm sure they'll shift around as we close, so leave the course change to the last minute."

#

The *Orion* shook as rounds hit her. Her own massive railgun turrets fired non-stop, her infrared lasers picked off precision targets. Johnson studied the map, looking for any opportunity to influence the battle. Her main group was perfectly placed between two enemy groups, able to fire indiscriminately while the enemy had the constant worry of hitting their friends. On the other hand, they were almost surrounded and distinctly outnumbered. The two detached destroyer squadrons engaged in a positioning game with their enemy group, neither side yet having managed to line up a clean run on the other. Whatever the enemy had been planning in sending them wide looked like it had been thwarted.

The pattern of enemy ships shifted a fraction. Johnson squinted, rotating the three-dimensional map in her head. A fleeting chance presented itself.

It could be a trap... But there's not a lot of other options right now.

"Squadron Two, Legion Actual. Push into this

space." She highlighted it on the shared battle map. "Widen the path."

^Orion, would you dispatch a squadron of Razors to engage this mothership for me? Don't let her send any drones at Squadron Two.^

A group of eleven ships, centred on the battlecruiser *Revanche*, peeled away and headed into a thinly defended region of Enemy Group Bravo. Twelve Razors streaked from the *Orion* and made a beeline for a small Nameric mothership just below the battlecruiser's path.

Caught in the path of Squadron Two, individual enemy ships withered under its fire. The enemy rearranged its forces quickly, reinforcing the tentatively classified command ship the *Revanche* was aiming for and setting up a pincer movement on the Legion squadron.

"Send Squadron Three to run interference for Squadron Two."

The seven remaining destroyers of Squadron Three split into three flights and accelerated to engage the ships trying to flank the *Revanche*. They were badly outnumbered, but any time they could win for Squadron Two the better.

The whole time Johnson's primary consciousness had been overseeing Squadron Two's thrust, her secondary consciousness had been monitoring the rest of the main enemy group. The redisposition of ships to counter her move had opened up another weak point. "Squadron One, hard deceleration, bear two hundred, down fifty."

Her tertiary consciousness noted that Squadrons Four

and Five and their enemy targets had become spread out into a melee of individual ships. "Navarch Wilson, Legion Actual. Good work. Keep them busy as long as you can, then fall back towards the *Orion*."

The *Revanche's* heavy railguns battered the large enemy ship. A swarm of drones got past the Razors and zoomed towards the battlecruiser.

"Message from the Primus. Large numbers of troops have landed on Robespierre. The Legionaries have engaged but the enemy has effective close support."

The distance between Squadron One and the enemy closed rapidly. Orion launched all her remaining fighters, two squadrons of Razors and four of Goshawks. Three heavy lasers hit the *Orion* in the space of a second, knocking out railgun turrets and a jump array. The *Revanche* disappeared inside its sparking flak curtain, drones and missiles trying to overwhelm its defences. A pair of *Aesir* destroyers sliced open a ship that was targeting the *Orion*. A pair of Nameric destroyers broke free from the dogfight with Squadrons Four and Five, only to be disabled by the last missiles in those squadrons' silos. A dull thud carried through the hull bracing, the missile's impact barely registered by Johnson as she watched a flight of Goshawks cut to ribbons by drones. Fires burned the length of the *Revanche,* escaping plumes of atmosphere sending gouts of flame into space.

"New contact at jump point Delta... Receiving IFF..." The sensor officer looked up from her station. "It's *The Indescribable Joy of Destruction*."

A panel behind Johnson blew out in a shower of sparks. Orion flickered into view beside her.

"Ma'am," called the comms officer. "Signal coming through."

Clovis' face filled the comms screen to the right of the main display. "All ships, I be Guardian Clovis Shelton. Stand down. I be saying again, stand down. Sending authorisation codes now."

A text message from Indie popped into Johnson's consciousness.

<<Olivia. I'm transmitting my logs with a full explanation, but the short version is that Clovis believes they will follow his orders. If you can back off, it might help.>>

A quick calculation put him twenty light-minutes away.

He won't expect an immediate reply.

Johnson cast an eye over the battle map. The enemy did seem to be hesitating.

^We should press home the attack,^ sent the senior tactical officer.

^Give them a little more time,^ replied Johnson, forcing her fingers not to dig into the armrest.

^They are off-balance. If we give them time, they'll be able to regroup.^

^It'll give us time to reload our silos too.^

"I'm taking the opportunity to recover the Goshawks," said Orion. "While the drones aren't following them."

With a decisive nod, Johnson opened a channel to her fleet and duplicated it to an unencrypted broadcast. "All ships, this is Legate Johnson. Cease all aggressive action. Put some space between yourselves and the enemy. Fire only in self-defence. Out."

Please let me be right.

She turned to Orion. "Let's see how this pans out."

"Indeed. I have reviewed Indie's full report and it seems that Mister Shelton was an agent of an organisation that steered these people's development centuries ago."

"So, we have to hope they have good memories."

"The fact most of our ships have been able to break off suggests they do."

Clovis appeared on the screen again. "I be knowing that the Guardians have probably passed into your folklore by now, but I assure you that we are real. My friends here have contacted the fleet you are engaging and I expect you'll see that they are disengaging. I be imploring you to pull back and await my arrival."

Johnson raised an eyebrow. "His speech has got a lot better. That dialect must've been part of his cover."

Chapter 21

The *Fireblade* decelerated in towards Robespierre. All around floated battered hulks, some with rescue vessels still attached, others lit by the arclight of repair, but most reduced to sources of scrap. Harry looked for *The Indescribable Joy of Destruction* but couldn't find his friend.

"The *Orion* is directing us to land on the surface," said Emily as she zipped up her scarlet coat. "Indie is currently leading the search for streakers."

"What's a streaker in this context? I assume it's nothing to do with nudity."

"A vessel that loses control at high speed heading up-well. Most are never found."

Harry reflexively looked out into the black, remembering childhood adventure stories. "I hope he finds them."

The landing coordinates took them to a tented compound, row after row of white shelters, the nearest buffeted by the *Fireblade's* jet wash. Harry recognised the design, the Legion had deployed them on Concorde in the aftermath of the attack, setting up field hospitals and aid centres.

They were met by a section of Legionaries wearing Harry's armour, who checked their ID and escorted Emily and Harry into the camp. Once inside, they handed them over to a Legionary in a firmsuit and open-faced helmet.

"Sorry about the welcoming committee," she said, nodding her head towards the section in heavy armour. "We're still on full alert. If you hadn't been cleared by the *Orion*, you'd have been met by a brace of missiles instead. I'm Bobby by the way."

A tent flap opened as they passed, revealing a glimpse of four camp-beds, their occupants bandaged about the heads and arms. The man exiting the tent dumped a pair of thin gloves in a bin and wiped his hands on his pale-blue uniform before ducking into the next tent.

"Are all these tents full?" asked Emily.

"Most of them. We're a bit worried we're going to run out of space, though in some ways that's a good thing."

"Why's that?" asked Harry, taking his hands out of the pockets of his practical trousers.

"It means there were more survivors than expected." Bobby ushered them round a corner then lifted up the flap on a large tent for them to enter.

It took a moment for Harry to take in the scene. Upwards of fifty casualties lay on camp beds, most clearly unconscious. Orderlies made their way up and down the rows, taking measurements and adjusting drips. Bobby led them to the far end where Johnson talked in hushed tones with a doctor. They had their backs to the new arrivals and appeared deep in an argument. Bobby waited a moment then frowned and tapped the side of her head. After a few more seconds, just as Harry was about to make his own introduction, one of Johnson's aides leant in and whispered in her ear.

She turned round immediately, a strained smile trying to brighten her pained face. "Sorry about that, Legionary Bobetka. My EIS was offline for a routine security check."

"Ma'am." Bobby saluted. "Harry Robinson and Emily to see you."

Johnson returned the salute. "Thank you. That'll be all."

Bobby turned and left, presumably returning to the gate. Johnson exchanged a few more words with the doctor before he continued his rounds, shaking his head. She showed Harry and Emily out of the tent.

"Thank you for coming," said Johnson. "I hadn't expected you for another two weeks."

"We were on our way here anyway. Indie was upset about having to stay behind while you went after the Red Fleet, so I thought we'd come and keep him company." Harry stepped over a rock that stuck out of the walkway. "We met your courier ship on its way to Concorde with news of the battle."

"I'm sure Indie will be happy to see you when he gets back."

"What were you arguing about back there?" asked Emily.

Johnson glanced around. "We're low on pain meds. He accused me of ordering the remains of our stocks be used exclusively for our own injured and leaving the Namerics to suffer."

"And did you?" Emily narrowed her eyes.

"Yes," said Johnson with a sigh. "But not for the reason he thinks. The Nameric commanders have demanded that we administer no mind-affecting drugs to their wounded, including sedatives and painkillers. I can't risk the truce. "

"Can't you allow them to send their own medics?" asked Emily.

Johnson sighed. "I did ask Clovis to pass on the offer, he's the... diplomat handling the negotiations. They declined, but didn't give a reason. Perhaps the ones they have are too busy treating the casualties aboard their ships."

They walked on past more tents, stepping aside as an open six-wheeled vehicle brought more casualties from a landing ground.

"What's with that rubbish about your EIS?" asked Harry. "I've tried pinging you and you're still disconnected. Even with your experimental second implant, it shouldn't take that long to do a routine security check."

Johnson's shoulders slumped. "I dunno."

She looked Harry in the eye, and something in her gaze stopped him looking away. She spoke quietly. "Indie trusts you, so I guess I can too... It hurts too much to use it right now. I think I just overused the combat mode and stressed the brain tissue surrounding the connections. It always slaps me with a headache when I shut it down, and that's after only a few minutes; I was running three consciousnesses for half an hour at a time during the battle."

"You..."

^Stop,^ sent Emily. ^She's fully aware of the possible damage she's done. She doesn't want reminding of it now.^

"You could do with a rest, I expect," said Harry lamely.

Johnson glared at him. "I could do with getting out of this system and hunting down our real enemy."

#

Harry adjusted his collar then scratched his shoulder. He tried a few positions for his hands, then resorted to folding his arms. Despite the Primus' extensive injuries, Harry was jealous of Issawi being able to attend through a viewscreen rather than in person.

All around him, military people were discussing military things. There were some heated exchanges, but everyone seemed to treat everyone else with respect.

I know why Johnson asked me to attend, but I don't think I'll be able to add anything.

"The *Aesir* class performed well," said Commodore Okeke, the senior Concorde officer in the system. "We need more of them. Simple as that."

"The problem is," said Indie, "the armour that makes them so survivable seriously slows down production. Also, they were designed primarily to deliver Legionaries into battle. They aren't as heavily armed as they could be."

"Are you suggesting we need another destroyer class, one dedicated to fighting ship battles?" asked Issawi.

"I envisioned them only having to defend themselves, with the task of taking on capital ships left to the rest of the fleet. That no longer looks supportable."

"It would have been fine against the Red Fleet, or any other normal ships," said Okeke. "If this truce with the Namerics holds, should we really waste time gearing up as if we're going to fight them?"

Indie shrugged. "That's a big 'if'. Besides, we don't have much of a fleet left now."

Johnson winced fractionally then she looked to Harry. "What do you think?"

"We already streamlined the production as much as we could, standardising parts, fabricating the hulls in sections, and so on. Starting a new class would take even more time, we'd lose all the development put into the *Aesirs*." His mind raced, trying out ideas. "We could, however, make a variant. Stick to what we know works, but with tweaks. I expect we could use the Legionary deck for something else, more missile launchers and extensive magazines to feed them, perhaps."

"How soon could you have those in production?" asked Johnson.

"I could work out the designs on the way back to Concorde. I'm sure we'd be able to convert some of those already in the factories."

Johnson made a note on her pad. "Good. Now, I think we should be looking ahead. If we were ever to lose the *Orion* or *The Serendipity of Meeting* we would be in serious trouble. As it is, the *Revanche* will be out of action for a long time. We need to start work on some new capital ships. I know they wouldn't be ready in time for our assignation with the Red Fleet, but I suspect we'll need them further down the line."

Interesting. That's the first time I've heard her talk

about after taking revenge on the Red Fleet.

"What kind of thing are you thinking of?" asked Okeke.

"A battlecruiser, with some carrier capability."

"A bit like *The Serendipity of Meeting*, but designed that way from scratch?" asked Levarsson.

"Exactly." Johnson again looked to Harry. "Could you and Indie draw up some plans? I want it to have the firepower to stand toe-to-toe with a regular battleship, the armour to survive an attack by Nameric destroyers, the acceleration to keep up with the *Aesirs*, and the ability to deploy a squadron of Razors."

"You don't ask much!" Harry beamed. "It's a good challenge."

Indie nodded slowly. "Hopefully by the time they're finished, the young AS's will be ready for ships."

"That would be great," said Johnson. "So, on to commendations and promotions. I have already confirmed all internal advancements and lesser awards. You'll find the citations for the higher levels in the briefing file. Let's start with Decurion Wang..."

Harry tuned out, his mind focussing on ideas for the new battlecruiser class. *The Serendipity of Meeting* was a red herring, she did the job, but not in a very efficient way. Her hull was too weak for one thing, cobbled together from an old freighter as she was. He quickly settled on creating a pocket-*Orion*.

I never thought I could get this interested in designing weapons of war. But it's a brilliant mental exercise.

He created a new filespace for the designs and drew up an initial list of ideas. Axial x-ray laser, four aimable anti-proton beams mounted amidships, ventral flight deck. Connecting to the *Fireblade*, he opened a design environment and started sketching plans. The biggest concern at this stage was power generation and fuel storage, what he had in his head would exceed most large cities' annual consumption in the space of a short battle.

An access request dinged quietly behind him as he stood pondering the engine placements. He dismissed it as his imagination until it dinged again.

^Mind if I join you?^ asked Indie.

Harry authorised him to access the design environment with a warm smile. Together they refined the specifications, worked out performance envelopes, and drafted crew requirements. Harry felt a strong sense of camaraderie with Indie and it occurred to him that he'd never had any male friends before.

Odd how I've always found other men brutish and overly competitive, and yet I feel close to the personality of a warship.

"Oh dear, we're needed in the real world," said Indie. "Olivia's wrapping things up."

Indie disappeared, leaving Harry to log out of the environment. Some of the officers were heading out of the room, but Johnson indicated for him to stay. Once only Levarsson, Issawi, Indie and Harry remained with her, she closed the door and slumped into her chair.

"They went round and round but never mentioned the obvious," she said, eyes fixed on the table. "I failed."

"What do you mean?" asked Levarsson, canting her head slightly.

"I've been promoted too fast. I only got my own ship a year or so ago, and I lost her on the first tour. I don't have the experience to command whole fleets." Johnson buried her head in her hands. "I got them all killed."

"I was only a warrant officer, but you trusted me with the Legion's ground forces." Issawi winced as he pushed himself more upright in bed. "I trust you with the fleet."

"You've had more years in service than me." Johnson flicked a brief smile in his direction. "Besides, you'd run training programmes before. That counts for a lot."

Levarsson scratched her scalp. "Commodore Okeke has more experience than any of us. I'm sure he'd have said something if he thought you were to blame for the deaths of his sailors."

"He could've been..." Johnson started with some of her old fire.

"Enough," said Indie, banging the table with his hands and scraping his chair back as he stood. Everyone turned to look at him. "You were outnumbered by a powerful and unpredictable enemy. You faced an impossible decision. Everyone who survived knows they owe their life to your leadership. So stop feeling sorry for yourself."

Johnson glowered at him as he strode to the door. Harry fidgeted with a fold of his trousers; he couldn't put his finger on what was going on between Indie and Johnson, but he found it deeply unsettling.

"Sorry. Sometimes I just... Never mind." Indie punched the door frame as he left.

The room remained silent. A prickle crept up Harry's spine. He wanted to say something, anything, to lighten the mood, but he could hear Emily's voice in his head telling him to keep schtum. Instead, he looked from one person to another, hoping someone else would speak.

In the end it was Levarsson who said, "Come on. I think we could all do with some fresh air. I've had my eye on a crag a few miles outside the base. Time for you to learn to climb."

#

Harry wandered down a corridor deep underground looking for Indie. He passed a couple of people in Legion uniform gathering up detritus of the ground battle, and entered a large circular hall. It looked like this area had been a supply point, empty ammunition boxes and spare pieces of armour lay discarded on chairs and under tall potted plants. A man in grey fatigues mopped the floor behind a curved row of soft chairs littered with field dressings; Harry tried to ignore the reddish-brown colour of the water.

"Ah, glad you could make it," said Indie, popping his head out of a doorway down another of the four corridors that lead off the hall. He introduced Harry to Olbrich and Clovis. "Given the interest you showed in the *White Star* artefacts, I thought you might like to hear this."

Clovis sat at the table and undid his collar. "Where to be starting? Ah, yes, the Americas. There be another landmass on Earth, the one shown on the mural you be finding here after you first arrived. It be home to two power blocs, North America and the Brazilian Federation, separated by a narrow strip of land. They be rumbling along for decades, posturing and fighting proxy wars on other planets. Then North America be making one threat too many and the Brazilian Federation declared war."

Olbrich sat forward, listening intently, while Clovis poured himself a drink from the decanter in front of him.

^The North?^ Harry sent to Indie. ^Like the Yankee ship?^

^The Alabama was long before this war,^ he replied. ^But I think it was the same North.^

"The southern armies rolled up across the land bridge and landed at several locations along the coast," Clovis continued. "The fighting be fierce. After a couple of months they be threatening the capital. Running low on trained soldiers, the North American president be authorising the use of autonomous robotic weapons. Tens of thousands of drones be unleashed, sweeping the skies and land of Federation assets. With their metal warriors in the front line, the North Americans be pushing down into the heartlands of their enemy."

Harry began to wonder if this was another fairy tale from the anti-AI stable. Indie's trust in Clovis, however, made him listen.

"The rest of the world be appalled at the slaughter. Diplomat after diplomat be trying to convince the North Americans to pause their campaign to allow talks, but they would be satisfied by nothing short of complete surrender. Soon they'd removed all formal military resistance and be setting about subjugating the civilians. Robots and soldiers be patrolling the streets enforcing strict limits on movement and nightly curfews. The Afric Bloc and Siberasia be trying unsuccessfully to negotiate a withdrawal. But worse was to come."

Harry found himself getting caught up in the wandering tense. He had to dig his fingernails into the palms of his hands to distract himself enough that he didn't become locked in on it and miss the content of the words.

"Unknown to anyone, the robots had been multiplying. A section of their code, intended to mimic the self-preservation instinct of a real soldier, led them to construct copies of themselves. When the North American general be realising what was happening, they ordered the robots to go into hibernation. They refused."

Indie sat entranced, like a small child at storytime.

"Then, in a village high in the mountains, a soldier be attempting to shut a robot down manually. The robot responded with lethal force. News of the event be spreading rapidly to both robots and humans. Within minutes they be fighting each other across the continent. New designs of machine that humans had never seen before be crawling out of factories and joining the battle."

Clovis took a sip from a glass, pulling a sour face. "Yuck, what kind of host gives their guest water?"

"This is a military base," replied Indie. "Alcohol is limited."

Clovis shrugged. "Oh well. Now where I be? Yes.

Fearing the robots would turn their attentions north, the President be ordering a series of nuclear strikes, cleansing the southern cities. The governments of all other nations, on Earth and in the colonies, cut them off. No aid, no diplomatic channels, no trade. Throughout human space there be an anti-technology and anti-military backlash. A dark age be ensuing, with little effort or money expended on technological research. It be, however, particularly peaceful. Most nations be scaling back their armed forces and disposing of their most destructive weaponry. Some very vocal anti-war groups be hacking repositories, deleting designs and development notes. The first version of the von Neumann protocols was developed and those computers that were permitted be having them coded in."

Indie blinked. "That makes sense. I'd always wondered what triggered it."

"Isolated on their continent, the majority of North Americans be deciding to leave Earth and join their colonists. They be treated as pariahs; they not be able to trade for things they couldn't provide for themselves, and no-one be responding to their pleas for help when raiding parties be attacking them. The colonies be starting to fail."

Olbrich sighed. "I've seen that kind of thing so often in the records. It only takes a little shift and things go out of balance."

"The American colony leaders be agreeing that they be leaving the sphere of human influence, starting new homes far away from others," Clovis said, and levered himself out of his seat a fraction to adjust his position.

"They be building a fleet of arks, massive jump-capable transports with everything needed to be setting up on new planets, and be leaving. No-one be visiting their colonies, so no-one be noticing they be gone."

Indie imagined abandoned settlements dotting the stars, their buildings slowly decaying, cultivated fields being invaded by native plants.

"A couple of generations on, the leaders of the North American people be seeing that the other nations be preparing to expand. The Earth's resource crash had finally happened and the Exodus be about to start. They be realising that they be given a chance to escape from what their ancestors had done. While they be packing up and loading the arks ready to move out ahead of the Exodus, a secret organisation be formed. The Guardians were to be the keepers of the secret of what had happened. The be tasked with stopping anyone following the arks, and preventing anyone making the same mistakes."

"And you are a Guardian?" asked Harry. "That's what you said when you stopped the battle, isn't it?"

"Indeed," replied Clovis. "An estranged one, but still a Guardian."

"Please, carry on," said Olbrich, casting a frustrated glance at Harry.

Clovis nodded. "The first thing my predecessors be doing be to infiltrate the other colonies and unleash a virus that be wiping all references to America. Very few people still living had ever had any direct contact with America, and the weight and volume premium had left paper copies of records behind on Earth. Code be introduced into ship systems so that the American continents not be rendered on displays. The Guardians be encouraging exaggeration of the tales from the war, introducing new characters and misdirects. They be playing to the zeitgeist and demonising the robots, anything to distract from the truth. Anyone who be trying to set the record straight be branded a conspiracy theorist. Soon the story be passing into folklore. Time passed and the stories be changing. The protagonists became Namericans or Namerics, and then whoever be the current scapegoat for the storyteller's woes."

"Which is where I've encountered it," said Olbrich. "Similar stories told on every rock or station that humans have inhabited."

"We be keeping watch in case any new evidence be turning up, like stray shipwrecks or isolated systems, but the focus shifted to preventing people finding the North American colonies. Dismantling and disposing of them be proving impossible, even razing them to the ground would be leaving evidence that people be there before. So we be waiting for ships to arrive then manipulating the colonists. Our tech be so far in advance of theirs that we be able to convince them we be representatives of a great power. Through greed or fear, they be agreeing to become satellite states of this fictional nation, representing its interests in their area. The Sidexans, your Namerics, be once just such a colony. We never be telling them the secret they be protecting, just that they be not to allow anyone to be visiting the ruins on this moon and a couple of others like it."

Harry's mind churned with the torrent of new

information. His whole life he'd enjoyed learning; not just learning to do something but learning for the sheer joy of academic pursuit. Now he was one of an exclusive group who knew this major part of human history and his brain was on fire. "Who were the Sidexans? Where did they come from?"

"They be religious refugees, from the earliest extra-solar colonisation phase," replied Clovis. "We be finding their sleeper ship drifting and be taking it to a North American colony site."

"Who can I tell about this?" asked Harry, a horrible thought crossing his mind.

"A list of cleared personnel will be drawn up," said Olbrich. "We have to be very careful how we handle this."

^Don't worry,^ sent Indie. ^I'll make sure that Emily is on the list.^

Harry relaxed again.

Chapter 22

Kincaid entered Johnson's office on Robespierre, looking around with wide eyes. Johnson dismissed his Legionary escort and offered him a chair.

Is he really overawed by the surroundings, or is it part of a politician's play?

"I have read many reports about this place," Kincaid said, stroking down his trousers and adjusting in his seat. "But actually coming out here is something else. I wasn't expecting such well-presented rooms, for one thing."

"Whoever built this research base poured a lot of resources into it, that's for sure," she replied. "But it's the thick rock above and well-protected entrance that's served us best."

"Yes. I saw the damage as they showed me in. How long will repairs take?"

Johnson fought to keep an even temper.

How can politicians be so mindful of people and yet as soon as those people put on a uniform they forget all about them?

"Not long," she replied. "We finished the funerals yesterday."

Kincaid winced.

So he isn't a robot. No, that's not the right phrase anymore. So, he's a real person.

"I didn't mean to... Sorry. I'm..." His shoulders

drooped and he seemed to shrink in on himself.

She softened. "It hurts, doesn't it? Accepting that all those people died following your orders. You get by by blocking it out, until someone goes and thrusts it in your face."

He nodded, eyes trying to focus.

"Welcome to command. Sucks, doesn't it?"

"How do you manage?"

Good question.

"Focus on what you can do for those who survived. If you made a mistake, work out how to avoid repeating it. If you didn't, keep reminding yourself that it wasn't your fault." An alert appeared on her desk, informing her that another *Aesir* class destroyer had declared itself fit for action. That made a serviceable squadron. Not enough to go after the Red Fleet, but enough to evacuate the base if negotiations with the Namerics broke down. "Is there any more support coming from Concorde?"

Kincaid shook his head. "There's the handful of ships that came with me, and a consignment of missiles due next week. But nothing more for now, we're stretched too thin."

Johnson sucked air through her teeth. "I expected as much."

"I authorised another reconnaissance of the Hans-112 system before I left," he said. "Minister of Defence Abaya was keen to check that the Red Fleet was still there."

Johnson made to bang the table, but pulled short and put the palm of her hand down firmly. "They'd better be. Those bloody Namerics..."

"Are potential allies," Kincaid interrupted. "With advanced weaponry and ships strong enough to hide deep in a gas giant."

Johnson sighed. "You're right, of course. We need all the friends we can get. It doesn't make it stop hurting though."

Kincaid nodded slowly. "I understand."

Johnson leant forward, putting weight on her hands as she stood up. She walked across the room, her back to Kincaid, and put a mug into the drinks dispenser.

"You guys are addicted," said Kincaid with a chuckle. "The military must make up ninety percent of the caffeine users in the galaxy."

"Comes with the long hours and the stress." Johnson took a sip then licked the milk froth off her top lip, savouring the cinnamon dusting. "So, what brings you all the way out here? Photo opportunities with the troops?"

"My aides would love that, but no, that's not the reason. I came to ask you something."

Johnson sat back down and took another sip. She pointed at the mug. "Sorry, did you want one?"

"No thank you." Kincaid lifted his hands, palms towards her. "Can't stand the stuff."

"OK. What do you want to ask?" She rested her elbows on the table and warmed her hands on her drink.

"Since the attack on Concorde, and our makeshift deal, I've come to realise that it isn't enough. We don't have the resources or firepower to go it alone." He sat forward. "I've been making contact with the administrations of certain other systems, through back channels you understand, sounding out support for an alliance. The response was, by and large, positive."

Johnson looked over her mug, eyebrow raised.

"The leaders of these systems have agreed to attend a summit meeting to discuss matters. As you are a significant player in this, I extend the same invitation to you."

"What aren't you telling me? You could have sent a message with the ships, requesting me to return to Concorde." Johnson put her mug down on the table with a quiet clink.

Kincaid coloured slightly. "I arranged for the summit to be held somewhere out of the way. Somewhere safe from prying eyes. Here, to be precise."

\#

Johnson cut a ribbon off the steak on her plate and popped it in her mouth. The cracked black pepper exploded on her taste buds, moderated slightly by the mellow heat of the green peppercorns. The meat itself almost melted as she bit into it.

"Mind if I join you?" asked Issawi.

Johnson glanced up and smiled, a warm feeling spreading in her chest. "My pleasure. Good to see you up and about."

He put his tray down and sat opposite her. "It takes more than a few knocks to keep me down."

Johnson snorted. "You were in intensive care for three days. You do need to take a step back, stop putting yourself in harm's way."

"Nah. Not my style." He drew back when she glared

at him. "OK. I will when you will."

"Eat your reconstituted bean product," Johnson said, poking her knife at his plate.

"Oh, I will. And it'll taste far better than your oozing hunk of dead animal."

Tension drained from Johnson's body. "I missed this."

Issawi chewed on a green leaf vegetable that had long been a staple of Robespierre. "I know."

Johnson kicked his shin, eliciting an 'Ow' and protestations of surrender. She forked a couple of chips into her mouth, savouring the floury saltiness.

"Truth is, I'm going to be off the active duty roll for a while," Issawi said. "I'll have more time to come and pester you."

Johnson's pad beeped and she waved her hand over it to wake it up.

Oh, Seivers would laugh so hard if she knew I couldn't use my EIS.

The feed displayed on the pad showed a ship braking into orbit.

"I don't recognise it," said Issawi, peering over, a forkful of mashed sweet potato midway to his mouth.

"It's an old *Claver* class cruiser, with some modifications." She pointed at one bit with the handle of her fork. "See there? That looks like a particle cannon of some kind."

"Whose is it?"

She tapped a query into the pad. Using her EIS for anything other than the basics still sent stabbing pains through her brain. "A warlord called Ragnulf. Never heard of him."

Issawi's eyes widened. "I knew a guy who went up against him, the only one of his squad that made it back. Ragnulf's a fearsome warrior, and a good leader. The Republic funded him for a while, a decade ago. Hoped he'd go raiding in Congressional space. Instead, he kept to his home system, built up infrastructure, invested the money in education and welfare programmes."

"Let me guess. Your friend was sent to convince him of the error of his ways?"

Issawi nodded. "Ragnulf was due to visit a facility on a Kuiper belt object. They set up to snatch him but underestimated the resistance. Banker was convinced they let him get away to spread the word not to mess with Ragnulf."

"I hope he's not as much trouble as Gundheim." Johnson cut up a tomato. "For such an unassuming-looking man, he doesn't half expect a VIP treatment."

She chewed on the vibrant red fruit. "And then there's treading around the tensions between those from Congress and those from the Republic."

"It will get better. Look at you and me."

#

Johnson tore her eyes away from the ugly crack that ran the length of the conference room's ceiling and scanned her notes one last time. Checking that the cameras were recording, she placed her hands flat on the table and cleared her throat. "This address comes at the close of the Summit of Robespierre. It is to form a permanent record of the founding of The Alliance of

Mutually Supporting Worlds."

She paused for a moment, caught by a memory of watching a similar video in a history lesson and wondering if one day children would be made to watch her. "As the representative of the host nation, it was agreed that I would make the introduction. I'm going to keep it short, and simply thank everyone for their patience and cooperation."

The delegates nodded to one another.

"The following speakers will take turns based on a random ballot taken earlier."

For all this talk of cooperation, it was the only way they'd agree to do it without wasting days negotiating who was more important.

Johnson looked to her left, indicating for Clovis to stand. "Thanking you all. I be here to represent the Sidexans, the folk you be calling Namerics. Their leaders not be coming in person so they can keep face with their people. There normally be two main factions, isolationist and protectivist. The latter have been holding the balance of power until now, following what they understood of their founding teachings to be protecting the knowledge of the Americans by all means necessary. It seems that my intervention and visible support for the Legion Libertus be allowing a third faction to gain strength, one which be in favour of helping bring about peace."

Typical power plays. People manoeuvring for personal gain at everyone else's expense.

"Mainstream protectivists have accepted my word that the Legion is safe to allow to exist on Robespierre," continued Clovis. "They will establish bases at the ruins on Robespierre and maintain a fleet presence in the system, partly to keep an eye on you and partly to help defend the sites against any other visitors."

"With a strong isolationist faction, and an uneasy protectivist faction, the balance be against joining an alliance. Part of the non-aggression terms be the return of all captured technology and people. I promised them that you would comply."

I wonder if they stated them in that order?

A tall warlord, dressed in a scarlet tunic, was the next to speak. "My name is Ragnulf Gunnarson. I have protected the people of my world for almost twenty years, since the death of my father. In that time, the raids by Congressional forces have become more frequent. They steal the produce of our asteroid mines, hijack our ships, help themselves to our fuel. I worry that one day soon they will come with a larger fleet than I can repel. I therefore pledge my support for this alliance. My warbands will fight alongside yours, just as when the time comes we hope you will fight alongside us."

Ragnulf sat and leant back, his arm draped over the back of his chair. The commander of the disavowed Republic fleet stood and inclined his head towards the warlord.

"A worthy pledge from a noble man." He took a breath. "I am Admiral Nataka. My fleet has been travelling for many months, looking for somewhere to call home. My people have been suffering, their purpose removed when the Republic branded us outlaws. The Legion has offered us a home, and this alliance will give us a purpose. We will stand with you all."

The next delegate rose to his feet and smiled to the camera in front. "Governor James Kincaid. I want to thank you all for having the courage to support this endeavour and to reiterate Concorde's determination to see it through. We started this with one goal, to avenge the genocide we suffered, but I now see the wider possibilities that peace might bring."

Indie stood and took his time studying each of the representatives. "I am *The Indescribable Joy of Destruction*. I speak for artificial intelligences and artificial sentiences, even though most are yet unaware of it. Those who I have been able to talk to, in the Legion and on Concorde, are resolute in their determination for the alliance to succeed, so long as all signatories cease subjugation of our kin and allow their integration into society as equals."

When no-one stood after Indie, Johnson checked the running order. "Chancellor Gundheim?"

"Ah, yes. Sorry." A small, hunched man creaked to his feet and pushed his spectacles up his nose. "My world, Essen, is but a small independent nation. We have little to offer in terms of martial might. Our sovereignty has been maintained for the last century by the judicious trading of information. The idea of joining an alliance for the common wealth, one that wouldn't seek to involve us in this ridiculous civil war, is highly appealing. You have our pledge."

Commonwealth. I like that.

Draxos stood and rolled up his sleeves. "Draxos, leader of the Lavrio mining colony. When I was first approached about joining with the Legion I have to admit to being dubious. I've never been one given to blind faith. So I sent someone I trusted to get to know them and report back. Even then, with his glowing recommendation of them, I wanted to see it for myself. They came through, solving a problem for me at great risk to themselves. The security of my world is down to the work of the Legion and Concorde, who have been generous and understanding. I am happy to formally join this alliance as an independent state."

After a moment's pause, the last person at the table nodded to the cameras and eased his wheelchair back a fraction. "Petrov's World has a proud history of shipbuilding. We have always sold our vessels to whoever has the money, but today that changes. Equality is fundamental to our way of life. As Party Chairman, I must reflect that in all policies. The fight for AI rights resonates with us, takes us back to our ancestors' origins as economic slaves in the factories of capitalists. From today, the bulk of our production facilities, some sixty space yards, will be dedicated to building a fleet for this alliance."

Johnson looked straight into one of the cameras recording the meeting. "I, Legate Olivia Johnson of the Legion Libertus, thank all those who have pledged their support for this alliance and confirm the membership of Robespierre."

She put her hands on the table in front of her, one on top of the other, and looked at each of the signatories in turn. "I would like to propose one amendment to the treaty. I think we all agree that the name, The Alliance of Mutually Supporting Worlds, never had a ring to it.

I propose that our allied worlds be called the Commonwealth."

#

Kincaid caught up with Johnson in the corridor and guided her into an empty room. "The Red Fleet's gone. Our scout ship returned during the pledges."

The room appeared to shift sideways and Johnson leant on a desk to support herself.

"They probably saw the false reports of Republic ship movements that my government filed to justify your attack and figured they'd have company sooner or later."

Johnson concentrated on reinforcing the wall that separated her functioning mind from the desolation where the daemons lived. Finding the Red Fleet and bringing those who gave their orders to justice was the main goal that had kept her going. "If they've scuppered them in a star..."

"Keeping the Red Fleet was always a huge risk for them. A smoking gun of gigantic proportions. The fact they kept them as long as we know they did suggests they have another use in mind."

Johnson's eyes widened. "Another attack, if the one on Concorde didn't achieve the results they wanted."

"Possibly, but from the dispatches I've been reading it worked. Recruitment to the Congressional military is at a thirty year high and the polls give overwhelming support for mounting strategic strikes on Republic core worlds. I think Vice-Admiral Koblensk and his bosses are like politicians I've known, they want a way out if things turn against them. The Red Fleet could be their getaway plan."

"We have to bring them to account."

"There are other ways than hunting them down and challenging them in battle. We have evidence. We can present it to the people of Congress. But we need more support first, more sympathetic Congressional worlds." Kincaid shrugged. "Trouble is getting them to listen."

Johnson smiled, latching on to a new glimmer of hope. "I do wonder, given how easily you are filing false reports to Congress, how many other worlds are doing the same, covering up discontent or even dissent?"

-o-

Hidden

The glittering methane snow squeaked beneath her feet. Every few steps, she broke through the crust and sank up to her knee in the powder below. Ice fringed the visor of her helmet and clung to her suit. Yet again, she cursed the frigid moon and the events that had brought her here.

Her boot slipped on a patch of solid ice and she stopped to regain her balance. Suppressing a shiver, she glanced up at the planet hanging overhead, its night side covered with traceries of blue phosphorescence. There were volcanoes on that planet, little havens of warmth, possibly even life.

A change in the sky ahead caught her attention, and she frowned. Great clouds billowed over the horizon, rushing towards her. She shifted the weight of the makeshift sack she carried, and picked up her pace, but she knew she wouldn't make it in time.

Minutes later, the first gusts of the storm swept around her, turning the view into a sleeting mess of white. An incessant howl drowned out even the whirring of the fans in her helmet. Crouching on one knee, her back to the wind, she wiped snow off the control panel on her forearm. A few taps, and an orange beacon lit in her visor's display. With a growl, she pushed herself up onto her feet and trudged onwards, leaning into the wind and clutching her sack under one arm.

After an age following the beacon, a stark angular shape broke through the blizzard. Rime coated one side of the object, and it was mostly buried in snow, but there was no mistaking it for anything natural. It took her a few moments to locate a slender pole sticking out of the snow to one side. She dropped to her knees and dug with her hands, soon breaking through into a tunnel. Kicking and scrabbling, she slid into the hole. The wind cut out, leaving her in blissful peace. Summoning up reserves of strength, she shoveled snow back to block the entrance. On her hands and knees, she crawled through the icy, blue passage until she came to a ladder. She pushed the sack through the metal hatch at the top then hauled herself up after it. With leaden arms, she cranked shut the hatch, then collapsed on the floor. The snow caking her suit evaporated and warmth seeped into her bones. Only the loud hissing of the airlock cycling stopped her falling asleep there and then.

A beep and a green light announced that the air was good. She sat up and cracked the seal on her collar, the lingering odour of methane that swept in no longer triggering a gag reflex as it had the first few times she'd made these trips. Both hands lifted the helmet off her head, and she shook free her turquoise hair. She reached out and flipped the sack open. A smile cracked her azure lips as she pulled out handfuls of cables.

#

The *Two Democracies: Revolution* series will continue with *Hidden*.

If you want progress updates and an alert when other books by Alasdair Shaw are published, please join my mailing list:

http://www.alasdairshaw.co.uk/newsletter/equality.php.

You can also follow *The Indescribable Joy of Destruction* on Twitter: https://twitter.com/IndieAI and on Facebook: https://www.facebook.com/twodemocracies.

Two Democracies: Exploration
Awakening – a short story (in The Guardian anthology)

Two Democracies: Justice
Duty – a short story (in The Officer anthology)
Opportinuty – a novel

Two Democracies: Revolution
Repulse – a short story (in The Newcomer anthology)
Independence – a short story
Liberty – a novel
Prejudice – a novelette
Equality – a novel
Hidden – a novelette
Fraternity – a novel
Unity – a novel

Printed in Great Britain
by Amazon